Bad Girl Blvd

Part 2

Erica Hilton

Buy

for Melodrama

Bad Girl Blvd

Part 2

Erica Hilton

www.melodramapublishing.com

Library of Congress Control Number: 2013946109
ISBN-13: 978-1620780398
ISBN-10: 1620780399
First Edition: November 2014
10 9 8 7 6 5 4 3 2 1

Interior Design: Candace K. Cottrell
Cover Design: Candace K. Cottrell
Cover Model: Luca Linn
Model Photo: Marion Designs

BOOKS BY

10 Crack Commandments
Bad Girl Blvd
Bad Girl Blvd 2
Bad Girl Blvd 3
The Diamond Syndicate
Dirty Little Angel
Dirty Money Honey
Wifey: From Mistress to Wifey (Part 1)
Wifey: I Am Wifey (Part 2)

PROLOGUE

The bright lights coming from over a dozen police cars parked haphazardly on the block and the ambulance in the middle of the night created a strong disturbance in the affluent Rockaway Park community. Neighbors pulled their drapes aside and peeked through their windows at the chaotic activity right outside their front doors. A few decided to exit their cozy homes, clad in pajamas and housecoats to get a closer look, maybe investigate the scene on their tranquil street now turned into some nightmarish horror show.

Uniformed officers and detectives swamped the entire area. The crime scene unit painstakingly gathered evidence, snapped photos of everything in the home, and hurried to identify their victims being rushed to the hospital. It looked like a home invasion in their eyes, maybe a robbery that had ended badly. Two victims appeared to have been shot inside the posh home. One male, in his late thirties, had sustained three gunshot wounds to his chest cavity and vital organs. He was bleeding out like a stuck pig while EMS workers fought doggedly to save his life as they wheeled him out on the gurney in the cold winter morning toward the idling ambulance. They were putting pressure on his wounds, trying to stop the bleeding. The female victim was young and beautiful underneath the blood that coated her skin. She was in her early twenties and struggling to stay alive, barely having a pulse. She was so bloody that it was hard to tell if she had been shot, stabbed, beaten, or what. Near both victims were two guns and spent shell casings.

When detectives combed the crime scene they noticed the badge in the bedroom and realized the male victim was one of their own. The situation, the crime scene became even more critical. An officer shot down in their city was a serious issue, and now the investigation intensified.

The looky-loos crowded around the crime scene, now looped with yellow tape. Fellow officers lingered in the area, upset and wanting revenge for a shot cop. He was from the city, but he was still an officer of the law.

The cop was rushed to the nearest hospital in one screaming ambulance, and the female victim was rushed to the same hospital in the second. Paramedic workers hastily fought to keep both victims on earth. During the ambulance ride, the female was in such bad condition that she flatlined twice. The workers rushed to use the defibrillator on her, delivering a therapeutic dose of electrical energy to her heart. She came through after a few trials with a weak pulse and was granted a second chance of life. The male victim wasn't as fortunate; he died due to his injuries while en route to the nearest hospital and was pronounced dead on arrival.

A cop dead. It caught the media's attention. It caught the city's attention.

Now it was a homicide of a police officer, and the NYPD wasn't going to rest until they captured the culprit or culprits.

They only had one witness, and she was in critical condition, induced into a coma because she had swelling around the brain, cerebral edema, and doctors needed to perform immediate surgery on her. The cops, however, needed her awake. They needed a name, and they needed a reason why an officer was dead and a young lady was dying.

1

Luca was groggy when she finally woke up out of a four-day coma and found herself handcuffed to the bed railing. She wondered why she was cuffed to the bed. She couldn't remember anything. She was disoriented and in severe pain. It felt like her body had been crushed by a steamroller. It was hard to breathe and hard to think. She was plugged in to several machines monitoring her vitals. The room was dark and felt still. She was alone for the moment. It was hard to move with the handcuffs around her wrist making it uncomfortable, restrictive.

Luca noticed the police officer posted outside her room. It was a clear indication that she wasn't going anywhere. They watched her closely. Even if she wanted to leave, her body felt fatigued and battered. Every movement she made, even slightly, ached like bones were breaking through her skin.

The nurse came into her room to check on her. She didn't know Luca had awakened from her four-day coma. She stood over the patient checking her vitals and noticed Luca's eyes gazing up at her.

"You're awake," the nurse said. "You've been asleep for a few days now. How are you feeling?"

Luca didn't answer her. She wondered how many days she'd been out, and what crime they were trying to charge her with.

The nurse continued talking to Luca while treating her wounds. She had a pleasant personality and seemed to really care about her job and the patients she attended to.

"You know you're very lucky to be alive," the nurse said to her. "But I'll get the doctor for you. He's ready to tell you about your condition."

Luca felt something was wrong. There was something she was missing or forgetting. Her memory was bad and had holes in it like Swiss cheese. Her heart felt really heavy for some reason. She felt afraid and alone. The nurse left to get the doctor. Moments later, her doctor entered the room.

He stood over her in his white lab coat, stethoscope around his neck and clipboard in his hand. Dr. Malone. He was tall, lean, and white with bushy hair. His eyes were warm, kind, and caring, which made Luca feel safe. He was ready to give her the grave news. It was obvious Luca wasn't aware yet.

"Ms. Linn, it's finally good to see you're awake. You were badly beaten and have been in a coma for four days. You've been hit on the head pretty hard, Ms. Linn, and we've had to put you to sleep for a while and do a small operation on you to release some of the fluid on your brain. You've been unconscious for four days, but you're a bit better now so we've woken you up," he explained.

Luca didn't understand what he was talking about. She'd been in a coma, she'd woken up and now her life was in shambles. She understood that part, but for some odd reason she felt the doctor had more grim news to tell her. It wasn't over yet. He looked down at her chart; his facial expression said it all—something was wrong. The nurse was standing behind him quiet as a mouse.

He sighed.

"I'm sorry for your loss," the doctor said, reluctantly.

"Loss?" *What loss is he talking about?* she wondered.

"You were pregnant, and we couldn't save the baby. It was lost due to the trauma of the beating you sustained," he continued.

"What?!" Luca uttered with shock. The news was overwhelming. Her memory finally flooded back into her like a strong gust of wind blowing. She reached for her stomach and found it flattened.

"No!" she cried out. "Not my baby! Not my baby!"

It was a painful feeling, and the pain of losing a child hurt more than the beating she'd received. She knew it was Squirrel's baby growing inside of her—now, nothing. Luca's sobs echoed from her room and out into the hallway. It was at that moment she finally remembered what had happened to her, and the painful memory came flooding back into her head so strongly that it almost took her sanity.

"Oh god," she hollered, clutching the doctor's hand tightly. "That fuckin' bastard! That fuckin' bastard!!!"

At that moment, Luca became temporarily insane. She ignored the pain in her body; the condition she was in didn't matter—she wanted to free herself from her restraints. She shook the bed crazily while screaming like a madwoman. The rage she felt couldn't be explained. The cop posted outside her door came rushing into the room to aid the doctor and nurse. Luca became violent. She snapped at anyone around her and at the same time tried to break her own wrist to free herself from the handcuff. Everyone gripped her and pushed her down forcefully on the bed while the nurse tried to inject her with a sedative to calm her down. The past week had been hell for Luca, and it looked like things were about to get worse.

***

BAD GIRL BLVD 2

Five days earlier

If Detective Charter hadn't seen it with his own eyes, then he wouldn't have believed it. Luca had lied to him. It was clear that she was the mastermind behind Bad Girl flooding the streets. The evidence was in his face. For months now, he had been sleeping with the enemy, and had fallen in love with a murderous queenpin. He simply stood in the undisclosed room aghast.

His heart sank like the Titanic. His mind started to spin wildly as the rage bubbled inside of him. Feeling played, Detective Charter felt like crying and tearing something apart with his bare hands. How was Luca going to explain the secret room behind the wall, filled with large amounts of kilos, money, and guns to him? There was no reasonable explanation in his eyes; possession was nine-tenths of the law, and what the detective stumbled upon in her home was enough to put Luca away for life.

In that split second, he lost himself.

He stormed toward the bedroom, scowling, with his fists clenched. He kicked in the bedroom door, startling Luca out of her deep sleep. Charter didn't hesitate, rushing over to her with cruel intentions. Luca looked at Charter wide-eyed, shocked to the bone. She was caught off guard by Charter roughly snatching her out of bed, shouting out, "You lying fuckin' bitch!" and dragging her across the floor by her hair.

Luca tried to fight him off, kicking and screaming, "Get the fuck off me! What is your fuckin' problem?!" However, he was too strong.

He roughly dragged her across the carpet, leaving carpet burns on her skin, and into the secret stash room where he harshly demanded a reasonable explanation from her.

Luca was dumbfounded that he'd found the room…how? It was hidden and protected with an intricate code. Charter was smart, but he wasn't a genius in her eyes.

"Explain this!" he yelled, pointing to the drugs, cash, and guns.

Luca gazed at him, terrified. She was speechless.

Charter wasn't in any mood to hear any of her lies or bullshit.

"I'm a fuckin' NYPD detective! A fuckin' cop, and you bring this shit around me. I loved you, Luca. I was in love with you. You blood-sucking, drug-dealing bitch!" he hollered.

"Charter, I can explain," Luca finally spoke out.

"Explain? Fuckin' how? How can you explain this shit to me, huh? How?!" Charter's eyes brimmed with anger.

Luca remained planted against the floor, staring up at her infuriated boyfriend. She breathed heavily. She found herself deep in quicksand and sinking fast.

"You fuckin' bitch!" he cursed. "I trusted you! A cop—I'm a fuckin' cop, and you think I'm supposed to ignore this? This is life in prison, Luca! Fuckin' life!"

"I can tell you the truth," Luca exclaimed. It was hard for her to speak over his loud screaming. She didn't know what to say or do at that moment. She wanted to tell him everything, but how?

"How, when you've been lying to me since day fuckin' one?" he spat. "I'm gonna send your black ass to muthafuckin' prison. You're a got-damn criminal, Luca."

"Just let me talk, damn it!" she screamed out heatedly.

"You definitely are going to talk before I lock you up."

Charter's pugnacious behavior grew like a deadly virus; Luca couldn't talk over his screaming and accusations. He stomped back and forth in the confined area, snatching kilos of heroin off the shelves and tearing them apart with his hands, spreading the potent drug all over the floor. He tossed hundreds of thousands of dollars everywhere while screaming like a lunatic.

Luca rose to her knees and locked eyes with him. She hated to see him like this. She hated more to see her product being destroyed and money thrown around. She had worked hard for everything in the room, and Charter was annihilating it. Tears trickled from her eyes, desperation displayed on her face. She knew how seriously Charter took his job with the NYPD, but she couldn't go to jail. It was hard to believe this was actually happening to her. She had always been cautious and prudent. This mistake had happened so suddenly, and it was about to become costly unless she could prevent any further repercussions.

Charter started to show tears in his eyes. He gazed at Luca for a moment. Her cop boyfriend appeared to be ready to listen to her story. He looked calm for a moment, but was still seething. He stopped destroying her product and turning her room into shambles, but his eyes burned into her. At first, he listened intently.

It was time to explain.

"It was Squirrel, Charter, not me," Luca lied to him. "These are all of his drugs. I didn't have a choice. I have nothing to do with this. He threatened me and our unborn baby, Charter. He's crazy. He's been stalking me, and I'm truly afraid of him. He's insane," Luca said.

She decided to play the innocent victim and put on a Broadway performance in front of Detective Charter. It was Squirrel or her, and she was ready to lie and fight hard to convince him she had nothing to do with the contents of the room.

Charter didn't say a word. His eyes hooded over in anger while he listened to Luca explain how Squirrel was going to put a hit out on Charter after he stalked and harassed him while executing a routine police stop in Harlem. Squirrel was also upset with Luca's newfound love, and he wanted revenge once he found out that she was dating and loved Charter, basically saying that it was Detective Charter's fault that she had to hold his drugs.

"If you hadn't gone messing with Squirrel, looking for trouble that night, then I wouldn't be in this mess with him, baby. I wouldn't have to involve myself with him on this level. I told you, I'm done with him and don't want any part of him anymore. He's my past, you're my future. I only love you," Luca pleaded in her sweetest and most girlish voice.

Charter still stayed quiet. He glared at Luca with his fists still clenched and his blood pressure rising. It was true love with her, but this . . . this was conspiracy.

Luca added, "All of his drugs and money are going to be gone first thing in the morning, baby, and Squirrel will be out of our lives forever. I promise you that."

Luca felt she was getting through to him. His face seemed to soften, but he was still silent—expressionless. The silence from him was the scary part. His eyes were still cold in her direction. His fists were still scrunched together like small boulders. She didn't know what he was thinking.

Luca walked toward him and outstretched her arm to take his hand into hers. He didn't resist. She was still nervous but tried to ease the tense situation with her intelligence, charm, and her sexuality. She knew despite the elephant in the room, he still loved her. She wasn't going to jail tonight, and this wasn't going to be the final chapter in her book.

She gently squeezed his hand and pulled Charter closer to her. "Let's just go back to bed and let me make passionate love to you . . . let me fuck you so good tonight, baby. Let's just forget about all this and enjoy each other like we always do. I'm having your baby, and do you really want the mother of your child to be in jail?"

Luca knew she was getting through to him. They hugged; his embrace against her was welcoming and strong. Luca smiled and added, "Your baby and I love you so much. We are a family."

Unexpectedly, Charter pulled himself away from her sweet embrace and scowled. He snapped. Luca worried greatly. Then it happened, the powerful hit came out of the blue. It felt like a brick had crashed into her face. She heard him scream, "You lying fuckin' bitch!" and then *POW,* another hard blow to the side of her temple, causing Luca to collide with the wall. More and more brutal hits were repeated to her face and skull, and Luca stumbled then dropped to the floor. Charter began beating the life out of her. The beating was violent and cruel as all of his frustration and humiliation manifested from being played.

"You think I'm fuckin' stupid?!" he screamed.

The sickening thought came to him that she wasn't carrying his baby, but Squirrel's. He had been a cop for too long not to know the difference between the truth and a lie, and his gut instincts told him she was lying about everything. Luca had been in love with the drug dealer for a long time, and he assumed she was still in love with him. And what kind of drug dealer gives any woman dozens of kilos to stash and millions in cash, and a small arsenal that would make a terrorist jealous?

The truth in Charter's eyes was that the woman he loved, his fiancée, the person who he thought was carrying his baby, was the infamous drug distributor of Bad Girl heroin. How could he have been so stupid, so naïve? His career could have ended had Luca gotten busted prior to him finding out. He would have been ruined and charged with a felony.

The visions of being played for a fool by Luca and Squirrel spinning wildly in his head only fueled his rage more. While Luca was on the floor crying and bleeding, he continued assaulting her. The heel of his foot came crashing down on her face. It felt like he had broken her cheekbone. He kicked and stomped her into the ground repeatedly. Luca howled from the pain. She tried defending herself, but she felt small and helpless underneath him. She begged him to stop, but her loud pleas for mercy fell upon deaf ears. The man was belligerent. He had gone crazy. It was the first time Luca prayed to God. Jail was suddenly a welcoming thought when she felt she was about to die tonight.

Charter blacked out. His mind started to play tricks on him. He yanked Luca by her throat, disheveling her hair while viciously pounding his fists into her, spewing her blood all over the room, dragging her body all over the place and tossing her around like she was a rag doll.

Was he a target? he wondered. Was he being used? Was Luca a plant in his life to get closer to the head detective investigating Bad Girl and the people who were overdosing on it? In his crazy state, he fell in love and forgot that she was once a suspect and he was pursuing her.

"I loved you!" Charter madly screamed. His dark eyes looked down at Luca's battered body.

"Please don't kill me. Please, I don't wanna die, not like this, not like this," Luca pleaded weakly. "I thought you loved me."

Her feeble plea and sad, defeated eyes did nothing to change the situation. Charter continued to go berserk. He knotted her hair around his fist, pulling it tightly, making it feel like he was about to pull out her hair from her scalp. Her black and swollen eyes gazed up at him, defeated. He punched her in the face again, and again, and again until her beautiful facial structure morphed into something mutant-like, her beauty contorted by swollen black eyes, a busted lip, and lumps across her face.

Luca couldn't fight back. He was just too strong and out of control. He beat her from the hidden room through the kitchen until they ended up in the bedroom. Luca's face and nightgown were coated with blood. Her body looked like it had been in a Mike Tyson fight. Charter beat Luca until there was nothing else to beat out of her. When his arms got tired and he became winded, he sat down on the bed to take a quick breather as Luca lay looking lifeless across the bedroom floor, battered, bloody, and bruised. Every inch of her felt broken. She couldn't move. It felt like she was dying.

Charter got his quick rest, regained his strength, and approached the beaten woman again to distribute some more punishment. He stood over Luca, sprawled face down on the floor, and disturbingly said, "You stupid bitch, you thought I was finished with you? I'm just getting started."

He started to beat on her again, telling her that he was going to kill her. Charter gripped the back of her head and slammed it into the floor with brute force. The blow knocked her out. He thought that he had finally killed her. Luca lay lifelessly on her stomach, her face turned slightly his way and eyes shut with blood oozing from her mouth.

Everything from the bedroom to the hidden room was in disarray. The place looked like a tornado had gone through it. Charter transformed into a monster and Luca was snatched into his horror show.

Charter showed no remorse for his actions. He simply went into the kitchen and poured himself a glass of Hennessy. He took a seat at the table with his hands and clothes covered in Luca's blood. As he sipped the cognac, he tried to think of his next move. He was an NYPD detective, and a scene like this was going to be difficult to explain to his superiors and internal affairs. A dead, beaten woman in the bedroom and a room filled with drugs, money, and guns—the truth would sound too farfetched, and the body would possibly warrant a life sentence behind bars. He was a decorated officer, and jail wasn't an option for him.

He decided that the only way out of his situation was to stage the scene and make it appear to be a home invasion leading to a homicide, and to make it look drug-related. He had fucked up by losing his temper. He had been on the force since he was twenty years old and had too much experience with crime scenes. The obvious was this: A woman beaten or stabbed to death multiple times usually meant it was a crime of passion, and he would be the number one suspect—cop or no cop. It was highly unlikely that a home invasion and drug case would result with the victim beaten to death.

Drug-related crimes usually consisted of a few shots to the head or body, maybe involving duct tape, or torture.

"Think, fuckin' think!" Charter said to himself, slapping his forehead while trying to keep his cool. He trembled a little knowing time was of the essence and his bad judgment could cost him everything he worked so hard for.

"What did I do?" the realization finally settled into him.

Charter gawked at his bloody hands and then became alarmed of the blood on his clothes. The first thing he needed to do was clean himself up. He had Luca's blood all over him. It was evidence against him. Everything was messy and potential trouble for him once investigators painstakingly ran through the entire home to deduce what had happened. He needed a shower. It was best to cleanse the blood from his skin, get rid of clothing or anything else leaving DNA that could trace back to him by burning it somewhere. For the blood in the home, there was always bleach.

Charter tried to brainstorm. He thought about more problems. There were the neighbors. Surely someone would say they saw his car in the driveway throughout the night. He wasn't a stranger to Luca's home. They were an item. So many things went through his mind. He didn't know where to start at first, but he needed to stage the perfect crime scene.

Charter decided the first smart thing to do was clean the house and cover his tracks. He quickly grabbed expensive jewelry from the bedrooms and then grabbed the electronics, iPads, iPods, iPhones, a Mac Air, and the DVR for the security system and tossed everything into a duffel bag by the door. He went back into the hidden den and reviewed the vast selection of guns. He opted for the .357 Magnum. He comprehended he needed to use it to help the scene of the crime appear believable to trained eyes.

With the gun in his hand, Charter marched back to the bedroom to shoot the bitch he believed was already dead and was supposedly carrying his child. He went from a good cop to twisted murderer like it was natural. He found himself traveling deeper and deeper into the rabbit hole. Once fallen, he wasn't about to get up.

However, the minute he stepped into the bedroom, he was shocked to see Luca gone. She had crawled away somewhere, staying hidden. She wasn't dead after all. Already, his plan was falling apart. She was still alive but she still had to die. It was too late to turn back now.

"This fuckin' bitch," Charter uttered with a scowl, annoyed.

He started to follow the blood trail to the far side of the bed, until he found a weak Luca pointing his police-issued service revolver at him. She was determined to live, recoiling in the corner like a leaf blowing in the wind. Her body felt like it was falling apart. She fought to stay conscious and keep her vision focused. The gun trembled in her outstretched hands, but it was still perfectly aimed at his chest. He couldn't get away after what he did to her. Charter was stunned and caught off guard.

"You bastard," she stammered.

It was a standoff, but Luca had the advantage despite her weakened condition.

"Look—" Charter started to speak.

Before he could react or speak, the gun went off six times in Luca's hands and Charter got hit three times in the chest before he collapsed by her feet and passed out on the floor, thick crimson blood pooling around him.

Luca finally lost consciousness and passed out next to the man she shot. The man she had tried to fall in love with.

2

The doctors declared Luca well enough to be discharged from the hospital. She was healing, but still broken down, and she had some complications to deal with since the severe beating she'd suffered from a dead cop. She lost a baby, her memory was still sketchy, her ribs were fractured, and her wrist broken, and she had to be wheeled out of her room in a wheelchair pushed by her mother, Lucia.

"You're going to be okay," Dr. Malone said to her.

Luca frowned. White boy didn't know shit about her life. Luca knew she was going to be far from okay—okay was farfetched in her vocabulary. Too much had happened in the past several days, and there were too many cops coming against her. She had to endure a week-long thorough investigation by a handful of detectives while going through her recovery. The cops didn't understand that she was the victim and killing Charter had been done in self-defense.

The police department had meticulously searched her home from top to bottom but apparently never found the hidden room of drugs, money, and guns. They never charged her with drug possession and distribution. The only charge they tried to hit her with was murder of a police officer. After a week of trying to gather evidence and deducing what had gone down that night in her home, it was evident that she was the victim and it was deemed self-defense and the case was finally closed.

It was good news for Luca. What was bizarre was—how had they not found her concealed room? Luca was confused, yet extremely grateful and relieved. Where were her drugs and money? Did Charter close up the room before she shot him dead? Or did she close it? Her memory was still sketchy.

She had given her deposition to the primary detective on the case, stating that Detective Charter came home as usual that evening, but on that night he'd decided he didn't want to become a father, saying he felt trapped. Luca went on to say to the primary detective on the case that she and Charter argued heatedly for hours, he accused her of cheating and proclaimed that the baby wasn't his, and without warning, he started beating on her. Luca went into vivid details about the fight and the severe beating Charter inflicted on her.

"He just kept on hitting me and hitting me," she had stated with tears tricking down her face in front of everyone. "I couldn't stop him and I couldn't run from him. I was just worried about my baby . . . and he took our child from me."

"Did you provoke him, in any way?" the detective had asked. He was six feet tall, a lean-bodied man with a narrow face and intense eyes.

"No, I didn't provoke him," Luca assured them.

She had to keep her story straight and not tell them she was thrust out of her sleep violently because Charter was upset about finding her room filled with drugs. The story she gave them was consistent, no matter how many times she told it—a domestic dispute ensued over assumed infidelity and over who was the baby's real father.

Why did she shoot him? The .357 Magnum they found next to Charter's dead body was unmistakable to her story, he was going to kill her.

"But why not with his own gun, Ms. Linn? Where did he get the .357 from?" the detective asked.

"How should I know?" she replied. "At this point I can only conclude he got the gun hot off the streets and was going to use an untraceable weapon to murder me."

"That's highly unlikely and inflammatory."

"Really?" she sarcastically replied. "Ya think? Your honorable detective came home and beat me until I saw stars swirling around my head like I was in a cartoon. He wasn't a dumbass. Why would he kill me with his police-issued weapon? He had the .357 so he could get away with murder."

Butterflies swam all around Luca's stomach while she was being questioned by the detectives.

"That's all for today." The detective stood up reluctantly. He really wanted to indict Luca for something, anything. However, her story was airtight. It was still Rockaway Park, Queens, and there wasn't as much loyalty to the deceased detective as there would have been in his Brooklyn precinct. Had this been in Charter's jurisdiction Luca's ass would be charged with involuntary manslaughter—just to fuck with her for killing a cop.

The only thing Luca wanted to do after her release from the hospital was go home and rest. During her time in custody at the hospital, she wasn't allowed any visitors except immediate family. Her mother stayed by her bedside the entire time, praying over her daughter and thinking that what Luca had done to that violent man was justice. Lucia had gone through her own horrible ordeal of domestic violence over the years from a handful of men, and she could relate to her daughter. It was a painful thing.

Lucia would continually hold Luca's hand and pray. It was a blessing that her daughter was expected to make a full recovery. She was lucky to be alive. Cop or not, and infidelity or not, Lucia strongly felt that the boyfriend didn't have any right to put his hands on her daughter. If given the chance, Lucia would have shot and killed Charter herself and took the full blame for it. Lucia had experienced prison life plenty of times, and it was the last thing she ever wanted Luca to go through. It was no place for a woman like her daughter.

Lucia slowly pushed her daughter in the narrow wheelchair like she was a cripple. Luca hated it. She frowned. She felt weak and vulnerable again, like when she was growing up. The doctors suggested she shouldn't walk yet, but be wheeled out into the lobby and toward her vehicle. Various parts of her still ached, especially her soul. She had lost her baby. It was her only connection to Squirrel. Luca thought about him while being pushed in the wheelchair. She missed him. The first thing she wanted to do was visit him, but things had changed between the two of them. Squirrel was still with his baby's mother and had warned Luca countless of times to stay the fuck away from him. But she was in love with him, and it was hard to stay away.

Luca had no remorse for shooting Charter. She had tried to love him, but he wasn't the man she wanted him to be. She did use him, kept him close and tried to substitute him for Squirrel, but it worked against her.

The ride on the elevator with her mother was quiet. They were on their way down to the lobby. Luca was expressionless as she thought about so many things. Where were Phaedra and Kool-Aid, and the rest of her crew? How come they never came to visit her in the hospital? She thought about Squirrel. She thought about her home and wondered about the condition of it. Also, how could she run her multi-million dollar drug empire in the state she was in? Her face was still a mess, her body fragile, and she was afraid that she'd lost everything. Luca wanted to rush to get home to get back to her business, pick up the pieces, and put her puzzle back together. She had come too far to lose everything now.

"I know you feel bad now, Luca, but everything will be okay."

"What is okay, Mother? Huh? Look at me. I feel like a fuckin' gimp," Luca said.

"No you're not, Luca, you're going to be just fine. Watch and see. Just thank God that you're still alive and you still have your freedom. That is all that matters."

Alive, yes, she was grateful to be alive, and having her freedom, yes. But if she didn't have her looks, her health, her crew and, most of all—Squirrel, then she might as well be dead.

Lucia continued talking to her daughter, encouraging her to dust off the pain and heartbreak and continue moving forward. But she wanted her daughter moving forward in the right direction.

"This is God giving you a second chance, Luca," her mother stated. "Take it."

Luca believed in second chances, but hers wasn't going to be used to become some spiritual or religious fanatic. Luca was a survivor, no matter what. She came up being bullied, laughed at, ridiculed, talked about, and tormented. And then almost overnight, she'd become a respected queenpin in the streets making millions of dollars and ordering contract hits on people. She was feared by most, in addition to achieving more success than all those who had laughed at and doubted her, even the late Naomi.

Thinking about Naomi put Luca's heart somewhere cold and distant. She had no remorse for murdering that girl. It took some time for Luca to understand that Naomi was never a true friend to her. Naomi liked to hang around Luca only to make herself look good. Who needed enemies when she had friends like that? It gave Luca insight though, never to trust anyone and not to quickly bring people into your inner circle. The only ones close to her were her mother, grandmother, and Phaedra.

Luca worried about Phaedra as her mother pushed her through the lobby and toward the exit. Phaedra had been her right-hand bitch since day one, but since the incident with Charter, she hadn't come around to visit her. It was told that she couldn't have any visitors because of the investigation against her, but Phaedra was that bitch that didn't care for rules and if she wanted to, she could have lied to come visit a friend in need.

"I had to park far, there ain't any spots around here, but I'll leave you in the lobby until I get the car," Lucia said to her daughter.

Luca didn't care. She was bundled up warmly in her sweater and winter coat. It was a chilling 32 degrees outside despite the sunshine. The wind was bone-cracking. It was early in the day and people moved briskly in the cold looking like Eskimos in their winter clothing, moving with their heads down, gloved hands nestled inside their pockets, trying to fight the frigid cold. It was the type of weather no one wanted to linger around outside in.

While Lucia rushed to get her Chevy hooptie, Luca was left alone near the glass lobby doors to wait. This was her low. She could barely move, and for a moment, she felt like her old self again, depending on someone to help her out. Luca sat in the wheelchair staring at the traffic coming in and out of the lobby. She didn't have her cell phone on her, so calling anybody was out of the question.

Twelve minutes passed, and finally her mother returned. She rushed inside the lobby, bringing the frigid cold with her. "I'm sorry it took me so long, Luca, things are crazy out there. Someone had me blocked in, and then it took a minute to get my car to start, and . . ."

Luca didn't pay her mother's reasons any attention. She just wanted to go home and recuperate. Lucia wheeled her daughter outside, and the cold instantly hit Luca like a hard smack to the face, bringing flashbacks of Charter's attack.

"Yeah, it's cold," Lucia uttered.

Luca suddenly froze up, but it wasn't because of the frostbite temperature outside, it was because she saw something that made her tremble slightly. She spotted her crazy and deranged cousin World standing across the street in only a hoodie and black jeans. It was definitely him; there was no mistaking it. He stood there like a statue, looking impervious to the cold. His presence was ominous and dark. Lucia didn't notice her nephew; only Luca saw him.

Luca and World glared at each other, but there was no exchange of words, only tension. Luca broke eye contact with him for a moment, hearing her mother say, "When we get home, I'll make you some hot chocolate." When Luca turned back his way, World was gone. He had disappeared abruptly like he was never there. His presence in Rockaway Park worried Luca greatly. It was a long way from Brooklyn. He was stalking her, and she understood that it was only a matter of time before she would have to deal with him. She owed him a lot, but wasn't ready to pay him anything. She had successfully avoided World since he came home after doing almost a bullet in Riker's Island right after he murdered Nate.

Luca knew what he wanted and why he was there in Rockaway Park. He wanted to extort money from her, and he also wanted Luca to buy him a Bentley Phantom so he could ride around the streets like he was Batman. Why was her cousin so obsessed with having a Phantom and wanting to be Batman? It was odd to her, but World had always been sixty cents short of a dollar. He had serious mental issues. He was a ticking time bomb, therefore Luca knew that sooner or later, he was going to become a serious problem—and problems from World were the last thing she needed in her life.

3

Luca insisted that her mother take her home. She didn't want to stay with her mother in Brooklyn; she wanted to be alone. Lucia tried to protest her daughter's request, stating that she was in no condition to be by herself, but Luca wasn't changing her mind. She had to get to her own home and survey the damage done there. She had to see what had happened to her supply, her money, and her guns.

"I need time alone, Mother, shit, to grieve for my lost baby. I'm going through a lot right now," Luca griped.

Lucia felt hesitant to leave her daughter's side, but Luca was adamant. There was a tiny confrontation, but at the end, Luca got her way. Her mother parked the Chevy hooptie in front of the posh Rockaway Park home where it was obvious that a crime had taken place, with the torn yellow police tape dangling from the porch and the place looking ransacked.

From the passenger seat, Luca stared at her lovely home that now haunted her with painful memories of the attack she'd experienced. She was strong and courageous, and in spite of what had happened inside, she wasn't going to be scared away from something she'd worked so hard to achieve, even though it was through illicit activity.

Luca moved with a crutch underneath her arm. Her mother helped her up the stairs onto the porch. Luca pulled away the remnants of crime scene tape from her porch with disgust and walked into the place. When they turned on the lights, it was evident that something was wrong in Luca's eyes. Her place was in shambles. Lucia was stunned at the sight.

"Ohmygod, Luca—you sure you want to stay here alone? Look at this place, it's a mess," Lucia stated.

Luca was enraged. If Charter wasn't dead, he would be after making her lose the baby that she'd hoped was Squirrel's and turning her home into a war zone. Luca and Lucia moved farther into the home and looked around. There was broken furniture, broken glass, and disarray everywhere. In the master bedroom, Luca gazed down at the bloodstained carpet and cringed.

The sight was haunting. Luca sighed.

"You okay?" her mother asked.

"I'm fine," Luca replied.

She was far from fine. Luca knew she could no longer live there. The stigma of a murder was just too strong to tolerate. The neighbors were gossiping about the domestic dispute and the murder of a cop, and they already had their preconceived notions about Luca. She was a young girl with a beautiful home and no job. How could she afford such a place? Her reputation in the affluent community was tarnished. Also, the fact that World was spotted in Rockaway Park made her worry and feel uncomfortable. How had he even found out where she lived? He was too close to home, and now it was time for Luca to dig up her roots and plant her seeds somewhere else.

Her main reason for going home was her stash. Luca faintly remembered being in the hidden room right before Charter assaulted her. She suspected that he might have closed the room before she shot him, since the cops never found the drugs. The one problem was that her mother was still lingering in the house, helping clean up. Luca didn't want to open the room in her mother's presence. Lucia was a changed woman, achieving a more spiritual level, talking about divine intervention. Luca didn't have time to hear about anything divine or intervention. She had other important priorities to take care of.

One, Luca had to get her mother to leave, and that took time. Lucia wasn't leaving until she was certain her daughter was fine and the house was cleaned and up to par. Lucia made her daughter some tea and soup, and then she tidied the bedroom. It took over four hours for Luca to get her mother to leave.

"I'm okay, Mother. I'm a grown woman. I don't need you babysitting me," Luca kept saying.

The minute Lucia left, Luca didn't hesitate to put in the code to her concealed room. She rushed inside to find the shock of her life.

The room was completely cleaned out.

Luca stood aghast, seeing all her drugs and money were gone. Everything she had worked so hard for had vanished into thin air. She couldn't help but panic. Luca could no longer stand—she dropped to her knees, teary-eyed, and felt her breathing shorten.

This couldn't be happening to her. She was thrust from one nightmare into another. The horror of falling into the pit of depression was too much to think about. Luca knew now wasn't the time to panic, but to find out who had stolen everything she had, and how. She rose from her knees and slowly in her injured state went through her entire house looking for her iPhone and other imperative electronics, but soon realized they weren't in her house and her DVR for her security system was gone.

Luca was infuriated. She wanted to see the footage of who robbed her, but there was nothing to view. It was at that moment that she knew she was dealing with a professional. Whoever robbed her wasn't leaving any stone unturned.

Luca was ready to wage war throughout the Tri-state area and God wouldn't be able to help those involved from her wrath.

4

"I s Brooklyn in the house?" the club DJ shouted though the microphone.
"Brook-lyn! Brook-lyn! Brook-lyn!" the crowd shouted back.

The Lemon Drop club was a seedy hole-in-the-wall spot that was packed to capacity on a Friday night. Clubbers moved to the latest hip-hop jams that DJ Kentucky threw on and downed cheap liquor like it was water. With wall-to-wall dudes grinding with the ladies in their scanty clothing and young hoods getting high throughout the club, it could never be confused with any upscale club in the city. The Lemon Drop was the bottom of the bottom, and anything and everything took place there, from drug dealing and drug use to prostitution and extortion.

While the people shouted out "Brooklyn!" and partied like it was New Year's Eve 1999, one particular hood moved through the club stoically with a dark hoodie draped over his head, concealing his identity. No one paid him any attention, like he was some invisible entity. Gangsters, thugs, whores, and drug dealers were prevalent in the place. Security was so lax that one wrong move into the wrong someone could set off a land mine and create a disaster. But a disaster is what Kool-Aid wanted to start. He had a motive. He was on a mission.

The crowd was thick and the music very loud. Kool-Aid was alone inside and felt no fear despite the many witnesses around. The men he glared at were also deadly and dangerous. They were seated at a corner table in the dimmed light, flanked by young hood rats getting drunk on Grey Goose and Hennessey.

Kool-Aid took a pull from the Newport between his lips, exhaled, and slyly watched his targets while being camouflaged by the many partygoers around him. He was cool but ready to stalk and then kill. Yeah, it was about to be on. Kool-Aid fixed his eyes on several men engaging themselves with whorish women, drugs, and liquor.

Since Luca had been hospitalized there had been talk on the street about her crew being weak and a hostile takeover in her Brooklyn area. Bad Girl heroin had been on the decline for a few weeks and eager, fledgling crews were waiting to step into the profitable territory and replace Bad Girl with something of their own.

Kool-Aid understood they had all worked too hard for muthafuckas to try and punk them. He had too much respect for Luca and the rest of his extended family to let anything happen to her and her empire. It pained him that she had been brutally beaten by her boyfriend. If she hadn't killed Charter herself, the nigga would have been a dead man anyway, cop or no cop.

Kool-Aid continued to watch their activity, lurking around the area like a vulture over a corpse. The one Kool-Aid wanted the most was a big-mouthed hotshot named Blade. There he was among his niggas, living it up with his crew like he was some Teflon Don. Kool-Aid was about to change up the elated atmosphere.

Blade had a big mouth that continually ran like diarrhea. He wouldn't stop slandering Luca's name in the hood. He perpetually called Luca a whore, a fraud, a dumb fuckin' bitch getting involved with grown-man business—he even threatened to pistol whip her. When word had gotten around that she was dating a cop, the character assassination intensified. Blade called her a snitch, a cop slut, and more. Kool-Aid warned him a handful of times to shut his big mouth about his boss, but Blade was too proud and arrogant to listen to the warning. Kool-Aid was only a kid in his eyes, and Blade didn't see him or anyone from Luca's crew as a viable threat.

Kiddie fuckin' gangsters is what he called them. He was a twenty-eight-year old hard-core thug coming from the roughest neighborhood, and he saw Kool-Aid as a cockroach underneath his shoe; easy to squash. However, he was about to learn the hard way to never underestimate anyone in the game. Kool-Aid was young, but he could kill like the best of them. Blade was just too stupid to know he had fucked with the wrong crew.

Kool-Aid kept cool. He had devised a plan. He removed a pack of loud fire crackers from his pocket and lit them like it was the Fourth of July. He tossed the firecrackers into the crowd and each one let off sounds like gunshots. The frightful sound echoed. Instantly, the crowd inside the club went berserk with full-blown panic. Screaming, pushing and shoving, and fleeing ensued. Kool-Aid's plan was working. While hordes of people rushed toward the exit, he removed the guns he loved carrying from out his hoodie; two chrome .9mms. The moment came while people's attention was diverted to finding safety; Kool-Aid went into action.

He catapulted his way toward his foes with his arms outstretched, looking like a gunslinger, and opened fire at the men by the table. They didn't even see him coming. The first few shots hit Blade's cousin. He went down rapidly. Kool-Aid moved with lightning speed and accuracy with both guns blazing in his hands. He loved doing this shit—killing. It was second nature to him.

Kool-Aid fired his two guns into the men repeatedly. His second victim went down fast with two shots to the head, and the third died quickly with a bullet slamming into his heart. The girls fled, the surrounding area transformed in turmoil, and Blade found himself dumbfounded. He was alone suddenly and gawked at the face of death, Kool-Aid. He scowled, knowing his time was up. Kool-Aid had him cornered and helpless, staring down the barrel of two pistols.

"Fuck you, nigga!" Blade screamed out.

Kool-Aid smirked, and then replied, "I warned you, bitch, to shut ya fuckin' mouth, right?"

It would be the last words Blade would hear. Kool-Aid fired, striking him multiple times in the head and chest, killing him instantly. He didn't even stay around to see the body fall. Kool-Aid was gone that fast, running toward the back exit and disappearing into the night. As long as he was alive, no one was going to ever slander Luca's name or his crew.

The message was undoubtedly sent.

5

The past two weeks had been essential to Luca. She was trying to regain her strength and re-strategize things in her life. Suffering a loss like that was heart-wrenching, and she remained holed up in her home like a hermit. She was devastated from the loss of her baby, the beating, and the robbery of her shit. She was a fan of playing chess and found herself in the checkmate position with no moves left.

Phaedra, Kool-Aid, Egypt, and Meeka were all worried about her. She ignored phone calls, stayed inside, and spoke to no one besides her grandmother and mother. Lucia was constantly coming by to check on her daughter regularly with food and medication. The trip from Brooklyn to Rockaway Park was long, and she even had to pay a toll, but well worth it for her daughter. Every day was hard and sad for Luca. Her injuries were healing, but not fast enough.

Luca stared at herself in the bathroom mirror. There were no signs of permanent damage on her face, but the indication of her being beaten still showed. It was hard to gaze at her reflection. It was difficult to remember, but she did. Luca would take her prescribed painkillers like she was popping Flintstones vitamins. It helped with her pain. But what would definitely help with her pain was being able to find out who was responsible for stealing her drugs and money and seeing them suffer.

With much time on her hands, Luca would lie in bed and come up with a million and one ways to torture and then kill the people who stole from her. She made up a list of potential suspects, even in her own camp, from Phaedra down to Kool-Aid. Someone was guilty, and someone had to pay. When she had access to her mother's phone, Luca logged into her online account to watch the footage, but she had the shock of her life: The footage stopped the day before the crime happened. It was frustrating; nothing was going right for her at all. She swore she would have the culprit or culprits dead to rights, but the joke was on her. In her mind, there had to be a mastermind out there beating her at her own game.

The heartache came when she tried to call Squirrel; his phone had been disconnected, and she had no other way of contacting him. She only wanted to hear his voice. She wanted him to care, come by and be with her, help her with her recovery. But that was unlikely. Squirrel had made it clear that he didn't want anything to do with her after she caused Angel to lose her baby.

In her dark bedroom, with the door shut and silence, Luca sobbed like she never sobbed before. Luca craved solitude—but too much solitude could be detrimental. Her crying bounced around the room as she nestled in the queen-size bed, underneath the covers, naked and shaking from the pain of defeat. With no evidence, no suspects, no drugs, no money, and no luck, her next move felt almost impossible.

There was a minor moment, after midnight, after a river of tears had run down her cheeks and her mind was spent from thinking too much, where she thought about killing herself. Maybe she could overdose on pills or cut her wrists in the tub or hang herself somewhere. Or what about a bullet to her head? Whatever method she decided, she just wanted to leave the world suddenly. It was too embarrassing to revert back to her old self again, when she was no one. She would be looked down on, bullied, and ridiculed on the regular. Luca loved the name and the power she had on the streets. It was intoxicating to have people look up to you and respect you, to make millions of dollars, and with the snap of your fingers, have people killed effortlessly.

It couldn't be all over—not now, not ever. She had an addiction to the lifestyle, and it spread like a virus inside of her. Luca cried herself to sleep and wanted to be alone for a long time.

✳✳✳

The next morning, her mother came to visit, as usual. Lucia stormed into Luca's bedroom and snatched the covers off her grieving and heartbroken daughter and cursed, "Luca, get your ass up. What, you expect to just lie there and die?"

Luca regretted giving her mother a key to her home. Now the bitch was coming and going as she pleased. Luca didn't respond. She remained glued to the bed, naked and silent.

"Luca!" Lucia shouted out.

"Just leave me alone," Luca returned.

"No, you're better than this. What is wrong with you? I'm here to help you get through this, but I can't help you if you don't want to help yourself," Lucia barked.

"It's all over for me," Luca muttered.

Lucia sighed heavily. She opened the windows for some cold fresh air, and had brought her daughter some fresh flowers to lighten her mood. She gazed at Luca lying in bed in the fetal position. There were minor bruises still showing on her body, but she was still beautiful.

Lucia sat by her daughter's side. It was hard seeing her own flesh and blood going through adversity. She took Luca's hand in hers, closed her eyes, lowered her head, and began praying for her daughter's immediate recovery. It was a slump hard to witness. The last thing Lucia wanted her daughter to do was fall into depression. The women in her family were always strong, been through hell and back, and though Luca had her weakness and flaws growing up, she had blossomed into her own and was able to say, "Look at me now!"

Lucia wasn't a fool though; she knew her daughter was mixed up in the drug game, and because she had once lived and experienced that lifestyle, Lucia wanted to be there as guidance for her daughter. She learned about the men in her life, and one particular name she heard Luca say in passing was Squirrel. It didn't take a rocket scientist to understand this Squirrel had Luca's heart. Love was a dangerous emotion. So many women had loved a man so strongly at one point in their life that it swallowed them up whole and made them go crazy. Lucia recognized not to ever let what a man brings to the table be all you have to eat.

The sad truth was that there are some people who will only be there for you as long as you have something they need. When you no longer serve a purpose to them, they will leave. Luca had to tough it out and weed the bad people out of her life. Her mother was going to help her.

"I'm going to give you some time to yourself, Luca," said Lucia. "But I'm here for you."

Lucia left the bedroom and started cleaning the house again. She even hired a carpet cleaning company to take care of the bloodstains on the rug, but they were too tough to get completely out, so Lucia eventually covered them up with throw rugs and planned on getting her daughter new carpet. In the kitchen, she made some hot chicken noodle soup for her daughter and really tried to establish their mother-daughter relationship, something they never had.

Lucia slowly fed her daughter the chicken noodle soup, which Luca devoured. And then Lucia brushed her daughter's hair tenderly and talked to her.

"Where you are right now, Luca, I already been there too many times in my life, and it never gets easier. I hate to see you like this, it hurts me," said Lucia with a long breath out. "But what hurts me more, is the mistakes I made in my past, especially with you. I smoked crack while I was pregnant with you. Before you were born, I was already neglecting your health and being selfish because I wanted to feel good, and every single day I hate myself for it. I just wasn't there when you needed me, and I know I haven't been the best mother to you, and I'm so sorry. I was caught up in that world—drug addiction, prostitution, going in and out of prison, and scheming just to make a dollar and never had time to raise my own daughter. I put the world first; I put boyfriends, the streets, and my drug use before my own child. I still carry the scars inside of me. I still feel that stigma everywhere I go despite the changes I've made in my life.

"I just don't want you making the same mistakes, Luca. I don't want you chasing behind these bad boys that will only bring you down and ruin your life. They're not worth it. You're a beautiful and very intelligent woman, Luca—you always have been—and this world you think is glamorous, the drug dealing, the money, the reputation, it's only transient."

Luca listened to her mother speak. She didn't reply. She lay in bed hearing her mother's voice and advice seep through her. For some reason, it felt good to hear her mother confess her past to her. Luca always grew up feeling alone and ugly. In reality, the motherly love was what Luca needed. She turned to peer up at her smiling mother. "Who was the man that you loved with all of your heart?" Luca asked.

"Easy, it was your father," Lucia mentioned.

"Really?"

Lucia smiled, thinking about the man. "Yes."

Lucia never spoke about Luca's father to her. She always kept that part of her life silent. Luca never knew her father and only heard fragments about him while growing up, but today, she needed to know something about him. She wanted her mind to drift somewhere else, something to take her away from the pain and sorrow that swamped her life. The only thing she knew about her father, whose name was Travis Roy, was that he was a very smart man who had a bright future ahead of him. Now he was doing life in Clinton Correctional facility in upstate New York. He had murdered a man.

Lucia gazed at her daughter. Luca was waiting to hear the story.

"I met him when I was sixteen. He was such a handsome man; tall, well-built with dark skin and curly hair, and was always dressed sharply. He had hazel eyes and an alluring smile," Lucia stated.

Lucia held her daughter in her arms while speaking, and Luca gazed up at her mother like she was a young girl again. Luca couldn't remember a time when her mother held her at nights and told her bedtime stories to put her to sleep. It felt like this was going to be her first bedtime story at twenty-something years old. Luca didn't care; she always wanted loving parents in her life, a mother and a father, someone to protect her when the world became too cold and the bullies seemed to be everywhere. She only had her grandmother, which wasn't enough.

Lucia continued on with her story. "We met at a house party. Back then, they used to be the shit. He stood with his friends and I stood with my friends, and I had caught his attention. You should have seen your mother back then, Luca. I was nothing to be played with. A curvy figure, a nice booty, long hair, and these girls today couldn't hold a candle to me back then."

"You're still beautiful now," Luca said.

Her mother smiled.

"But your father was the finest thing in the room, all the girls wanted him, but he was looking at me. I was hanging with a bunch of wild girls and we called ourselves, the Pussy Pack—"

"The Pussy Pack?" Luca repeated with a raised eyebrow.

"Hey, we were young and the only thing we had that was gold was our pussies, and all the boys wanted to play in our backyards. There wasn't one ugly girl in our clique, we made sure of that, but your mother was the baddest bitch," she said proudly.

Luca smiled. All of a sudden she felt like a twelve-year-old little girl sitting up late listening to her mother's tales instead of a murderous drug queenpin with a tainted past. This was what she wanted while growing up, a normal childhood with her mother. But not everyone was always dealt a good hand in life.

"And your father, Travis, he couldn't take his eyes off of me. It took at least fifteen minutes for him to get up the courage to come over to speak, and when he broke away from his friends and came my way, I felt so excited, but then Daniel Crocker tried to intervene. He was this neighborhood tough guy that had this crush on me, but I didn't like him. He was a thug and everyone was scared of him. I was sure your father was going to turn away and mind his business. Surprisingly, he didn't. Like a warrior, he continued marching my way, then tapped Daniel on his shoulder and said to him, *'Yo, my man, I think she was waiting for me.'* He glared at Daniel with no fear. Right then and there, I fell in love with him.

"The two got into a heated argument over me. Daniel was taller, but your father didn't back down. They didn't fight; I guess the look in your father's eyes said he would kill someone over me, and that night, he probably would have. Well, we talked and laughed, and what attracted me to your father even more, was he was so smart. He knew things that were far out of this world. He recited poetry to me. He gave me black history lessons. He always told me I was beautiful. He charmed my panties off and we had sex that night. Yeah, I was fast back then, and it didn't take long for me to become pregnant with you. I was in love with him and I thought our fairytale would never end, because I was truly happy with your father.

"But life happens and reality replaces the fairytale daydream. When you were born, things got really rough. Travis wasn't working. I wasn't working. We both got hooked on crack, and our lives spiraled downhill from there. I was terrible back then, crazy, and didn't care at all. It was always about having a good time and living day by day no matter what."

"Who did my father murder?" Luca asked.

Lucia knew the question was inevitable. She remained silent for a moment, looking nostalgic. She held Luca's hand and said, "Your father, he was a very jealous man, and no matter how bad I became or looked, he was still in love with me and wanted nobody to have me. But crack became more important to me than anything else, and I did whatever I needed to do to make sure I got high."

Lucia exhaled. She hated to relive her past, but she continued.

"Well one day, there was this young hustler named Tucker, very attractive, had money, had drugs and despite my condition, he took a liking to me. I was a crackhead, but I wasn't a waste like so many became. I still had my beauty and shape; I was just down and out. Tucker, he was one nasty muthafucka—a damn freak. He got off by taunting the young fiends in the neighborhood. He had what we wanted, drugs, and we had what he wanted, sex. He would make the girls suck his dick for hours, sometimes in front of his friends, and then share the girls with his crew. He loved the girls. He loved pussy, and he loved embarrassing and torturing some of the girls when he had the chance. He liked to burn bitches with irons and hot combs, or beat them, and as fiends, we tolerated it.

"He liked me, though. He craved me, and when I was at my low, I would succumb to some of his twisted desires."

Lucia paused for a moment, remembering the horrors as if it were yesterday. Her eyes became watery, her mood somber. She went on with, "You have to remember, Luca, I was a different person back then. The only thing I had on my mind was getting high. So one day, I'm in his house, and I'm butt-naked in front of all his homeboys, and each of them had this lewd grin aimed at me. They had their pants around their ankles, dicks in their hands, and were ready to have their way with me. Tucker promised me an eight ball after the show. So I did what I had to do for that eight ball, I fucked every guy in that room for hours. They did things to me that no one could imagine. I became their personal sex slave for a damn eight ball. And then when they were done with me, Tucker beat me just for his own personal enjoyment and I was tossed out like trash.

"Your father found out about it and he went berserk. I didn't know it, but he bought a gun and went hunting for Tucker for days. He finally found Tucker in his car with a young woman. He went crazy and rushed the car and emptied the entire clip into Tucker, shooting him eleven times. He was arrested right there on the spot. You were only two years old when it happened."

Luca knew it was a painful memory. She finally heard the story, and hearing about the love between her father and her mother made an impression on her. She wanted that same love with Squirrel.

"We all make mistakes, sometimes over and over again, but it's what we learn from making our mistakes that turns us into better people," Lucia stated.

They continued talking. Luca opened up for advice about a few things and confessed that she loved Squirrel more than she loved her deceased boyfriend, Nate.

"Why?" her mother asked.

"He's just different. He's exciting," Luca said.

"But he's already taken, Luca. Why do you want a man that someone else has?"

"Because I do. I love him a lot, and I know he loves me."

Love should have been the furthest thing from Luca's mind. She still didn't understand how money and drugs just walked away from a room without a trace. She felt that it was highly unlikely that any of the first responders on the scene took it. It was just too much stuff to walk out the door with in a duffel bag.

The gnawing feeling that one of her underlings robbed her wouldn't leave. It played over and over again in her head like a bad movie. She couldn't shake that eerie feeling of betrayal. And it was now time to get to the bottom of the problem and expose the truth. It was time to call a meeting with her peoples and see who was lying and then dying.

***

The second body for Kool-Aid came two weeks after the Blade hit. A stickup kid and drug dealer named Vincent Perry took it upon himself to push an inferior product stamped Bad Girl on the streets of Brooklyn. It was far from the potent heroin the customers were used to receiving, and Bad Girl's brand was plummeting.

When Phaedra and Kool-Aid got word of this, they were incensed. Vincent Perry was fucking with their upscale reputation by peddling his bootleg heroin with their infamous brand name attached to it, and something needed to be done about it.

Vincent was a goon with no problem implementing violence to prove his point. He was notorious on the streets of Brooklyn for sticking up well-known drug dealers and carrying out hits for the Blood gang, and recently decided to dabble in the drug business. He was considered the type of fool to take from the rich and give back to the poor, but he was about getting rich by any means necessary. He got his product from the Colombians in Washington Heights and brainstormed up the idea to name it Bad Girl, knowing once the name was out on the streets again it would sell like crazy, turning a profit of hundreds of thousands of dollars, even though he stepped on it several times.

Vincent was known to always be heavily armed, carrying no less than two guns on him at a time, and he was putting together a small yet violent crew to help him push his product. Kool-Aid yearned to put a stop to it. There was only one organization that had the right to sell Bad Girl, and any kind of infringement or fraudulent product meant death.

Kool-Aid hit the streets trying to find this Vincent Perry. He made it known through the grapevine that he was looking for him, and once Kool-Aid found the muthafucka, it wasn't going to be pretty.

Soldiers on both ends tooled up for war. With Luca out of sight and out of commission, someone had to hold down the fort.

A few shootouts between the crews ensued, and Brooklyn was hot. Vincent Perry was a force that was hard to bring down, but Kool-Aid was determined. He and some goons would hit the streets night after night, searching for the problem and anxious to eradicate the threat. The longer the fraudulent Bad Girl stayed on the streets, the weaker the real Bad Girl's reputation became. And it wouldn't take long before customers moved on to a more potent product.

After two weeks on the hunt, Kool-Aid got his chance when he stumbled unto Vincent Perry picking up an attractive prostitute on the corner of Pennsylvania Avenue and Dumont. It was well known that Vincent Perry had a thing for young whores and liked to get his dick sucked while reclined in the front passenger seat.

He was in a black-on-black E-class Benz, draped in jewelry and eager to bust his nut into the whore's mouth. From a few cars away, Little Goon—one of Kool-Aid's henchmen, with a good eye and accurate memory—spotted Vincent's Benz turning the corner in the desolate area of Brooklyn.

"There that nigga go right there," Little Goon had pointed out.

Kool-Aid gazed keenly at the Benz passing from the opposite direction. He uttered, "Bingo," and got ready to take action.

They watched the leggy teenage prostitute clad in a short skirt exposing her thick thighs in the winter cold and high heels with a bright yellow bubble coat climb into the front seat of the Benz. The car pulled away from the curb, Kool-Aid, being behind the wheel of a Dodge Caliber, an inconspicuous vehicle, followed his target.

After several turns and a few blocks later, the Benz unobtrusively parked down a dark alleyway. Vincent paid the young whore her fifty-dollar fee, unzipped his jeans, pulled out his hard and average-size dick, and waited for her lips to bless his shit. For safety measures, he wrapped his hand around a loaded .45 and kept it near and visible.

"Go ahead bitch, start suckin' my dick," he gruffly said.

The pretty whore leaned into his lap, palmed his dick and slowly wrapped her full, glossy lips around the mushroom tip and started sucking him off. Vincent Perry groaned and closed his eyes from the overwhelming pleasure. He gripped the .45 loosely, thinking more about busting a nut than any lurking danger. Pussy was making him slip. It was one of his weaknesses.

As the prostitute's head went up and down in the driver's seat, her lips coaxing the cum from his balls while Vincent got lost in the fleeting moment. His Benz was angled in the alleyway where he was able to see anyone coming in the one direction—one way in and one way out. Behind his vehicle was a towering brick wall that supported the passing train tracks and a slew of Dumpsters and debris.

"Oh shit, damn, that feels good. Ooooh yeah, suck that dick. I got a li'l sumthin extra for you if you make me cum real good," Vincent said.

She made sure to give him the best blow job of his life, deep throat, licking and sucking his balls while jerking him off, willing to swallow his babies.

At the other end of the alleyway, Kool-Aid and Little Goon were parked and waiting. It was too risky for them to run up on Vincent. He would have the advantage, being nestled too deep from the entryway, and one slipup could cost them their own lives. Vincent Perry was a shoot-first type of nigga, no questions asked later. So their only option was to wait until he finished with his nut and catch him driving out. By then, his guard would be down and Kool-Aid could catch the nigga slipping.

A half hour went by. The two killers stood lingering by the entrance to the alleyway with several automatics on them. Kool-Aid wanted it to be messy. He wanted a strong statement sent out, and he wasn't about to miss his shot. They heard the ignition to the Benz start up, indicating Vincent Perry was done sexing the bitch. Kool-Aid rushed into action, throwing up the lift to the Caliber and removing a black Uzi.

He looked at Little Goon.

"What about the bitch?" Little Goon asked.

Coldly, Kool-Aid responded, "Fuck it. Casualties of war."

The E-class Benz slowly emerged from the dark alleyway. It was a cold night, and that industrial part of Brooklyn was desolate of any traffic, cops, and residents. When the nose of the Benz came into Kool-Aid's view, there was no hesitation. He and Little Goon opened fire. The bullets tore into the vehicle. Glass shattered, the prostitute screamed, and the engine revved loudly. Under attack, Vincent pressed down on the accelerator and thrust forward, away from the danger. He was suddenly inundated with heavy gunfire. His pistol fell from his reach. He cursed heatedly. His attempt to escape from the danger was unsuccessful. The blaring Uzi screaming from Kool-Aid's hands was just too powerful and sent him and his passenger into a full-blown panic.

The Benz careened off the road and hit a utility pole. The front end was smashed around the pole. Kool-Aid and Little Goon ran forward and continued to spray the vehicle with a hail of bullets. Vincent and the prostitute jerked violently from the blaze of bullets tearing into their bodies. Blood splattered everywhere. Kool-Aid glared at the body slumped over the steering wheel, Vincent's brains on the dashboard. The prostitute suffered the same ghastly fate: She was lifeless in the passenger seat, her head smashed against the window, her eyes wide open.

The threat had been neutralized. The message sent.

Kool-Aid and Little Goon ran back to the car and sped away. Kool-Aid was pleased with the outcome. He couldn't wait to inform Luca about the work he'd put in to keep her empire alive and her name from being slandered.

He called Phaedra to give her an update. When she picked up, the first thing Phaedra said to him was, "Luca called me, and she wants us to meet. She sounds upset about something."

"About what?"

"I don't know, but she wants all of us to meet at her place in Rockaway Park. It sounds important," Phaedra stated.

"A'ight, I'm there," Kool-Aid said.

6

Day by day, Luca regained her strength and was becoming her old self again. Her wounds, physical and mental, were healing with a big help from her mother. Lucia became her biggest supporter and motivator. Lucia tried to encourage her daughter to move into a different direction and away from that treacherous lifestyle. Luca had plenty of time to think about things—and giving up was the last thing on her mind. She couldn't stay around the house moping and crying over spilt milk. It was time to go back to the grocery store and get a bigger gallon, maybe more groceries. Several weeks had passed since the incident with Charter. The investigation against her was closed, deemed justifiable homicide, but now she was ready to do her own investigation. With millions of dollars in drugs gone and millions in cash missing, it wasn't anything to sneeze at. People needed to die and die fast. Luca's heart was colder than before.

It was time to call an emergency meeting with Murder Inc. and resolve some critical issues. She had spent too much time away from her crew and the streets. Phaedra was the first person Luca contacted, and her right hand bitch was elated to finally hear from her. But on the phone, Luca wasn't as cheery.

"I want you to contact everyone for a meeting at my home, Phaedra," Luca sternly said.

"No problem, I'm on it, Luca," Phaedra replied. "It's good to hear from you again. We were worried about you."

"No need to worry. I'm a grown woman, Phaedra," Luca returned with aloofness in her tone.

"I know, but things haven't been the same without you," said Phaedra.

Luca didn't have time for small talk. She was only concerned about finding her product, questioning her crew, and then murdering muthafuckas. She didn't trust anyone. In her eyes, everyone had the potential to set you up and let you down, from Squirrel to Charter. And when it came to greed, anything was possible.

Detective Charter tried to break her in her own home, but he couldn't. Before, she had been young and naïve, but due to her intelligence and her cleverness, she quickly climbed the ladder in the drug trade and became a force to be reckoned with.

It's a new day, Luca said to herself—*a new and improved me. Fool me once, shame on you, fool me twice, shame on you and all those you love.*

The next day, Phaedra, Kool-Aid, Egypt, and Meeka sat around her modern dining room table looking like a council. It wasn't the welcome they all expected from Luca. She walked into the room with a cold chill in her eyes. No smiles, no explanations. It was strictly down to business. Everyone sat in silence, feeling the tension. Instantly, they saw and felt the change in her.

Before she spoke, Luca glared into the eyes of each and every one of her peoples. Clad in all black, she was irritable and annoyed.

"A lot has happened to me in this world that has me questioning what's real and what's surreal. Our lives are only a small spec on the map of eternity. Life is a vapor that can dissipate in a nanosecond. Whether we're careful or not, we die. Knowing what I know and what I've been through, it behooves me to say that my heart has now imploded."

The sudden crazy testimony coming from Luca flew right over her crew's heads. They were dumbfounded by the sharp statement. They all had street smarts, not book smarts. Fortunately for Luca, she had developed both.

"What are you sayin'?" Phaedra asked.

"We supposed to be a family, right? When I found you all, y'all had nothing, but because of me, we gained everything," Luca continued. She circled the table, walking heavily around her subordinates and scowling like she'd sucked on a rotten lemon. "So who in this room would have the fuckin' audacity to steal from me, when I gave y'all everything?"

It was blunt and to the point. Her peoples were stunned. The accusation against them was harsh. Luca continued circling the table and stopped behind Phaedra. She placed her right hand on her friend's shoulder and pushed down slightly. "The way I see it, no outsider would have known about the contents of that room. The only ones that knew about it are the ones seated in this room. And the only outsider that stumbled across it is now dead. So since I've been in this house healing, I've been doing a lot of thinking. Why none of y'all came to visit me in the hospital?"

Phaedra sat still and stoic. Luca wanted an answer.

"We tried to come visit you, Luca, but you were heavily guarded, and police were everywhere," Phaedra spoke up.

"I find that bullshit, Phaedra!" Luca shouted. In her fragile mind, she felt that if the shoe was on the other foot, she would have found some way to come visit any one of her peoples in the hospital. She felt rejected. But being visited in the hospital was the least of her worries.

She went on to gripe about how everything she worked so hard for was gone. She accused them of being thieves and disloyal to the organization. Phaedra grimaced heavily at the accusations.

"This is bullshit, Luca, and you know it!" Phaedra exclaimed.

"What?"

"Out of all people, you blame us; especially me. I would die for you, Luca, and you know this. You are my sister, the one I never had, and after everything you did for me, you think I would take from you?" Phaedra exclaimed.

The two locked eyes and glared at each other.

"Luca, I'm out there every day bodying muthafuckas and keeping your name strong, making sure everything was on point when you got out the hospital," Kool-Aid chimed in with zeal. "Niggas that came out their mouth sideways about you, best believe they ain't talkin' anymore, and muthafuckas that tried to bootleg our product, they taking permanent dirt naps for their transgressions against this organization."

Luca looked into the faces of her crew. Her mind was running rampant. She was desperate to find out the truth.

"Anyone could have come in here and stole from you, Luca," Phaedra said. "You were in a coma for four days, cops in and out of your home, paramedics—"

"Neighbors, too. Who the fuck knows who came up here being nosy and who was watching you on the down low?" Kool-Aid offered the possibility. "Just because they're white, don't mean they're right."

"He's right, Luca," Meeka added. "It could be anyone."

"And Charter, you're a hundred percent sure he's dead, right? No conspiracy with the police investigating you? Cuz lots of money, and lots of drugs, could tempt anyone to go corrupt," Kool-Aid mentioned.

They all had Luca thinking. "I'm sure that bastard is dead," she uttered.

"What do you remember after you shot that muthafucka?" Phaedra asked.

She couldn't remember anything. Then Kool-Aid asked the million-dollar question.

"Who the fuck called 911? Now that's the nigga you need to be talkin' to, and the nigga I need to get at."

Luca knew he was right. Who had called 911? Was Walter Charter even dead? Had she actually hit him with the bullets? She was dazed and confused. Maybe she imagined killing him. And did the NYPD pull off some elaborate hoax to conceal their wrong—raid her home and steal her shit? She knew anything was possible.

Everyone was conjecturing some sort of conspiracy theory that involved everyone from the police department down to the neighbors. Nothing was too farfetched. Luca started to relax more, beginning to believe that her crew didn't snake her. The loyalty they showed was comforting. How could she doubt them? With Phaedra and a handful of killers at her beck and call, Luca was in full mode to start investigating the detectives who had investigated her, including the EMS workers that had come into her home; Charter, to confirm that he was not pulling off a Machiavelli by faking his own death; and the neighbors.

With her council by her side, she drafted a hit list of potential suspects, and whoever didn't check out innocent was dead. Kool-Aid was ready to wage war against the police and all of New York. He had already started by killing Blade and Vincent Perry, now it was time to extend his wrath. In the meantime, Luca needed heroin so she could generate money and get back on her feet, and her only source was Squirrel.

Whoever had robbed her came off with millions in product, millions in cash, and a treasure trove of guns. She was worse off now than when Nate was murdered. When Nate died, she had money and drugs to build off of; now she had nothing but her reputation, and she was flat broke. There was no packing up and leaving her rental home that now hosted the horrible memory of her being brutally beaten and almost killed.

"We starving out there, Luca," Phaedra blurted out, crying broke. "We need to do something. Kool-Aid is out there holding the fort down, but without any work, we can't push away the wolves for too long."

"She's right," Kool-Aid chimed in. "It's drying up out there, and crews are coming in the droves tryin' to stamp their weak-ass shit wit' the Bad Girl logo."

"Do you have a new connect or sumthin'?" Meeka asked.

Luca knew she needed to do something and do it fast. She was barely holding onto hers and felt her reputation and lifestyle pulling away from her. The look in her people's eyes showed they were desperate to do anything. None of them had any savings plan, nor did they know how to budget their money and save it for a rainy day. They spent their fortune as soon as they earned it. They never predicted it would come crashing around them. The day Charter beat up Luca was the day the troubles started.

Luca needed to regroup.

She needed to think and get her priorities back in order. She had several eager young faces looking up to her, respecting her and waiting for further instructions. It was her move on the chessboard. She was the queen—dominant, powerful, able to go anywhere on the chessboard without any restrictions.

"I'll make something happen, I promise y'all that. However, in the meantime, I want y'all to be on the lookout and on the hunt," she commanded. "I want ears on the streets everywhere. There were a lot of drugs taken out of that room, so that means someone's going to be eager to move it, and probably move it fast."

Everyone nodded.

Luca continued, "This isn't the end of us, just a minor setback. Y'all understand me?"

"We definitely understand you, Luca," replied Kool-Aid with a nod.

"Good. We put together a list, and everyone, and I do mean everyone gets profoundly interrogated, I don't care who the fuck they are, from the police captain on down. Muthafuckas take from me, they get their life snatched away from them."

"We on it," everyone said simultaneously.

She dismissed the meeting and everyone stood up to leave the room.

"Phaedra, stay behind. I need to talk to you," Luca said.

Phaedra nodded.

Luca shut the door, giving them some privacy. She then looked at Phaedra and said, "I'm sorry about the way I came at you. I got a lot on my mind."

"It's cool, Luca. You went through hell these past few weeks," Phaedra calmly replied.

"I trust you. You've been by my side since day one, and there's no reason I should have doubted you."

"Luca, after everything you did for me—from helping me with my situation in the Simpsons' home and removing that asshole from my life, and making me somebody in this world when I was a nobody. I will never forget that and will be by your side until the day I die. You are my sister, Luca, and I would go to hell for you," Phaedra declared with tears streaming from her eyes.

Phaedra's statement warmed Luca's heart. Her words were reassuring and earnest. Luca nodded and smiled. "You and I, together, we will definitely own this fuckin' city," said Luca.

"We will."

The two ladies hugged each other in private, showing their affection and admitting their devotion. The way Luca placed her arms around Phaedra; it was such a strong welcoming for Phaedra, she didn't want to release herself from her friend's arms. She was in love with Luca, but kept her feelings a secret.

That evening, both friends talked with normalcy. It wasn't about drugs, killings, the streets, or millions, but about life, the future, and love. Luca felt fortunate to have a friend like Phaedra in her life, and there was no replacing her.

7

The cocaine-colored BMW traveled across the Brooklyn Bridge in the heart of the evening rush hour pouring in and out of the city. Traffic on the bridge was a nightmare—a parking lot from Brooklyn into Manhattan. The cold evening wind whisked against the bridge. Luca sat comfortably in the backseat of her Beamer reading the latest issue of *Fortune 500* while Phaedra drove her to see her attorney, Dominic Sirocco. Luca had to see about some investments she made. Money was tight and she figured one of her investments needed to pay off.

Luca wore dark shades to cover her puffy eyes and a long, blue wig to appear like her natural self. The last thing she needed was anyone asking questions. She just wanted to focus on business.

It took a staggering forty minutes to cross the bridge and arrive in lower Manhattan. Traffic was heavy all over, but Phaedra maneuvered the BMW through the streets of Manhattan like a professional. It was almost sunset when they pulled up to the towering glass building on the west side of town. Phaedra parked out front and remained behind the wheel while Luca exited the car and walked into the soaring chalice of a building just blocks away from the newly constructed Freedom Tower.

She hurried through the fulsome lobby and took the elevator to the eighteenth floor. Luca walked into her attorney's office with business heavy on her mind. Dominic Sirocco sat in his high-back leather chair with a picturesque view of the Hudson River and the New Jersey skyline via floor-to-ceiling windows.

"I need to cash out on some of my investments, Dominic," Luca said to him. "I need some quick cash. Liquidate something."

The look Dominic gave back indicated things weren't going to be that feasible. "Luca, it doesn't work as easily as that."

"What do you mean? It's my money, I made some legitimate investments, and I want to cash out on it right now." Luca sounded desperate.

"Luca, you do get dividend checks quarterly and you could use those checks to either reinvest in other stocks, mutual funds, bonds, gold or other supplementary things, but right now, things are tied and it's late," Dominic said to her.

"Look, I'm in a serious bind right now. I tried to transfer some of the money from the overseas accounts you had set up for me, but the passwords aren't working," Luca explained to him.

"Those offshore accounts have a minimum of twenty-four months to mature before anyone can begin making withdrawals."

"You got to be fuckin' with me!" Luca barked, almost going berserk in his office. It was the most ridiculous thing she had ever heard.

"Let me remind you, Luca, I told you all about this since day one when you came into my office with a duffel bag filled with money. You were a high-risk customer. Laundering your money was going to take time, and a profitable return wasn't going to happen overnight. And this desperation in trying to expedite any of your money from any accounts, offshore or inland, it will raise red flags with not just the IRS, but the feds too," Dominic reprimanded.

Luca couldn't remember what was said to her during their first meeting. It was hard to think rationally when she had so much going on.

Her beating caused a few memories to go sketchy, but she was sure she couldn't have fallen for such foolishness.

"Luca, you are a very smart girl and I always had respect for you—"

"If you had respect for me, then you would get me my money when I need it and stop bullshitting me."

Dominic tilted back in his expensive leather chair and clasped his hands together while trying to talk some sense into one of his lucrative clients. He tried to be all smiles with nice words and gestures, but Luca started not to trust him. It was hard to trust anyone. First, millions of drugs and cash were taken out of her home, and now her attorney was telling her that there was going to be a lot of red tape involved in trying to cash out one of her investments.

Dominic sighed. "Look, the most I can do for you at the moment is move around a couple annuities and you should be able to receive a check in the mail in a week or so. But it won't be much, maybe fifteen, twenty thousand."

It wasn't quite the news she wanted to hear—fifteen, twenty thousand in a week or two was peanuts. She needed twice or triple that to remain functioning on the streets and keeping up with her bills.

Frustrated with the news from her attorney, Luca excused herself from his office, fuming. She had nothing else to say to him. She needed to make other arrangements and climb her way out of the difficulty she was thrust into.

Luca stormed out of the building and jumped back into her BMW. Phaedra saw the look on her friend's face and knew that things had not gone too well with the meeting with her attorney. It was none of her business, so Phaedra didn't ask any questions.

"Just take me back the fuck home, Phaedra," Luca commanded.

Phaedra nodded and started the ignition. Luca sat slumped in the backseat, gazing out the window, watching the city pass her by and feeling her life spiraling out of control. She tried not to look defeated, but today, she was. Today, it felt like the world was coming against her.

* * *

The soothing warm shower cascaded down on Luca in her rich bathroom. It was the only comforting thing in her life at the moment. The water cleansed her body, and she wished it could cleanse away her pain and troubles, too. Under the showerhead, Luca sighed heavily with her mind going on about so many things and so many occurring problems. How could she be broke? She was smarter than the average man, and she made all the proper provisions to not succumb to this type of situation. The investments she made, the product she distributes, her tight knit crew, her connections and other things, it all seemed to gone to hell overnight.

Luca planted her hands against the wall, lowered her head, and exhaled. She then folded her fingers into a tight fist and, without warning, punched the wall in front of her. She hit it repeatedly as tears trickled from her eyes. Angry and furious was an understatement of how she felt.

She cried in the privacy of her home and lingered in the shower for an hour, washing herself, her tears mixing with the soothing shower water. Luca stepped out and toweled off, staring at her image in the mirror. Even though she had Phaedra and Kool-Aid by her side, as well as her mother and grandmother, for some reason she felt alone. What could get her mind away from the pain and loneliness? There were some days where Luca felt the urge to sample her own product, just a taste to see what all the fuss was about. Her clientele went bananas over Bad Girl. Escapism was what she was thinking about.

Luca wanted to block out her problems, and the thought of getting high off her own supply scared her. It was tempting, but she had to be the better woman—becoming a drug addict wasn't becoming a better woman but a damn fool. She wanted to continue getting rich off of drug dealing, not let it bring her down even more.

Luca moved from the bathroom into the bedroom, butt-naked and frowning heavily. She had money on her mind thinking about the measly fifteen to twenty thousand her lawyer promised to arrive in a check sometime next week. Her woman's intuition said somebody was playing her. When she got near her bed, she felt a sudden ominous presence behind her. She spun on her heels and caught the shock of her life. Luca staggered backwards, screaming out, "What the fuck!"

It was World unexpectedly standing in her bedroom. He was alone and gazing at Luca's naked body like she was fully dressed. His eyes didn't show a hint of any sexual interest. He just stood looking blankly at her.

"Hey cuz," World greeted with a low drawl.

He was clad in all black, his hood draped over his head, looking sadistic. His stint in jail had made him more muscular. He didn't have a weapon in his hand, but that didn't mean he didn't have a pistol on his person. It was probably concealed.

"World, how the fuck did you get into my home?" Luca shouted. She looked around her bedroom for a weapon to protect herself, but nothing useful was in sight; besides, World had the advantage. She was helpless.

"Cuz, you ain't gotta worry about that. What you need to be worried about is my money and the car you owe me," World said.

Luca grabbed the long robe off the back of the chair and quickly donned it. World didn't care about her nudity. He just wanted what was his.

"I don't owe you shit, World," Luca shouted.

"You do, cuz, and if ya don't give me what is mine, then there will be hell to pay. I don't give a fuck, cuzzo, how you get it, but I need to receive it. I do you a favor and you fuck me? We supposed to be family, cuzzo. Why you do me like that?" World said calmly.

"Fuck family!" Luca retorted.

World chuckled creepily. "Cuzzo, I'm nobody to mess around wit'. You know I'm crazy and I ain't been takin' my fuckin' medication, so I got voices in my head sayin' 'Fuck it, do this bitch, family or not,' but we family, cuz, right? I did you that solid a while back and kept my mouth shut, a nigga ain't no snitch, but a nigga is a killer, you feel me, cuzzo?"

"Are you threatening me, World?"

"Yes," he replied frankly.

World stepped closer to Luca. His beady eyes narrowed in on her and he frowned. He lifted his shirt, revealing the .9mm tucked snuggly in his waistband and said, "Don't make me go against family, cuzzo, because if I do, I damn sure won't regret it, but you will. I just don't give a fuck. You understand me, cuzzo?"

Luca glared at him, standing frozen near her bed. If World wanted to, he could easily kill her, and there wasn't anything she could do about it. It was his move; she felt like a pawn about to fall. World was strong, fearsome, and crazy. They were first cousins, but they were never close. His mother and her mother were sisters, but his mother died of cancer when he was just a boy.

"Okay, I get it. You're crazy and I owe you big time. Just leave. . . let me get my shit together and I'll hit you off." Luca's heart was skipping several beats.

"I'm leaving, cuzzo. Yeah, I'm leaving. I want my fuckin' money and I want my Phantom," World said.

He started walking backwards toward the bedroom door. He kept his attention on Luca, smiling devilishly. He finally made his way out of the bedroom, appearing to vanish in the dark. When he was out of sight, Luca took off running in the direction where the only gun in her house was located—a .380 under her pillow. She quickly snatched it into her hands and went chasing after World in her opened robe. She stormed out of the bedroom and went flying down the stairs. She wasn't going to hesitate to shoot him dead and explain the body later.

Frantically, she ran out of the house with the gun in her hand and looked everywhere for World, but he was nowhere to be found. It seemed like he had disappeared into thin air. There wasn't even an unfamiliar vehicle parked on the street. Where could he have gone so quickly?

She ran through her house looking in every room, every closet, and in every crevice, but no World. How did he get in and how did he get out? It scared Luca to the bone. World was a scary dude and nobody fucked with him in the streets. Most times he minded his business, but then when he didn't, he became a tornado mixed with an atom bomb tearing up everything in its path. He could be useful or he could be hazardous; it depended on which World you were dealing with that day.

Luca meticulously went through her entire home and made sure every door was locked and every window shut and sealed. She wouldn't let the gun out of her hand at all and chose to sleep with it. Better safe than sorry.

Now with World stalking and threatening her, Luca felt completely trapped into a corner, as if the room were caving in on her. She went berserk in her home and out of the blue, started knocking things over and tearing stuff apart. She smashed her flat screen TV against the floor, tore pictures off her wall, turned over furniture, threw things erratically, and screeched so intensely that the neighbors probably heard her.

Two hours after her rampage, Luca sat on the floor in her disastrous-looking bedroom with her hair in disarray, completely naked. It felt like she was going mad herself. She held the .380 loosely in her hand and wanted to shoot holes in her wall. Her tear-stained eyes were zoned out and her mind was going crazy. How could she come back from this type of fall? It felt like the trouble wouldn't end. Who could she go to? What did she need to do next?

"Keep it together, Luca. Keep it together, just keep it together," she chanted to herself.

The bedroom seemed to swallow her up, and the darkness and silence gave her comfort for some strange reason. If anything moved wrong in her room, she was going to shoot to kill. Luca took a deep breath, closed her eyes, and sat there for hours until she ended up falling asleep on the floor, gun in hand and drifting into a deep sleep. She wanted to wake up in a new life, a new place, a new beginning. This one chapter in her life felt like it was never going to end.

***

"Wake up, bitch. Wake up," a voice called out to her.

Luca stirred in her sleep and refused to listen. Sleep was the only peace she had. She felt a strong presence standing over her and felt someone kicking her side repeatedly. It didn't hurt, but it was becoming annoying. Luca was lying in the fetal position on her bedroom floor with her eyes closed and mouth drooling. She thought it was morning and the person nudging her side with the tip of her shoe was her mother. She was wrong.

"Luca, I said wake up!" the voice said again.

"Stop it, I'm fuckin' up!" Luca cursed.

Luca lifted her head and stared up at the person towering over her in her bedroom. Luca's eyes widened when she recognized who it was. The person smiled. Luca was shocked.

"You miss me?" Naomi asked.

"You're dead," Luca exclaimed.

"Yes, I know, and you killed me," Naomi replied.

Luca was speechless. Naomi was smiling down at her and looked so stunning. She was more beautiful dead than she had ever been alive. Luca gawked at the dress Naomi was in, an exquisite form-flattering dress. Her hair was almost golden; her eyes sparkled like diamonds, and her complexion was radiant. Luca couldn't believe her eyes.

"I look great, don't I? I always been a bad bitch, even more of a bad bitch dead," Naomi boasted.

"But I killed you."

"Yes, you did, and thank you for that. Death did amazing things for my figure and complexion," replied Naomi.

Taken aback, Luca slowly stood up with her attention fixed on every part of Naomi. It was like she was an angel in all white. Where were her wings, though, and how did she get to heaven with all the sin she committed?

Luca stretched out her hand to touch Naomi to make sure she was real. Luca felt her skin, and there wasn't anything transparent about her dead friend.

"Why are you here?" Luca asked.

Naomi smiled. She didn't appear to be a threat to her, not yet anyway, and she didn't look bitter about being shot in the head with a .357. Maybe a bullet to the head caused amnesia.

"Why am I here?" Naomi said, "Now that's a good question. Maybe you can answer that one for me, Luca."

Luca didn't have the answer. As smart as she was, this was truly bizarre. She had to be dreaming, but when she touched Naomi, it felt so real.

"Don't I look great, Luca?" Naomi said, twirling around in her dress like a ballerina, showing off her figure. "Look at me. You always did when we were growing up. You always envied me, even after my death."

"I fuckin' hate you," Luca spat.

Naomi laughed. "Hate. It's such an ugly word, but you were always such an ugly girl."

Naomi then stared at Luca with a steely glare. "You see Luca, even in death; I'm still prettier, smarter, and a better bitch than you'll ever be. You had to kill me because I was better."

"I killed you because I had enough of your bullshit. Since we were growing up, you paraded me around like I was your flunky, like I was a charity case to you. But I wasn't!"

Naomi frowned.

The bedroom abruptly altered into a cloudy mist and it appeared to linger around Luca like a skin disease. It enveloped everything in sight, until Luca was unable to see her own hands in front of her face. Naomi vanished, but Luca heard her enduring laughter; loud, chilling and contemptuous.

"What the fuck do you want from me?!" Luca shouted.

The cloudy mist covered everything. Luca felt she was about to suffocate in it. She collapsed to her knees and closed her eyes tightly. It seemed to transport her in time. When Luca opened her eyes, there was Naomi again, looking back at her with contempt. By some phenomenon, Luca found herself back in Nate's Canarsie house and nothing had changed. It was lavishly decorated and had the latest amenities.

"Why am I here?" Luca asked.

She looked around, remembering how it used to be. Just being there brought back painful and disturbing memories. Luca was in awe. What was happening to her?

Naomi, still showing off her lovely white dress, repeatedly twirled around in it like a young girl in a dance recital. She abruptly stopped, looked past Luca, and fixed her attention somewhere else. An unknown presence was approaching. Luca pivoted on her bare feet and looked behind her. She nearly had a heart attack when she witnessed her late ex-boyfriend, Nate, approaching them from a distance. Luca stood aghast at the sight of him. He was handsomely dressed in an all-white suit, white shoes, and fresh haircut. He looked remarkable. He had been dead for a long while, but death did him some justice too.

Nate seemed to glide their way, like he was on ice. Luca's heart beat rapidly. Had he come to harm her? His look was stoic. Luca stood frozen with fear, her eyes glued to his every movement. He came closer, but he passed her by without any acknowledgment and thrust himself into Naomi's open arms. Luca stood there watching the two kiss passionately with their white on white attire pressed into each other.

Once again, Naomi was seducing her man—or more accurately, her dead ex-lover—while Luca could only helplessly watch. Their tongues danced as they peeled away each other's clothing. Naomi positioned herself inside of Nate's masculine exposed arms. He started grabbing her ass and rubbing his hard dick against her. She was ready to be his all over again. Their ghostly spirits intertwined with Nate ready to slam his dick into her back door.

As the two spirits romantically enticed each other in front of Luca, she felt a sudden cold seep inside of her. Her breath released an icy mist and it felt like she was about to freeze to death. She couldn't turn her head away from the sexual rendezvous happening right in front of her. Luca watched them fuck. She watched the immoral affair occur once again, but this time in her presence.

Naomi moaned while Nate thrust himself into her glorious insides. The more heated it got between them, the colder Luca became. It felt like her insides were frozen with ice. Her breath was arctic. She wrapped her arms around herself to keep from freezing to death. She was naked and afraid.

She watched Nate pleasure himself and Naomi. This time, Naomi was on her back, looking up at his face, holding her legs up while he pumped into her from above. Nate finally turned to acknowledge that Luca was in the room, but the minute he looked at her, his features altered into another man, someone she was truly in love with. Unexpectedly, it was Squirrel and Naomi making passionate, hot love in front of her.

Naomi stared up at Luca, smirked and said, "I'm taking him too, Luca. He's mine. He never loved you. He never will. No one ever will. They always loved me, not you. I will always be better than you."

All of a sudden, Luca found herself under attack by an invisible force that thrust her into the ground and compelled her there. Standing over her were Gloria and Tanya. Their faces were mangled in a blur, but she knew it was them. They were in all white also, and stronger than ever and angrier at Luca.

As Squirrel fucked Naomi like he was in love with her, Luca felt herself being ripped apart by these two demonic forces. The thought of Squirrel being with another woman was tearing her apart, literally. She tried to fight it off, but the force was too strong. Luca helplessly watched Naomi ride Squirrel's big dick in position after position as the two enjoyed each other. Naomi continued to mock Luca as Gloria and Tanya ripped her apart piece by piece.

Luca shouted. The pain was just too unbearable.

"Look at you, you're ugly and pathetic, and you will never have anyone love you. You will always be a loser, and you'll be dead like me, and alone forever. You will always be ugly . . . you will always be ugly . . . the pain has only just begun," Naomi tormented.

"No! No! No! NOOOOOOOOO!" Luca screamed out.

Swiftly, Luca was plunged out of her wretched nightmare and thrust awake. She found herself back in her bedroom, on the floor, alone and still naked. She was in a cold sweat. It felt like she couldn't breathe. Luca looked around and collected herself. It was only a nightmare.

Luca sighed with relief. It had felt so real. The vivid and horrid images of Squirrel and Naomi fucking were still embedded into her mind. She loved Squirrel, and she didn't want anyone else to have him.

The dream made her realize she had stayed away from Squirrel for too long now. She needed his help, and she needed to see him despite his warning.

8

There were so many games being played between Dominic Sirocco, World, and the streets that Luca started to feel like a walking Xbox. She finally received a check from one of her investments for fifteen thousand dollars instead of twenty. It was a damn shame and an insult. She had invested millions into different avenues, but could only access a tiny payout from it all.

Luca was tired of the games.

It was time to make moves. She felt a hundred percent better. Her wounds were completely healed. Now it was time to get her business accelerated again, and there was only one person who was able to make that happen: Squirrel. Despite how he felt about her, they undisputedly did good business together and made millions of dollars. Squirrel loved making money, so she was positive Squirrel would want the wheels greased again and continuing to turn.

Phaedra drove Luca into Harlem in the cocaine-colored BMW with dusk settling over the city. Luca made sure to get dolled up in her finest attire and makeup to see Squirrel; even though it was unannounced and she was uncertain he would even be there. She had to try though.

Dressed in thigh-high boots and a black minidress under her $8,300 double-breasted mink jacket, Luca looked top-notch seated in the backseat of her BMW. Though she was broke and going through trials and tribulations, Luca still made time to look good and expensive. It was about image—never let anyone see you sweat. They were parked inconspicuously on the cluttered block, across the street from the towering projects and one of Squirrel's prominent stash houses.

Phaedra sat behind the wheel and conversed with her friend. Lying on the passenger seat was a loaded Glock 17, and in the backseat with Luca was a double-barreled, sawed-off shotgun. Luca was in love, but she wasn't stupid. Stepping into enemy terrain was a high risk for them. Squirrel was one unpredictable muthafucka, so it was better to be safe than sorry.

Luca and Phaedra watched Squirrel's young soldiers lingering in the cold in front of the project building from a short distance. The goons outside seemed to be impervious to the frigid cold, wrapped up in their thick winter coats, ski hats, Timberlands, and gloves, moving about from the courtyards to the lobby. In the New York City cold, hustling never stopped. It was a twenty-four-seven grind.

Luca staked out the area. Her mind was continuously on Squirrel, wondering what he was doing and who he was fucking now.

"I know he's up there with some bitch," Luca said.

Phaedra sighed with frustration. She was always patient, but tonight, she constantly looked at the time and sighed time after time. She wanted to be somewhere before it got too late. Even though she was Luca's right hand-bitch and owed her boss a lot, she still had a life of her own. Being the loyal lieutenant that she was, she always put her boss first. Loyalty was her entrapment. However, this was business, and they needed product—a second coming.

"Why you sighing for, Phaedra? You in a damn rush to go somewhere?"

"No rush, Luca. I'm good," Phaedra lied.

Phaedra glanced at her boss in the rearview mirror and then turned away. She was pissed that Luca continued to play herself with this fool

Squirrel. They seemed like idiots in the cold, but Luca was determined to reconnect with Squirrel when it was obvious he wasn't trying to reconnect with her.

It didn't take long for one of Squirrel's soldiers to spot the cocaine-colored Beamer parked on the block and figure out who was inside. Word traveled from the soldier to one of the block's lieutenants and then a phone call to Squirrel who was laid up naked with one of his side bitches in a faraway bedroom while pulling on a blunt.

"Yo, what you need?" Squirrel answered.

"I know ya busy, boss, but I thought you might want to know that bitch from Brooklyn is parked out here. You know, the Einstein one," his lieutenant informed him.

Squirrel smiled. "What she want?"

"Don't know, she just parked, her and that young bitch, sitting there watchin' shit. They ain't make a move or nuthin'. What you need me to do?"

"Don't do anything; just let that bitch sit there. Fuckin' bitch don't listen, but she'll learn," Squirrel said.

"A'ight."

Squirrel hung up and focused his attention on the busty, big-booty hood rat that had been fucking him for hours. Luca wasn't even on his mind or of any concern to him.

Two hours passed and the two ladies still lingered in the car on the block. Luca watched the area like a hawk. There was no sign of Squirrel, just niggas coming and going, and fiends being served. Luca was tempted to get out of the vehicle and daringly walk into the project, but she had no sign if he was around or not. The more time went by, the more pissed off Phaedra became.

After five hours of waiting, Luca finally felt it was time to leave. She'd gotten dolled up for no reason at all. It was a waste of time. However, Luca was persistent, and this wasn't the last time she would come around.

The next day, Luca came back with Phaedra into the Harlem hood with the same results—no Squirrel—and the day after that, the same thing. Luca did this for six days straight and she was going to continue stalking Squirrel until he got the point. She wasn't going away. She didn't care what it looked like and wasn't scared of any of his soldiers.

Phaedra, on the other hand, was fuming that they had to subject themselves to such a humiliating act, stalking like fuckin' schoolgirls with a stupid crush. She would smoke her Newports repeatedly or try to get high, but when Phaedra would tempt to roll up a blunt while waiting for hours, Luca would scold her and remind her that they needed to stay focused.

Phaedra would pout and frown, but she always followed orders. Also, Phaedra couldn't help wonder if her boss was losing her damn mind. Luca had gone through a horrid ordeal not too long ago and her memory got twisted and cloudy some days. Speculations came about if Luca was right in her mind to continue leading and running the empire.

Six days straight, driving to Harlem from Brooklyn and sitting in the idling car in the winter cold for heat—lurking and watching like they were cops.

On the sixth day of parking on the cold street, Luca dressed in black leggings, highlighting her luscious curves, and a low-cut top underneath the same double-breasted fur jacket. Luca and Phaedra smoked a Newport apiece in the car and watched the block, observing the same soldiers come and go in the freezing cold. It was the same faces and the same routine. Squirrel's goons made sure to taunt them as they sat idling, sometimes quickly banging on the hood or trunk of the car while passing by; or firing warning shots into the air; tossing items at her car; or flipping their middle fingers in their direction. Luca didn't budge, though. She was determined to see Squirrel by any means necessary. She knew they were fucking with her; Squirrel would never allow any harm to come to her, especially since he thought she was pregnant.

On this day, there was a sudden knock on the passenger window. One of Squirrel's soldiers was at her window. Luca gripped the pistol in her hand and Phaedra did the same thing with her weapon. Slowly, Luca rolled down the window, allowing the cold air to rush in. She looked at the baby-faced thug squarely in his face and asked, "What you want?"

The young thug glanced around the car, noticing the gun in Luca's hand and said, "I come in peace. Squirrel wants to see you."

"He does, huh?"

The man nodded.

It was what she'd been waiting for. Luca collected herself and stepped out of the car, her six-hundred-dollar Jimmy Choos hitting the pavement and knowing it was only a matter of time.

"You want me to come wit' you?" Phaedra asked.

"No need, I'm okay, just stay here. I'll be right back."

Phaedra nodded.

Luca followed behind the kid into the project building. As she moved through the lobby, all scowls were on her from a handful of thugs. They didn't like her and didn't trust her. The word was out that she was dating a cop, and Squirrel's goons felt she was bad for business. If it was up to them, they would have killed her where she stood.

Luca followed behind the kid into the elevator and they rode it up to the eighth floor. Getting off, Luca gripped her gun, but it was inevitable she was about to be searched and have the weapon taken from her. The beefy ruffian standing guard outside of apartment 8C made sure of that.

"She's good," the bearded ruffian assured the kid.

The door opened and Luca slowly walked inside. She was nervous and excited about coming face to face again with the man she loved. The apartment was dimly lit, the windows painted black and the place loaded with kilos of pure heroin stockpiled in the corner of the living room and duffel bags filled of cash on the opposite side of the place. The minute Luca stepped into the living room, the hit came out of nowhere and she dropped to the floor, shocked. Squirrel had smacked the shit out of her. He stood over Luca frowning. The smack brought about a flashback of the beating she got from Charter.

"You're persistent, I give you that, Luca. Stupid for coming here when I warned you to stay the fuck away from me, but persistent," Squirrel said.

"You know I couldn't stay away from you, Squirrel. I love you so much," Luca replied wholeheartedly.

"You love me? Bitch, you are drama, and your cop boyfriend, he's even more drama and lucky I didn't blow his fuckin' brains out," Squirrel shouted heatedly.

Luca stared up at a furious Squirrel and wiped the blood that trickled from her lips. He was clad in a wifebeater and jeans, a .9mm tucked in his waistband. He clenched his fists and was ready to tear into Luca, but when he looked down and noticed her flat stomach, indicating that she was no longer pregnant, he became bewildered by it.

"What happened to the baby?" he asked.

"You mean your baby," she corrected. "And I lost it."

"Lost it…how?"

"Charter beat it out of me, and now he's dead," she blurted out.

"Dead?" he uttered with a raised eyebrow.

"I shot him three times for putting his hands on me."

Squirrel didn't believe her. He felt she was saying anything to save her own ass. She was always cunning and smart, sometimes too smart for her own good. She had lied about so many things before, that it was harder for

Squirrel to believe she was even pregnant, and even harder to believe she had killed an NYPD officer. He scowled nonstop at her and was tempted to beat her to death. But you never shit where you eat; Squirrel was too smart to bring any unwanted attention to one of his hubs that contained over sixty kilos of heroin and cocaine.

Luca went on to explain everything to Squirrel. She went into details about the violent incident that occurred in her home and how she had been in a coma for four days, losing her baby, their baby, thoroughly investigated by the NYPD and healing. Squirrel didn't believe it was his baby. He didn't believe her story. She wanted to make him believe.

Squirrel removed the .9mm from his waistband and pointed it down at Luca. She didn't even flinch. It was a bluff. She knew it. She locked eyes with the killer drug boss.

"You should have stayed the fuck away, Luca."

"You're not going to kill me," she gallantly stated.

"And why the fuck not?" he asked.

"Because you never been that stupid, Squirrel. A gunshot, and a body in one of your places of business, it would be detrimental. And besides, I know you love me."

"Love you?" he laughed. "Bitch, you're a fuckin' vortex of trouble, like a plague, and I need to rid myself of any plague, especially one that lies to save her own life."

"I'm not lying about this, Squirrel. I was pregnant with your baby and I killed that cop," she exclaimed.

"You killed a cop. I don't think your blood runs that cold," he replied.

"I can prove it."

Squirrel looked blankly at her. Luca stood up and walked over to the Mac laptop on the table. She logged in quickly and did a Google search which pulled up the story online. Squirrel walked over with the gun in his hand and started to read it. Although her name was withheld from the main article, he realized it was her. She was telling the truth.

"I love you, baby. And you know I would do anything for you…even kill for you," she stated wholeheartedly.

"You're a killer now, huh?"

"I am."

Squirrel chuckled lightly. He gazed at the young beauty and he did notice the change in her. It took heart to come at him the way she did—stay parked outside the projects for six days to get his attention. He remembered when they first met, he thought she was naïve and getting over her head in this business. Now, she was one of his best clients, moving hundreds of kilos a month and making millions.

Luca's eyes were cold and changed, and the thing that mattered the most, she was determined—determined to do whatever it took to get back on top and regain her reign in the game.

"They stole everything from me, Squirrel, all that I had…every last ki and every penny," she told him.

"And what the fuck you expect from me?" he asked, scowling heavily.

"I need your help."

"My help? And why the fuck would I help you?"

"Because I can rebuild this, Squirrel. Even better. You know me, baby. You know I'm smart and determined, and I got the means, the crew, and the brains to make you so much money, you'll be wiping your ass with hundred-dollar bills and blowing your nose with fifties," Luca proclaimed.

Squirrel laughed.

"I'm serious, baby."

"And this rebuilding, what's it goin' to take?"

"I can't afford to get any work from you directly, so I need at least thirty kis on consignment," she said.

"Consignment, bitch you done bumped your head and lost your muthafuckin' mind. You come to me without a dime to your name, a dead cop, stalking my shit, problems in your house, and you have the audacity to want shit from me on consignment. I should throw you out that fucking window," Squirrel hollered.

Squirrel's loud and furious voice echoed out into the hallway. Luca stood looking at him like a deer caught in headlights. She didn't know what she was going to do. She needed this favor from him, and she was willing to do anything to get back into his good graces.

"You can kill me if you want, Squirrel, you have the power to, I never doubted that… but to let you know, I have power too…"

"You threatening me, bitch?" Squirrel exclaimed, stepping toward her and ready to put the gun against her temple. He wasn't going to shoot her, but if he had to, he would have pistol whipped her into the floor.

"Baby, I love you too much to threaten you, and I'm not stupid," she replied in a civil tone.

Squirrel looked at her fiercely. His hesitation to destroy her where she stood was a small indication that he was listening and still had some feelings for her. The room was tense and Luca needed to play her cards right. She understood what hand to play when dealing with Squirrel. He had the streets on lockdown, but Luca had something else he definitely would need in the future. One thing she understood is that power came to those who knew how to take it and were willing to risk everything to get it.

This was her risk. There was no turning back.

Luca didn't avert her eyes away from his strong glare. She simply said to him, "I need you, but one day, you're going to need me."

"And why?"

"Henry MacDonald, Andrew Gilligan, Holland Lemansky, Samuel Duncan, James Levy," Luca recited the names coolly to him.

Squirrel was dumbfounded. "Who the fuck are they?"

"State prosecutors, judges, district attorneys, cops, detectives; people I have in my back pocket—powerful men I have incriminating and embarrassing dirt on. Men I control and men who will help me out when I get into a difficult situation," Luca explained to him evenly.

Squirrel couldn't help but to be impressed. "I'm not gonna even ask you how you was able to secure that. You're a smart bitch; in fact, you're one of the smartest people I ever knew."

Luca was flattered, but she remained cool and stoic. "You're going to always need protection from the law and the IRS, any wise person understands that."

"And this benefits me, how?"

"For thirty kis on consignment, my list becomes your list too. I'll update you about their transgressions, and they're in your pocket too," said Luca.

Squirrel nodded. He was definitely fond of the idea.

"Now that sounds promising, but I'll give you half on consignment, fifteen kis, nothing more," Squirrel replied. "But I want my money within the month."

Luca quickly thought it over. She wasn't in a cemented enough position to negotiate with him, and so it was a deal. She nodded to it. She could flip those fifteen kilos in less than a month, most likely a week or two. Luca was more excited about getting back into business with Squirrel. She knew in her heart that he still had feelings for her. Behind the coldness in his eyes, she saw some sentiment, though he tried to put up a front. And she knew he was conflicted between her and his baby mama. The bitch was always in the way.

Luca fixed her eyes on Squirrel's strapping physique, barely covered with the wife-beater, tattoos showing. In her eyes, he looked too scrumptious, and she wanted to devour him right there, get on her knees and take his big dick into her mouth and suck him off until her lips became numb. She missed him so much and wanted their reunion to be a hot and steamy one.

Though she wanted to feel every inch of him inside of her, tonight was about business only. She decided not to come on too strong and just be glad that she was back in his good graces. Luca knew that he would soon come around to her, knowing where his true love was at, and things would rekindle to how they were.

Luca walked out of the apartment with fifteen kilos of pure heroin concealed in a black bag slung over her shoulder. She lingered in the foyer for a moment, looking back at Squirrel. Their eyes locked deeply. She smiled, but he didn't.

Luca walked out of the projects a proud woman. It wasn't going to take long for her life to get back on track. She climbed into the backseat and smiled at Phaedra.

"I assume that everything went okay," said Phaedra.

"It went more than okay. Like how I planned, Phaedra," Luca replied.

Phaedra nodded. "So I assume that Squirrel is back in your life again."

"We're on somewhat good terms."

It was certainly good news for their organization. However, Phaedra felt uncertain about Luca getting back into bed with Squirrel, both literally and in business. She didn't trust Squirrel and she knew the stranglehold he had on Luca's heart; sometimes her boss couldn't think straight because of him.

It wasn't her business. It was about getting money. Phaedra and Luca rode silently back into Brooklyn. Fifteen kilos was going to profit them a great deal.

9

Phaedra and Kool-Aid walked into the small, brand-new lounge called Paradise in SoHo, New York. The lounge, with its full bar, music background, outdoor seating, and classy ambience was as relaxing and soothing as a Caribbean beach. The crowd that came was young and trendy, the food was good, and the drinks were strong.

Kool-Aid followed behind Phaedra with his guard on high alert; his pistol tucked snugly in his waistband and concealed beneath the large winter coat he wore. His presence spoke out young thug, but Kool-Aid didn't care what people thought of him; he wasn't about to play fake for no one, even in a tasteful lounge like Paradise. Phaedra, on the other hand, was there for a reason, and her reason was Clyde.

She couldn't explain why she'd been going to the lounge for the past month with Kool-Aid. And she couldn't explain the black skirt and tight top she wore that highlighted her young and curvy physique. For a while now, Phaedra had stopped dressing like a boy, a young hood—she had started to wear dresses, tight jeans, and revealing shirts. Hanging around her boss, Luca, had a profound influence on her. And up until Clyde, she'd been certain that she was a lesbian for life.

Phaedra had an unexplainable crush on Clyde. She had liked pussy for a few years now, but seeing Clyde made her pussy throb. He was a handsome Panamanian man in his early thirties. He was dishy, tall with a dark goatee, and looked like he once had a bleak outlook toward life, but now had a positive aura to him. With his Roman nose, wrestler's shoulders that were part of his strong physique, and his tiger-like tread, Clyde commanded attention wherever he went. He was once a heavy hitter in the Baltimore drug game, but got out a few years ago after getting shot several times. He survived the attempt on his life and invested his drug money into a legit business in New York that was thriving.

Phaedra and Kool-Aid took a seat by the bar and produced their fake IDs to order their drinks. She and Kool-Aid visited the lounge at least twice a week and spent lots of money there, sparing no expenses when it came to drinks, food, entertainment, and having a good time. Their business caught the attention of the owner, Clyde. Phaedra was too inexperienced to realize that she and Kool-Aid looked like a couple.

Phaedra sipped on her drink and nodded her head to the jazzy beat playing. It was great to get out of Brooklyn once in a while. The game could lay heavy on one's heart and mind, and even thorough gangsters like Phaedra and Kool-Aid needed a break from it sometimes. Phaedra looked around for Clyde, but didn't see him anywhere. Kool-Aid noticed her behavior and said, "What's up wit' you and that clown-ass nigga?"

"What you mean?"

"You know what I mean. Why you hawking him for? I thought you didn't swing that way, Phaedra. I thought you and me like the same thing; pussy. When did you start riding the broomstick?" Kool-Aid laughed.

"Stay out my business," Phaedra said.

"I ain't worried 'bout ya business, ya business ain't shit to me," Kool-Aid replied.

"As long as we got that understanding," said Phaedra.

"Whatever. Let me just get my drink on and look for my next baby mama in this bitch, cuz I is seein' some fine-ass honeys up in this joint, and I'm ready to let the dog loose."

Phaedra laughed.

Kool-Aid was a calm dude for a Brooklyn killer; he was a jokester, a comedian behind the gun and violence. His smile and young features masked the dangerous muthafucka that he was. He was a killer on an elevated level. But this evening, he was just a normal nigga in a Manhattan lounge having a drink with a close friend.

"So I heard we back in business," Kool-Aid said.

"We are."

"It's 'bout fuckin' time, fo' real. It's time to lock these fuckin' streets down wit' that pure shit again and wash out these punk-ass muthafuckas. Too much talkin' and bullshit out there."

"You anxious, ain't you?"

"Hells yeah, I need to get that money and I need some action."

"You need fuckin' Ritalin, that's what you need."

"I need some pussy," he joked.

Phaedra laughed. She took a sip of alcohol and glanced around the place for the second time. The crowd was coming in gradually from the cold to enjoy drinks and good music. Paradise was becoming well known in the SoHo neighborhood.

The conversation died down for a minute, both Kool-Aid and Phaedra were in their own thoughts. Kool-Aid downed his beer, looked at his friend, and asked, "So Luca, how she making out?"

"I think she doin' good, besides that jerk coming back into her life."

"You mean Squirrel?"

"I just don't like him."

"That's because you want to fuck her."

"Fuck you, Kool-Aid."

"What? You know it's true. I see how you look at her sometimes, starry-eyed and shit," Kool-Aid commented.

"I respect her."

"Yeah, I do too, but—"

"But what?" Phaedra interrupted him.

Before the conversation went on into uncharted territory, Clyde walked up to the two with a smile. He was becoming familiar with Phaedra and Kool-Aid frequenting his place of business.

"I see the two of you can't get enough of Paradise. I can't blame y'all, I can't get enough of my own place either," Clyde spoke with a smile.

Phaedra grinned. She felt like a woman around him. He always complimented the diamond-in-the-rough Phaedra and made sure to make her and her friend feel at home whenever they came into his place. His charismatic personality and deep voice were a big part of his allure. He always wore expensive suites and his pricey cologne was appealing.

"It's nice in here," Phaedra said.

"Yeah, it's really nice, drinks ain't watered down, I ain't gotta watch my back up in here and the ladies are fine as fuck," Kool-Aid stated.

"I try to make it paradise for everyone," Clyde replied.

"And that you do," Phaedra chimed in.

"Yeah, that you do, Clyde. I respect your hustle, cuz you doin' it big wit' this place. Shit, when I retire from the game, I want to open a business just like yours, make that money and shit," said Kool-Aid, who was not shy in telling anyone about his occupation.

"You could do whatever you want, my friend," Clyde encouraged with a smile.

"Yeah, I know, and I am." Kool-Aid smirked.

The two men looked at each other. It was no secret that Clyde used to be a gangster and in some way, he felt Kool-Aid was slyly challenging him. Clyde was old-school, though, with respect going as far west as L.A., south of ATL, and more bodies on his hands than a mafia hit-man. He had seen plenty of young boys smell themselves and challenge him during his time in the game. They were all dead now. He just hoped that Kool-Aid was never that stupid.

"Put your mind to whatever you want, my friend. Just make sure it's the right decision and that it don't come back to haunt you or bite you later on in life," Clyde advised.

"Nah, I always do and I got a bigger bite," replied Kool-Aid with a sharp smile.

"I bet you do," Clyde replied coolly, unperturbed by the young hood's words. "But anyway, I'm very grateful for y'all's business. Enjoy the evening."

"We will," Kool-Aid said.

Clyde removed a cigar from the pocket of his inner jacket, cut off the tip with his cigar clip, and placed it in his mouth like he was a don. He lit it, took a few puffs, and exhaled the smoke in Kool-Aid's direction.

He smiled at Phaedra, and then said to the bartender, "For the rest of the night, drinks are on me. You and your friend have a great night."

"Thank you," Phaedra said.

She watched Clyde walk away and definitely wanted to be with him. He was the one man who was able to create butterflies in her stomach. While her eyes were fixed on her male crush, she heard Kool-Aid say to her, "And you like that nigga, Phaedra? You must be out ya damn mind. Stick to being a fuckin' lesbian."

10

The Ford Taurus rounded the corner, sped up the brick driveway, and parked in the one-car garage nestled in the backyard of an old two-story corner home in Queens, New York. The garage door shut, shading out any sunlight. Meeka and newcomer Egypt stepped out of the car looking more like prostitutes than drug dealers. A lean, clean-shaven man with a neck tattoo stood by the garage door, smiling and nodding. He unquestionably liked what he saw: tight skin, tight clothing, protruding tits, and phat ass. He took a drag from his cigarette and turned on the single bulb dangling above the garage, anxious to see the product he paid for. He licked his lips, thinking perverted things about the girls, but he knew they were connected to some heavy hitters and were not to be fucked with.

Egypt and Meeka stood in front of him with serious scowls. Both of them were armed and dangerous and had each other's back in case anything went wrong. So far he was only one guy, not a threat to them. Smiling like he'd won the Lotto, the man clapped his hands together and said, "So, show me yours and I'll show you mine."

Meeka looked at Egypt and nodded. Egypt walked over to the trunk, popped it open, and lifted it to show off what they had. He walked over and peered into the trunk. There it was: six kilos of Bad Girl, stamped with the signature pink mark and ready to be sold off.

The man smiled broadly.

"I like, I like," he said. "So Luca's definitely back in business?"

"Yes she is," Meeka assured.

"Great to hear, cuz shit was drying up out here."

"Well it won't anymore," Meeka said. "Now that we showed you ours, show us yours."

"No doubt, fair is fair," he replied.

He walked over to a cluttered area in the back of the garage and reached for something. Meeka and Egypt were on high alert, their hands near their weapons for fear that he might be setting them up. They both breathed a little easier when he handed them a book bag filled with cash—all stacked hundred-dollar bills.

"Yo, tell your boss this ain't gonna be enough, though. I'm gonna need more by the end of the week. This shit sells better than pussy," the man said.

"We know it do," Egypt responded.

Meeka tossed the book bag of cash into the backseat of the car. The deal with the new guy had gone smoothly. Bad Girl was the talk of the town; every hustler wanted their hands on it. It was pure gold, and moving faster than cars at 2 a.m. on the expressway. Within the week, Luca had flooded the streets once again with genuine Bad Girl. Now her reach extended into Queens, Far Rockaway, and as far east as Suffolk County, Long Island. The white kids out there couldn't get enough of the stuff, and they spent their parents' money on it like it was water.

Luca was becoming a rich woman again.

Meeka gazed at the man. He looked okay, but there was something about him that she felt was off. He went by the name Xavier. He looked sophisticated and business minded, and didn't come across as a drug dealer. One of Luca's clients vouched for him, said he was good peoples, ran coke and dope twenty-four-seven upstate to the college kids in New

Paltz, Albany, Syracuse, and Buffalo. He had a profitable thing going for him. He'd heard through the grapevine about Bad Girl. The competition was putting him out of business and it put his dope to shame. Xavier had lost an extensive number of clients because of the competition, so if you couldn't beat them—not yet anyway—you might as well join them. And he did so, but under orders from a superior force.

Meeka and Egypt climbed back into the Ford Taurus. Xavier lifted the gate to the garage. He looked at the two passengers. If he wanted to, he could have had them killed instantly. He was smarter than that. He knew they weren't the masterminds or the sharpest knives in the drawer. He stood off to the side as Meeka slowly backed the car out of the driveway.

He watched the girls disappear from his sight and uttered, "Stupid fuckin' bitches."

To meet in Queens, a foreign place to the girls, and in the shaded garage of a backyard carrying six precious kis of Bad Girl—Xavier knew these bitches were asking to get themselves robbed and possibly murdered. It was tempting, but he and his superiors looked at things in the long-term. It was better to walk down the hill and fuck all the cows in their time than to run down the hill only able to fuck one cow because they scared the others away.

When the car was out of sight, Xavier pulled out his cell phone and dialed up his bosses. They answered right after the second ring.

"Yeah, it's me, Xavier. I got what y'all need," he spoke through the cell phone.

"Good," the heavy baritone voice uttered. "It went smooth?"

"It did, they didn't suspect a thing. Those bitches were more thirsty about business than anything else."

"Okay, continue on with the plan. This Bad Girl is good product, it sells very well, but it will soon become our product," the man said.

Xavier smiled. He was ready to get all that money and continue making a name for himself.

Bad Girl wasn't just becoming infamous on the New York streets, but growing to be infamous in other areas as well—upstate New York, Connecticut, Rhode Island, and as far south as Delaware and Baltimore. It was also catching some wrong attention. The haters were jealous and wanted in so badly that they were ready to wage war against the Brooklyn crew.

A young girl like Luca having control over such a prominent and potent drug and making millions from it made the old heads in the game and the young wolves on the streets stir. Restless and crooked cops were ready to do a takeover.

Bad Girl had become the number-one draft pick in the game.

11

Luca and Phaedra had just finished counting a pile of money in front of them. Two-point-six million was stacked on the long folding table in the private room. The big bills were separated from the small bills, and every bill was accounted for and packaged tightly for re-up, payroll, and profit. It was a substantial profit from the streets in such a short time, and it needed to be cleaned. However, she still had her trust issues with her attorney, and wasn't giving him another dime until he proved himself to her once again. She wasn't going to make the same mistakes twice. She lived and learned. Dominic was on thin ice with her.

Luca had got into the habit of smoking cigars. After counting money all night, she pulled out a pricey Cuban cigar and lit it. The flavor from it seeped into her system, and she sat back in a cushioned chair and exhaled the smoke, trying to blow smoke circles like the ones she saw on TV. Her business with Squirrel was going really well: She had paid off her debt to him, regained some of his trust, and she was able to purchase a shitload of kilos from him at a reasonable price. Like she'd said, fucking with her, Squirrel was able to wipe his ass with hundred-dollar bills and blow his nose with the fifties.

No one brought in as much money as Luca did. She was his best client. She made herself too valuable to lose. Luca did her business with him directly, no middleman to meet. Luca interpreted this as Squirrel still yearning for her, wanting to constantly see her. It made her smile. It made her feel so good, because every time she went to see the nigga, she would be dressed in her finest and sexiest outfit, showing off her ample cleavage or her nice curves and phat ass. She saw the way Squirrel would gaze at her, trying to keep his composure and make it only about business between them. She knew she had some good pussy and she was his biggest freak. No bitch could suck his dick better than she could, or fuck him better than she could. No bitch and no nigga could bring him a vast fortune like she could. Luca understood that she was hard to come by—sexy, savvy, business-minded, ambitious and also a freak. His baby mama, Angel, didn't have shit on her. If she and Squirrel were ever a couple, they could run the East coast and perhaps become billionaires.

Luca sat in her chair for a minute, smoking her cigar, feeling like a diva—a boss bitch. As the money and power came pouring in, she didn't forget about being robbed of a fortune. She frowned at not yet knowing who had taken her shit. It had been a few months, and still no clues. She continued to investigate every person who was in her home the night she shot Charter.

She spread some money around for information and made a few connections with some detectives from Queens. Like always, money talked and bullshit walked. The paid detectives allowed Luca to have a copy of the case file to go over scrupulously. Now it was time for Luca to do what she did best: use her wits and computer savvy to pull up any kind of information.

She spent the entire morning going over the police report, hacking into personal files and thoroughly checking out everything. She used her hacking skills to pull up all their information, bank records, credit scores, and any kind of financial information from cops, detectives, the paramedic workers that treated her, and even her neighbors. She wanted to see who would be stupid enough to deposit large sums of cash into their accounts, or see if anyone made any big purchases or took an exotic trip somewhere—perhaps paid off an outstanding debt or suddenly quit their jobs. All morning, Luca went through file after file, checking account after accounts but nothing. Everyone seemed to check out clean. It irritated her that these people were so clean. But she didn't give a fuck; someone wronged her and she had worked too hard to be played by some mediocre city worker who probably didn't have half the intelligence she had.

Ego became a factor, and Luca wanted revenge—if they were guilty or not, a statement had to be made. You don't cross Luca and her crew and expect to live your life—no fairy-tale endings, no happily ever after.

Luca sat behind her computer pulling on her Cuban cigar, and the computer screen glared with a list of names—a list of potential thieves. Liars who were about to become dead men and women. The room was still and she was alone, thinking about murder. She didn't care who, as long as it got done and she felt some satisfaction for the loss of product and money she endured.

The first two on her murder list were two Queens detectives—Justin Cannon, an aging veteran with over fifteen years on the force and some questionable items in his jacket, and Clinton Trotter, a man with an attitude and ten years on the force.

Luca wanted them both dead.

She called Phaedra on a throwaway cell phone to greenlight the hit.

"You sure you wanna kill a cop? That's gonna bring down a lot of heat on everyone," Phaedra said.

"I don't give a fuck what heat it's gonna bring. I just want them dead, Phaedra. They were in my home when my shit went missing. They are suspects in my eyes. They need to go," Luca declared.

"I'm on it then, Luca."

"I want Kool-Aid and yourself the only ones handling this hit. You understand me?"

"I understand."

"And make the killings clean, Phaedra. No torturing because they probably won't talk, and not up close and personal; it's too dangerous. Just make them dead."

"Okay," Phaedra continued to acquiesce.

"And one last thing, Phaedra. Go through their homes and do a good search of the houses. If you find something interesting, don't hesitate to call me about it."

"I will, Luca."

She hung up.

Luca didn't give a fuck about rational thinking when it came to killing cops and the heat it would bring down on everyone. She just wanted to take action and make herself feel good. She wasn't getting fucked properly, or at all, and her way of getting off was murdering people. It was sadistic, but after the day Charter beat her into a coma and she took his life, Luca had woken up a completely different woman.

She sat in her comfortable chair, puffing on her cigar and feeling like a female don. For some strange reason she thought about the dream she had about Naomi. It felt like even in death, Naomi was still winning. Luca sensed she had to still put on a show for that bitch, despite her being dead. It wasn't time for Luca to crumble. It would never be time for Luca to crumble; even when she was winning, she still felt she had something to prove.

***

Kool-Aid slipped into the modest three-bedroom home in the quaint and quiet suburban Rockaway Park area. With no alarms to worry about and the family out for the evening, he skillfully picked the lock to the back door and made his way inside. He moved like a cat burglar. Breaking and entering homes had been his forte in his preteen years, and he knew the drill: lights off, use a penlight in the dark, wear latex gloves, try not to disturb anything, and carry a .9mm in case he ran into unwanted company.

Kool-Aid started off with the downstairs area. He did a clean, stealthy search all over, opening up drawers and cabinets, and then made his way upstairs. The place was nicely furnished, cozy, with a few high-end amenities, but nothing excessive. Kool-Aid shined his penlight on a few pictures on the wall, and there he was—Detective Clinton Trotter in a family photo. He was all smiles with his arm around his wife, a fat brunette, their three kids surrounding them and everyone dressed in their Sunday best.

Kool-Aid laughed softly at the photo. "Fuckin' family affair here."

He continued upstairs and went into the bedrooms. Each room was neat and clean; the beds were made and everything was in its place. Kool-Aid searched through the master bedroom inch by inch. He was looking for any kind of expensive jewels, documentation of pricey vacations, or paperwork indicating the detective's guilt.

Kool-Aid spent an hour inside the house, intruding on the family's privacy, rummaging through their belongings. Unfortunately, he didn't find anything. It was clean. The detective lived an average and modest life. And by the many family pictures spread out through the home, he enjoyed being with his wife and kids. Kool-Aid didn't care how the man lived his life and about his family, he still had to die. Luca greenlit the murder, so Kool-Aid was ready to carry out his job. The question was, how?

He slipped out of the house the same way he came in. Half an hour later, the Trotter family's burgundy Buick pulled into the driveway. The detective, his wife, and his youngest son exited the car carrying balloons and a few doggy bags. The family laughed and made their way inside, unaware that their home had been invaded.

From a distance, Kool-Aid smoked his cigarette and watched the happy family walk inside from behind the wheel of his Black Acura Legend. Kool-Aid exhaled the cigarette smoke and smirked. Killing a cop was going to be a high-profile murder, and he was anxious to do it. Luca paid him handsomely for his services, and his loyalty to her was unquestionable.

Tonight wasn't the night for the cop to die, though. He had to come up with a plan to make it clean and not up close. He sat on the quiet block for a moment and watched the house. It was the Brady Bunch all around. These people were food to him, and he was hungry.

Kool-Aid took one last drag from the cigarette and flicked it out the window. He started the car and drove away. He had one last stop to make, and then it was time to put the cop's death into motion.

Detective Justin Cannon's luxurious four-bedroom house was just two miles away from the Rockaway Park country club, and the veteran cop made sure to take advantage of the golf course every Sunday morning. He was a diehard golf player with a zero or less handicap, and considered a scratch golfer. He always wondered why he'd become a cop instead of becoming a pro golfer.

Kool-Aid parked outside the detective's home in his Acura Legend in the quiet and chilly night. As he waited, he started on a second pack of Newports, kept his gun close to him, and listened to the radio. It was a tedious task, but someone needed to do it. Luca trusted only him to get the job done right.

Two hours went by, the night getting colder the longer Kool-Aid sat and waited in his car. The bedroom lights were on the longest, indicating detective Cannon's presence there. Kool-Aid itched to get inside and search around, but the cop was in for the night, and Kool-Aid didn't want to keep coming back. It was now or never. He decided to wait until it got later, and then break in while the man slept and creep through his place. It was risky—maybe just too risky. There was no doubt the detective had guns in his home and wouldn't hesitate to shoot a young armed black man. He would have been justified, especially being a cop. Kool-Aid was always about risks, though. He was Luca's number one enforcer.

After midnight, the lights to the bedroom went out. To be on the safe side, Kool-Aid allowed an extra hour to fly by before he proceeded. He stepped out of his car smoking his umpteenth cigarette, flicked it into the street, observed his surroundings, and headed toward the cop's house.

He moved like he was the dark, clad in all black, wearing latex gloves, his pistol stuffed in his waistband and his attention on how to break into this bitch. Kool-Aid was stealthy moving from his vehicle to the two-story home and scaled the fence with swiftness, like Superman leaping over tall buildings. He crept up the driveway toward the back of the home and made it to the backdoor.

Crouched low in the dark, constantly watching his surroundings, Kool-Aid removed his lock pick and started to pick the lock. It took a while to open up, but five minutes later, he was creeping into their home like a shadow under the door. Removing his penlight, Kool-Aid found himself in the kitchen. It was clean, dark, and smelled of Pine-Sol. From the kitchen he slowly moved into the living room. It was another well-furnished home with flat screen TVs, a high-end stereo system, nice artwork hanging on the walls—no family portraits, no wife, no kids, just a lonely aging cop who had spent too much time on the police force, chasing bad guys and forgetting about having a social life.

When Kool-Aid got to the foot of the stairway, he removed his pistol and made his way upwards. Reaching the second floor, he heard the TV playing. The door to the master bedroom was ajar and a speck of TV light shone into the hallway. He wanted to see if the cop was asleep. If so, then he could search around and leave. Luca wanted it clean.

Kool-Aid slowly walked toward the bedroom with his gun down by his side. He heard ESPN playing and thought he heard loud snoring behind the noise. He had to make sure. He tiptoed toward the bedroom door, ready for anything. When he got a few feet away from the door, out of the blue he heard a toilet flush. It caught him off guard; someone else was in the home. A golden light exploded into the hallway from the bathroom, exposing his cover. A slim woman exited the bathroom clad in her panties and bra. She froze in her steps, seeing the intruder and then seeing the gun. Her eyes widened with fear. She screamed.

"Justin! Justin! Ohmygod . . . Justin!" Her shriek echoed like thunder.

Kool-Aid had no choice; he pivoted with the gun outstretched in his hand and fired twice—*Bam! Bam!* She dropped dead with two in her head.

"Shit!" he shouted.

The shot ricocheted through the house. Without a doubt, Justin Cannon was awakened by the chaos. Kool-Aid burst into the bedroom, and instantaneously four shots went off at him, barely missing him by inches. Kool-Aid dropped and rolled behind the heavy dresser. Detective Cannon may have been aging, but he was still accurate with his firearm. It was a miracle that Kool-Aid didn't get hit by all four gunshots.

"I'm a cop!" the detective shouted. "What the fuck are you doing in my home?!"

Kool-Aid didn't acknowledge him. Things had gone bad in a matter of seconds. He'd fucked up. He suddenly felt he should have waited until the house was empty, but he became impatient. Now he was pinned down in the corner and caught between a rock and a hard place. The detective was on his phone calling for backup with the intruder trapped in his bedroom.

More shots slammed into the dresser Kool-Aid hid behind. He couldn't stay there for too long. He wasn't about to panic, though. Being in a gunfight wasn't anything new to him. He just needed to think. It was always his dream to go out in a blaze of glory, but tonight wasn't his night to die.

Kool-Aid reached for a lamp near him and tossed it at the door. The detective took the bait. When he jumped up to fire, Kool-Aid sprang into action and had the man dead in his sights. Before the cop could react, Kool-Aid opened fire on his ass, striking him multiple times in the chest. The cop was dead, but backup was coming.

Quickly, Kool-Aid ransacked the house to make it look like a burglary gone bad. He wasn't worried about his prints because of the latex gloves he wore. Within minutes, the place looked like a tornado had gone through it. Kool-Aid snatched up some jewels and cash and hurried back to his car. He jumped inside and sped away, just minutes before two police cars with their lights flashing and sirens blaring came to a halting stop in front of the home. It wasn't the way he had planned it, but the job was done. Next was Clinton Trotter. This one had to go down a little more smoothly, and fast.

***

Kool-Aid was a psychotic genius, and his plan to cunningly kill Detective Clinton Trotter was a masterpiece. He got the idea from watching the documentary of one of his favorite hit men of all time: Richard Kuklinski. The mafia hit man claimed to have killed over a hundred people from 1948 to 1986. Kool-Aid idolized the man and had picked up some of his methods of killing people. Using cyanide to poison victims was one of Kuklinski's favorite techniques. The poison was hard to detect during an autopsy and it was a clever way to execute a hit. Kool-Aid decided to use the method on the detective.

For a day, Kool-Aid followed the detective from his home to various parts of Queens, watching the man run errands for his family on his day off. Trotter picked up the dry cleaning, went into Best Buy to buy a few things, pumped gas in his car, stopped by a friend's and so on. Kool-Aid was bored out of his mind following the man around.

When Trotter went into the local store to purchase a few things, Kool-Aid saw his opportunity to strike. He stepped out of the car with a nasal spray bottle in his hand and his jacket draped over his forearm. Inside the bottle was the deadly cyanide. Kool-Aid calmly walked toward the store and waited for his victim to exit. The day was brisk and the streets were quiet and free of much traffic, vehicle and pedestrian.

Kool-Aid took one final pull from the Newport between his lips and tossed it. He looked around to see if anything was out of the ordinary, but everything in his surrounding area seemed cool. He had to strike now. There was no way he was about to let Luca down. She ordered the kill, and he was like Burger King—have it your way.

Five minutes went by before the detective walked out of the store with a bag in his hand. He walked toward his car, unaware of the danger coming his way. Kool-Aid walked toward him, looking remote and expressionless. He hid the nasal spray under the jacket he carried. As he walked toward his victim, he slightly raised his forearm with the hidden bottle, not to raise any suspicion. His prey was approaching closer; Kool-Aid watched him from his peripheral vision and acted normal. The last thing he wanted to do was alert the man that he was in danger. When they were about to pass each other on the sidewalk, Kool-acted swiftly, but cunningly. He pretended to sneeze into the man's direction, spraying the nasal bottle precisely into the victim's face. The detective quickly reacted and was livid.

"What the fuck, man!" he shouted heatedly.

"I'm so sorry. It's this weather, it got me under the weather," Kool-Aid respectfully apologized.

He let out a fraudulent cough.

"You spread germs and shit like that, man! Cover your fuckin' mouth."

"I'm so sorry. It just came suddenly," said Kool-Aid.

The detective frowned intensely at Kool-Aid, but he wasn't about to overreact. It was just an improper sneeze from a fool who seemed harmless, but had no manners at all. Kool-Aid backed away, still apologizing and looking like a regular, harmless kid in his preppy attire. One could never guess that the boy wearing the wire-rimmed glasses and beige khakis was an advanced killer. Therefore, detective Clinton Trotter didn't give him a second thought.

The two went their separate ways. The detective repeatedly wiped his face from the handkerchief he removed from his pocket. He continued to curse as he walked toward his car. Kool-Aid trotted across the street. He was out of the danger zone, and now it was time to watch his work take effect. The poison had already absorbed into Trotter's skin.

Before Kool-Aid could get into his car, he already noticed the poison taking an effect on his victim. The toxin could kill within minutes, maybe sooner. The detective started to stumble while he walked, and then he fell against a wall. He looked dazed and confused. He clutched his throat. It appeared that he was choking on something, gasping for breath. He then collapsed on his back, dying slowly.

It looked like the man was having a seizure on the hard concrete. People in the area noticed the detective in some kind of distress and they immediately came to his aid, calling 911. It would be too late; he was already dead.

Kool-Aid smiled. His job was done.

It was clean and subtle.

He turned the ignition and drove away.

Two detectives dead within forty-eight hours. It was surely going to make the news and raise some suspicion.

12

Luca was dressed to the nines in her black, short, double-breasted Ralph Lauren peacoat, sporting boyfriend jeans and a corset with leather boots. She was bejeweled in diamonds and platinum bling. She was making a statement; she was back, wiser than before; moving fifteen kilos a week and grossing millions of dollars for herself. She stood in silence over the gray granite tombstone of Walter Charter in the well-kept cemetery in Queens, New York. The granite tombstone reflected the sunlight, and tall trees inundated the grassy area. The cemetery was eerily silent for a moment.

Luca didn't come to the cemetery to pay her respects or grieve over Charter's death. She had other intentions. She needed to see the truth for herself even if she *had* been the one to pull the trigger and take his life. Luca had to cover every corner, turn black into white. It was better to be safe than sorry. It was the reason why she paid two caretakers ten thousand dollars each to illegally exhume the body of Walter Charters.

The Hispanic caretaker sitting in the backhoe started to disturb the earth and slowly dug down into the grave. Luca stood patiently as the backhoe removed mounds of dirt from the grave and came closer to the bronze casket nestled inside the earth.

Within the hour, the casket was brought up and ready to open. Luca stepped closer, watching the caretakers handle everything with care.

"You ready for this?" the Hispanic man asked.

"I'm paying you both a good fuckin' amount of money for this, so shut the fuck up, do your job, and let me see the body inside," Luca barked.

The man shrugged. "Hey, I was just asking, lady."

"Don't ask. I'm a big fuckin' girl."

He didn't reply. Luca was a hard bitch that didn't want to be looked upon as weak. She had seen death before, so it offended her when the man asked the question. If it was a man instead of a pretty woman standing there, would he have asked him that too? she thought.

The caretaker slowly opened the casket, revealing the corpse inside. Luca stepped forward with a cold stare. She looked down at the body inside and confirmed that it was Walter Charter's body. He was dressed in a dark blue suit, and his body hardly looked decomposed.

The sight of him again put a bad taste in Luca's mouth. She stared down at him for a moment and remembered that awful night. Did she ever love him, she asked herself, or was the detective nearly a pawn in her chess game? The sight of the body somewhat disturbed her stomach and in front of the caretakers, she gargled up a chunk of spit inside her mouth and spat on the corpse, disrespecting the man's final resting place.

"Fuck you!" Luca cursed.

The two caretakers looked dumbfounded at her despicable action toward the body, but they kept their silence and minded their business. Ten thousand dollars lining their pockets was more money they ever saw at one time. The crazy woman could do whatever she wanted to do with the body; they assumed it was maybe her late husband that did her wrong.

Luca spit on the body again, this time in his face, and cursed again. If she could kill him again, she wouldn't hesitate. What he had done to her was unforgivable. Because of Charter, she had lost a fortune from her home. Luca was so heated, she was ready to wrap her hands around the man's neck and choke him, but it would have been useless, he was already dead.

"I hope you burn in hell for eternity, muthafucka!" she exclaimed.

She had seen enough. She looked at the two caretakers and said, "Throw his black ass back inside that hole."

If she could, she would have taken the body out of the casket and tossed him into the hole as is—would've hacked him up and then buried the body. He didn't need to be resting in some bronze, cushy casket. He needed to be eaten by worms and maggots. Luca yearned to desecrate the body by any means, but it was too much to do, and she had other places to be.

Luca pivoted on her heels and walked away. She had gotten her assurances. Charter was no longer a threat to anyone. She exited the cemetery with the sun gradually vanishing behind the horizon, the weather becoming colder as night descended onto the city. Luca looked at the time and it was almost six in the evening. She removed a cigarette from her pack and lit it up before she climbed into her black-on-black Audi S8, one of the newest toys that she treated herself to. She started the ignition and the car purred silently. It was sleek and it was fast, and Luca loved every bit of it.

She sped away into the evening looking like a diva behind the wheel. Her comeback in the game was swift and subtle like Michael Jordan on the basketball courts in his heyday. In fact, she considered herself to be the Michael Jordan of the drug game. No one could touch her or compete with her. She was too smart, connected, computer savvy, and business savvy, and she had a handful of killers in her pocket who would kill anything at a mere snap of her fingers. It felt good to have that type of power and that type of money to buy and do anything she wanted—for example, illegitimately exhuming the body of a dead cop.

Luca, just recently learning how to drive, shakily bent the corners like the newbie driver she was, which didn't stop her from hitting 80 mph. She was having some fun inside her new car, pushing the pedal to the metal and showing off like a kid with a new toy. It didn't take long for glaring blue-and-red police lights to shine in her rearview mirror. She was tempted to take them on a high-speed chase, but she thought better of it. Luca nearly cursed, "Fuck me," and slowly pulled to the side, thinking it was just a routine traffic stop.

She was alone on the quiet and serene street in Rockaway Park. Luca put the car in PARK, leaving the Audi idling, and sighed heavily. She was armed with a .9mm in a stash box in the center console. The last thing she needed was a gun charge and some time in jail.

Luca gazed into her rearview mirror and suddenly noticed the car pulling her over wasn't a marked police car, but an unmarked car. She looked sharply, seeing both doors open up and two men in plain clothes stepping out of the vehicle with the police lights still shining. They both approached her car with extreme caution with their hands placed on their holstered weapons on their hips.

What is this about? Luca wondered.

She kept her cool, but she knew a single black woman in a private suburban area getting pulled over by two white cops could be trouble. Luca right away pulled out her cell phone and pushed the record button. She wasn't taking any chances. Both men approached the vehicle, scowling; one went toward the passenger side and the second came toward the driver's side. They were white males, each standing six feet tall. The one on the driver's side had a lean body with a narrow, clean-shaven face and intense eyes. The cop on the passenger side was stockier, with a thick goatee and bald head. They were dressed in blue jeans and jackets, their badges displayed over their clothing. It was no mistake that they were official.

Luca rolled down her window halfway, not risking anything. The detective came to the window and peered inside. Luca felt tense. She looked at the man and asked, "Why did you pull me over?"

"Ma'am, we need for you to step out of the car please," he said.

"Why?"

The man looked like he was ready to become a hardass. "Look, we can do this the easy way, or we can do it the hard way. It's your choice," the detective stated in a stern tone.

Luca wanted to become defiant, but she was in a bad predicament. She sighed with frustration and stepped out of her car. She felt her heart in her throat, and though she kept a cool demeanor, she was extremely nervous. The detective on the passenger side walked over to stand next to his partner. They looked like two rednecks ready to conduct a lynching.

"We know who you are, Luca," the lean cop said. "You think you can fuck with us and get away with it?"

"I have no idea what you're talking about," she replied.

The cop scowled heavily and stepped closer to Luca in a threatening manner. Luca took two steps backwards and found herself pinned between her car and two menacing-looking cops.

"You nigger bitch!" he growled through his clenched teeth. "You think you can kill two of ours and live your life peacefully?"

"I have no idea what you're talking about, Detective," Luca replied calmly.

"Detective Cannon and Detective Trotter, both dead within forty-eight hours of each other, I find that fuckin' ironic—especially since they were the two detectives investigating your case."

Luca repeated once again, "I have no idea what you're talking about, Detective. I'm a law-abiding citizen. I pay my taxes. I pay my dues. I'm no criminal."

The casual and condescending tone coming from Luca infuriated the detective in charge. He abruptly wrapped his hand around Luca's slim neck and pushed her against the car with force. She was stunned and scared.

"Look, you black bitch," the detective screamed out, "you fucked up, and we know it was you who set up the hit."

His nostrils flared and his eyes burned into Luca. He squeezed harder, craving to choke her to death or simply break her neck. He was strong. He was furious and wanted revenge for his fallen brothers. His partner looked enraged also, but he saw that his friend was taking things too far, and especially in the public view. With his free hand, he removed his issued Glock 19 and pressed it into her forehead. Now with a gun to her head and his hand wrapped around her neck, Luca thought he would be crazy enough to kill her.

"I can kill you right now, bitch, and no one would give a fuck."

Luca gasped in his grasp. He squeezed harder.

His partner stepped closer to the incident and exclaimed, "Detective Stagger, that's enough!"

"Fuck this black bitch. I want her dead!"

"Now it's not the time or place, Stagger. Look around you. Too many loose ends everywhere," his partner said reasonably.

The detective lowered his gun from her forehead and loosened his grip around her neck. Luca caught her breath quickly and shot a murderous look at the cop. If she'd had the chance, she would have killed him where he stood. But for now, the cops had the upper hand.

Detective Stagger glared at her and through his yellowing, clenched teeth, said, "You want to start a war with the NYPD, and I'll make sure you will lose. I'll stick my fuckin' gun so far up your black, nasty twat that you'll spit bullets from your black lips. You don't fuck with us. You're going down, bitch; that's a guarantee."

Detective Stagger holstered his weapon and stepped away from Luca. He had made his point clearly. Luca scowled but kept quiet. It was a tense situation, but she kept her cool. The detectives walked back to their unmarked car and climbed inside, leaving Luca standing in the street. She was highly perturbed by their harassment, but it wasn't going to deter her from moving forward with her plan. They didn't know who they were fuckin' with.

Luca climbed back into the driver's seat and picked up her cell phone. She smiled seeing it was still recording. She stopped it and pushed play to hear how clear it sounded, and no doubt, she heard the cop's voice and his threats clearly. She smiled, saying to herself, "Yes, fuck with me if you want, and I'll have both of y'all badges."

✳✳✳

Luca's run-in with the two racist detectives didn't bother her too much. They came with their idle threats, and that's what they were, idle threats. They didn't have any hard evidence against her. She did fume that the detectives had the audacity to harass her in public. And that one muthafucka who choked her and put his gun to her head—she was tempted to sic her dogs on him. Fortunately for the detectives, enough cops' blood had been spilled in Rockaway Park, where things were starting to heat up to a boiling point. So Luca needed to calm things down for the moment.

She needed some stress relief. Unfortunately Squirrel wasn't around to provide her with the good dick she needed, so she had to settle for a quick substitute. She was becoming sexually frustrated and needed some intimacy to escape the stress of the game. She had her needs, and with her pussy itching to be scratched, she found the right guy to scratch it.

She navigated her Audi S8 to Yonkers and came to a stop in front of a three-story condo on a busy boulevard. It was home to a young buck she had met in the club last week. His name was Rondo, and he was nineteen, six-three, and fine from head to toe. His astonishing physique protruded from his shirt and his gleaming bald head, baby-face features, and hazel eyes made him a definite cutie. He boasted about playing basketball overseas and hopefully making it to the NBA someday. His pipe dreams bored Luca when she only wanted one thing from him: her pussy eaten out and a good fuck. He wasn't Squirrel, but he would temporarily do.

Luca stepped out of her ride in the winter cold with her double-breasted peacoat buttoned up to the top, and underneath it, something lovely for Rondo to peel away in whatever fashion he wanted to claim the prize underneath. She strutted into the atrium and toward the stairway like a bitch on a mission. No one knew about her boy toy in Yonkers. It was her business, and her business only. Tonight, after everything she'd been through, she needed some playtime to herself. She needed to spread her legs to the towering eye candy and forget about the game, Squirrel, and all her troubles.

She definitely needed to forget about Squirrel. Every day without him in her life made her heart grow heavier and heavier. Their business arrangement was working out perfectly, but her love life with him was still a shaky place. Angel had all her man's time, and Squirrel only became business. Luca yearned for the day when things became sexual and hot and heavy between them again.

She wanted to be Squirrel's personal nut that he would always crack.

Rondo's place was on the third floor. It was an attractive place, quiet with a beautiful hilltop view of five miles of Yonkers, and at night, from Rondo's terrace the picturesque view was breathtaking.

Luca knocked on Rondo's door. She took a deep breath and waited for him to answer. She tried to erase her memory of her earlier disaster with the police. It would be forgotten for now because they were only fishing to indict her on something. It was the only pass the detective would get, if they kept on roughly pushing then it would be inevitable that she would push back.

The door opened and a smiling Rondo greeted her. Luca didn't have time for the foreplay or pleasantries; she wanted to feel some sexual gratification quickly. She pushed the young boy into his apartment and invited herself in.

"We got to make this quick. I have somewhere to be tonight," said Luca.

Rondo smiled. He replied, "Okay. I missed you, though."

The sentimental reply flew over her head and she acted like he had sneezed or burped. His feelings for her meant nothing; like a fleeting thought, like ocean waves crashing against a deserted shore.

Rondo, clad only in jeans, couldn't wait to lay his hands on the beauty in front of him. He walked toward her with a strong sexual twinkle in his eyes. Luca undid her coat and removed it like a banana being peeled.

They went into the bedroom where she undressed for him and then she placed her light brown skin against the softness of his king size mattress and spread her legs widely so he would be able to enjoy her. Her shaved slit looked delicious enough to eat. And Rondo was ready to eat her out.

Rondo tore away his jeans leaving his dick dangling and his chiseled chest looking more alluring than anything else. He climbed between her opened thighs and started to kiss her breasts softly and worked his way down her soft skin.

"I need you," he said. The words flowed sweetly from his lips like honey dripping on her.

He was ready to love her and please her, unaware that she was a murderous drug queenpin. In his eyes, Luca was a beautiful flower, so innocent and pure—a rose without any thorns. But her thorns were sharp and prickly and able to cut like razor blades.

He wanted to taste her sweet nectar as he kissed his way down her body. She invited him to taste her, lick her, to eat her sweetness. She cried out as his lips worked her sweet spot. Her breathing was labored. Luca's spread legs were trembling as she felt her climax approaching.

The way he ate out her pussy was mind-blowing. There was no doubt that Rondo truly enjoyed tunneling his tongue inside of her, tasting and boxing her clit with his tongue, his lips clamped around her pink walls. She held his head in place and prepared to flood his mouth with pleasure.

The man ate, and ate, and ate, he wouldn't stop, he couldn't stop; he needed her sweet juices to run down his face like the juices of a sticky, sweet mango on a hot summer's day. Rondo craved her body, and it was her hot, wet core that was calling out to him. He covered her body with his strapping frame with beads of perspiration forming on his cinnamon skin. He rolled a condom back onto his erection, then took careful aim and made his descent. Luca's silky walls caressed him, bathed him, their bodies collided together as their passionate lovemaking turned into heated fucking. She needed to feel a big, strong man inside of her. She needed her pussy devoured and stroked heatedly. His flesh pressed into hers and it took her breath away. They moved together in unison, two bodies, and one soul.

He gripped her hips hard and buried himself deeply into her glorious-feeling insides like a Mandingo warrior.

"Oh please, don't stop," Luca cried out.

"I damn sure won't…"

They fucked vigorously. He roared inside of her, with Luca cooing, "Ooooh, I needed this. Fuck me! Fuck me!"

Her cries, her moans and groans were a soundtrack of transcendent pleasure. Being with Rondo, having him deep inside of her, she felt that temporary escape, that feeling of bliss. Her mind was somewhere else, but then it all changed. As Rondo had her legs vertically in the air, her legs spread like eagle wings and pounding his dick inside of her, her phone rang out of the blue. She wanted to ignore it, but she couldn't. It was probably important. It was easy for Rondo to ignore her ringing phone. He wanted to finish off with a bang.

"Stop," Luca said.

Her phone rang and vibrated against the dresser. Rondo continued going, his ass and pelvis grinding and bouncing up and down between her thighs.

"You feel so fuckin' good, baby."

She wasn't his baby. He was only a piece of dick.

"Stop!" she commanded.

She felt too good to stop suddenly. Luca pushed him off of her before he angered her. "I said stop. I need to answer it." No matter where she was at, her business always came first.

Luca rolled off the bed naked with her body glistening, and pussy tingling. She picked up her cell phone and had the shock of her life. It was Squirrel calling her out of the blue. Her eyes widened with excitement. Usually, she was calling him and it was always about business; now here he was calling in the night. Luca didn't hesitate to answer, even with Rondo watching and listening. It was highly important to her to find out what he wanted.

13

Squirrel frowned heavily at Angel lying on the floor with her black eye; bottom lip split open and blood trickling to the floor. He hadn't meant to hit her so hard, but his temper had gotten the best of him. He clenched his fists and was ready to strike her again if she continued to disrespect him. He'd had enough of her mouth and bullshit. Angel's feisty attitude always brought out the worst in him.

"You just don't know when to shut the fuck up, you dumb bitch. I told you I'm not fuckin' her anymore," Squirrel shouted.

"You're a liar, Squirrel! A stupid, muthafuckin' liar!" Angel shouted heatedly. "I don't trust you at all."

"You're a dumb and insecure bitch," he retorted.

"I hate you! I fuckin' hate you!" Angel shouted. "Go to hell!"

Squirrel's eyes brimmed with anger. He was sick and tired of Angel accusing him of still having an affair going on with Luca. It had been a long while since they fucked. He tried to explain to his baby mama that when she came around, it was only for business. She was his number-one client, producing millions for his empire. Luca was a strong and profitable commodity. Now Angel was giving him an ultimatum: Luca or her. Squirrel wasn't about to choose between his baby mama and money. It pissed him off to the point where he beat her down, blackened her eye, and busted her lip.

"Who the fuck you think you are telling me what I *need* to do? Remember who the fuck I am and what I'm capable of doing, Angel," he spat.

Squirrel charged over and grabbed his baby mama by her long hair and dragged her across the floor and toward the door. Angel kicked and screamed. She cursed him like she never had before. Squirrel was ready to set an example.

"Get the fuck out my house, you unappreciative bitch!"

Squirrel tossed her out of his apartment like yesterday's trash.

"Fuck you, Squirrel! You fuckin' bastard!" Angel screamed. "You can't keep doin' me like this."

"Yes I can," he boldly replied.

Angel jumped up and tried to attack him. Squirrel swung and knocked her squarely in the jaw. She dropped abruptly with pain shooting through her face. He then kicked her in her stomach and Angel doubled over from the pain. One of Squirrel's goons watched the argument and assault take place. He stood like a statue knowing it wasn't his business. Angel continued to curse and create a scene in the narrow project hallway despite getting assaulted. And what was most humiliating, she was in her panties and T-shirt, but didn't seem to care at all.

"Get the fuck out my face, you jealous fuckin' bitch!" Squirrel shouted.

"Fuck you! I ain't goin' no-fuckin'-where!" Angel retorted with tears streaming down her face.

"You think you not—"

"You a bastard, nigga! You put your hands on a woman, you think that makes you a fuckin' man. You fuckin' coward! You pussy!"

Squirrel looked at his towering goon standing not too far from them and said, "Mack, get this bitch outta my sight."

He didn't care if Angel was in her panties and bra or that it was cold outside; Squirrel just wanted her gone. Mack walked over and finished what Squirrel started. He effortlessly grabbed Angel with brute force and forced her into the stairway kicking and screaming.

"I told you, bitch, don't fuck with me." He was finally fed up with her.

Squirrel slammed his door shut, and still heard Angel's loud, vengeful voice echoing into his apartment. He needed to forget about his baby mama. It had been a stressful week. Just the other night he had to murder one of his soldiers because of his disloyalty, now he had to beef with his baby mama. He turned over the kitchen table in rage. He needed to calm down, but how?

If Luca wasn't on his mind then, she was now. Squirrel thought about her and that pussy, how good it was and how super wet it got for him; the way it contracted around his big dick when he was inside of her.

Fuck Angel!

Squirrel decided he had been away from that good and sweet pussy for too long. It was time to go back to it. He picked up his cell phone and dialed her number. He was determined to speak to her, and he let the phone ring repeatedly until she answered.

"Hey," Luca answered, knowing it was Squirrel calling and trying to contain the excitement in her voice.

"What you doin', you busy or sumthin'?" he asked.

"No," she quickly answered.

"Good, then you and me, we need to talk," said Squirrel.

"We do."

"Tomorrow night, meet me in the city, Midtown. You know that restaurant where you sucked my dick for an hour in the front seat of the truck?"

"You remember that, huh?"

"I remember a lot of things about you, Luca. You were fun, and we were good together," Squirrel said.

"We were definitely good together," Luca replied. She was tempted to say it was good times until his baby mama raised hell. But why bring that bitch up when they were having a civil conversation for once and it wasn't about business?

"I do miss you though, Luca."

She blushed when she heard Squirrel say he missed her. She was ready to jump through the phone and take him there. However, she kept her composure, even though hearing his voice made her pussy wet and tingly. She missed him so much.

"What time do you want to meet?" she asked.

"In the evening, say around nine. And wear something sexy."

"I will," she assured him.

"A'ight, I gotta go, and don't keep me waiting tomorrow."

"I won't, Squirrel. Love you," she asserted happily.

Squirrel didn't reply to the *love you* remark. He hung up with a smug look on his face. He had that bitch in his pocket. It was guaranteed pussy from Luca tomorrow evening. Just thinking about how he was going to freak her off made his dick hard. His baby mama wanted to act up, then fuck her, he thought. There were women lined up a block long ready to be with him, and Luca was the first in line.

Yeah, Luca was the right type of bitch to take his mind off of things. Forgive and forget, for the time being anyway.

***

The minute Luca hung up with Squirrel, she was ready to leave Rondo's apartment. Suddenly she wasn't feeling him anymore. Her main love had called to rekindle their relationship and she was ready to jump into it like a girl playing double Dutch.

Rondo looked at her with a strong unease in his eyes. His dick was still hard like concrete and he was ready to continue where they had left off.

He was ready to bust a nut. The aloof look Luca shot back said otherwise.

"You still ready to do this?" he asked.

"Something suddenly came up and I need to go."

"Now?"

"Yes, now," she shot back.

Luca didn't care about his feelings. She collected her things throughout the bedroom and started to get dressed. Rondo stood butt-naked and dumbfounded with a hard dick and anger simmering inside of him. He couldn't believe it was going down like this.

"What are you, a fuckin' cocktease? You get a nigga started and then just leave. A nigga can't get a blow job or something?"

"Blowjob," she returned coldly. "Nigga please."

"Oh, so it's like that, after I done ate out your pussy you ready to bounce on a nigga," Rondo exclaimed heatedly. He stood to his full height, still naked, and glared at Luca. "And what if I don't let you leave?"

Luca glared back and returned, "Believe me sweetheart, you do not even want to go there with me."

Rondo clenched his fists and locked eyes with Luca. He was so horny that it hurt. "So the next nigga calls and you go running to that nigga like some thirsty bitch?"

"You hardly know me, and for your sake, let's keep it like that."

"You know what, fuck you!" he shouted. "Get the fuck out my house before I throw you out."

Luca smirked. He was skating on thin ice with his disrespectful insults. Lucky for him, Squirrel calling her to meet up put her in a really good mood and she thought against siccing her dogs on Rondo.

"Gladly, lose my fuckin' number, nigga," Luca replied and walked out of the bedroom.

Rondo seethed with both hurt and anger. When he heard the door shut, he released a few tears—that fleeting sexual experience with Luca was some of the best pussy he'd ever had.

✳✳✳

The following evening couldn't come fast enough for Luca. She wanted to fast-forward time so she could go on her date with Squirrel. She stepped out of her Audi S8 with her six-inch red-bottoms touching the concrete in the bustling neighborhood of Midtown Manhattan. It felt like the perfect day and she felt like the perfect woman.

Elegantly clad in a wool trench coat, a stylish halter top with the deep plunging neckline, and a pair of Stella McCartney harem pants, she couldn't wait to see her man and grab his undivided attention.

The restaurant where they were meeting at was called Dovetail, located on 59th Street. The upscale gem was secluded on week nights, but on the weekends you had to book weeks in advance for a table.

Luca looked around to see if Squirrel was standing anywhere outside, but he wasn't. She assumed he was inside already, seated at a table, dressed handsomely and waiting for his queen to show up. She proceeded toward the entrance, striding in the winter cold like she was a figure skater on ice. It was hard to contain her smile. It was hard not to be happy.

Before Luca entered the restaurant, she stopped dead in her tracks when she saw her standing in a distance, grabbing her attention—Naomi.

Was Naomi haunting her, or was it just part of her crazy imagination? It wasn't her guilt; she was glad the bitch was dead. But why was she having visions of her? Especially now?

There was Naomi, scantily clad in a white nightgown, her impassive look aimed at Luca through the bustling crowd. No one saw her. Luca coldly stared back. She refused to go crazy, not now when she was about to have a lovely dinner with Squirrel.

Naomi stepped closer, and as her transparent figure walked toward

Luca she peeled away her nightgown, revealing her chocolate-brown skin, and smiled like she knew a dirty little secret. She was Luca's first kill, and they say your first kill always comes back to haunt you, especially when they were a friend. Naomi was never a *true* friend.

Luca closed her eyes for a short moment, praying the frightful image would go away, and when she reopened them, the bitch was finally gone. Luca breathed with relief, but the hand placed on her shoulder from behind startled her greatly. She quickly pivoted and screamed, thinking it was Naomi. To her embarrassment, it was Squirrel.

"You okay?" Squirrel asked.

Luca quickly collected herself and smiled. Seeing Squirrel made her feel at ease.

"I'm okay."

"You sure?"

Luca nodded. There was no way she was going to allow some bitch from her past to ruin the moment she had longed for with Squirrel. She gazed at her king. He looked so good in his leather jacket, boot-cut jeans, and beige Timberlands. The one-carat, round-cut diamond stud earring shimmered in his left ear like a small sun. It was easy to see Squirrel was someone important. He looked like a platinum selling rapper with his bling showing and domineering stature. Luca noticed the fleeting looks he received from some of the ladies passing by and decided to claim her prize. She stepped closer to him and planted her lips against his, and he didn't resist. They kissed in public for a moment.

Dinner was five stars in Dovetail. They each had a charred sirloin accompanied by beef cheek lasagna layered with paper-thin slices of turnips. The dish was hearty and delicious. It was just them, engaged in an intimate moment and lengthy conversation.

Squirrel was funny and sweet. He made her laugh and smile. Luca didn't want the evening to end. They were meant to be together. She couldn't take her eyes off of him as they dined and talked. There was no question about it, she was hardcore, head-over-heels in love with him. She never had feelings like this for any man, not even Nate. Squirrel had her heart in his hand, and the majority of the time, he bounced it around like a basketball—playing games.

"You do look great, Luca," he complimented with a smile.

"And you always look great, baby. I'm glad you called me—you know, about something other than business."

"I've been thinkin' about you, Luca. I fucked up, and I regret treating you the way that I did. It was wrong of me."

"Baby, I been forgave you," she revealed.

"You did?"

She nodded.

She took a sip of wine and wore her heart on her sleeve. It was really going good this evening, but there was one thing that still bothered her, and she needed to know. The thought of it was like a bad taste in her mouth.

"So what's going on with you and Angel? Is she still in your life?" Luca asked. She was nervous to hear the truth.

"I've been done with her, Luca. That bitch is no longer in my life. The only thing that bonds us is our children, and that's it," he replied with a straight face.

"So no more Angel? Just us?" Luca asked with hope.

"No more Angel, baby. That bitch is just a baby mama in my life," he said with conviction. He rose slightly out of his chair and leaned across the table in her direction.

Luca lifted her buttocks out of the chair too and they kissed in the restaurant, across the table like heated lovers. She felt such a connection with him that a spark of electricity shot through her when her full lips smashed against his. Her pussy throbbed and she was ready to melt.

"You love me?" she asked.

"I love you," he lied.

Luca was a genius with a superior IQ of 134, but sometimes when it came to love, she was known to ride on the short yellow bus. She longed to be loved by someone, but throughout time, love had done her wrong so many times. She remembered the story that her mother told her about her father and their love for one another—how her father loved her mother so much that he actually killed a man for her. Her parents might have been two penniless junkies, but they had actual unquestionable love for each other. It was the same love she wanted from Squirrel.

After dinner, the two of them left the restaurant hugging and kissing on each other like two love birds. She was happy. She couldn't wait to feel him inside of her once more. If only he would ask her to marry him. She was ready to say *I do* at the drop of a hat. Every woman wanted to feel loved, even cold-hearted female drug dealers. She wanted his baby inside of her again. She craved to have his son, to give them both a parental bond—a life they both created. She wanted a life with him. She wanted happiness and joy. Luca only wanted him. Somehow, Squirrel became her core, and it was hard to exist without him in her world. But for now, sex with him would do.

"Damn baby, this is you?" Squirrel asked, pointing at her parked Audi S8.

"Yes, it is." Luca smiled.

"You coming up, baby. I love your style."

His compliment warmed her heart and made her feel butterflies in her stomach. Any love and praise she got from him was like receiving diamonds; they were just that precious.

In separate cars they drove back to her place in Rockaway Park. He followed behind her. During the drive, Luca swam in excitement. She wanted to push the accelerator to the floor and hit 100 mph on the highway, but was afraid she would lose Squirrel in the process or get pulled over. He closely drove behind her in his red Corvette, and every minute she would check her rearview mirror to see if he was still following behind her. She didn't want to lose him again.

In her luxurious home, Squirrel and Luca took their time, exploring each other's bodies and capitalizing off of each second of sensual pleasure. They kissed for what seemed like hours in the bedroom, and Luca was ready to surrender herself to him. However he wanted her, she was ready to give it. She was over the moon excited. It was the first time Squirrel had ever kissed her like that, so passionate and so deep. She was softened by his touch and moaned against him. He kissed and licked her neck, finding her sensual hot spot and making her moan in pleasure. He kissed her ears and whispered the sort of naughty things he wanted to do to her. Luca responded by spreading her legs and grinding her body in time with his. Her hands roamed without restraint over his big strong chest, washboard abs, and muscular back, caressing him and unbuttoning his shirt at the appropriate intervals.

At some point, her clothes ended up on the floor, and Squirrel could do nothing but stare in amazement. He never got tired of seeing her naked. Her curves went everywhere, her skin was soft like cotton, and her pussy looked so delectable. Her beautiful breasts were round and full and capped off by the most delicious pink, suckable nipples. It was no contest, she had a much better body than his baby mama. Over the years, Angel had gained weight and developed stretch marks across her stomach. She was still sexy and pretty, but she couldn't hold a candle to what Luca was packing. Luca's astonishing body with her tiny waist and big ole booty that made women envious and men weak with lust, and the freak she had inside her was what always brought Squirrel back.

Squirrel laid her down on the bed for more room to stretch out and get comfortable, and he began exploring her body with his mouth. Luca closed her eyes and moaned; she enjoyed everything he was doing to her. For once, things were passionate and not rushed between them. They were on a bed instead of the front seat of his truck, or with her curved over the bathroom sink in one of his stash houses, or sneaking a fuck on the couch before someone walked in. They were together, intimate and passionate with each other, just how Luca wanted it.

Squirrel parted her soft thighs and gaped at her magnificent looking pussy. She took her manicured fingers and spread her lips, and her inner pink lips opened to reveal themselves like a beautiful orchid. Squirrel touched her pussy gently, exploring her hardened clit, and watched her body respond to his soothing touch.

They shifted into different positions on the bed, with her face hovering over his big, fat dick. Squirrel grabbed his cock and fed it to her. Luca wrapped her full, glossy lips around it and he felt her hot, wet mouth enveloping him as she swallowed him up. She paced herself while sucking his dick, using her mouth like a vacuum, trying to suck the cum from his balls. He gripped the sheets and arched his back. Luca was the best that ever did it to him. She sucked his dick for a moment, and then she wanted him inside of her.

In the missionary position, the heat was intense and he could feel the muscles of her pussy grabbing him before the head was even inside of her. He gripped her thigh and pushed forward and once he was completely inside of her, she straddled him tightly and dragged her manicured nails down his muscular back.

"Ooooh, fuck me, Squirrel. Fuck me, baby, fuck me so good. I missed you so much," Luca cooed.

Squirrel pumped his engorged dick in and out of her wet, hot pussy. He stroked and thrust and drove every single inch of his hard meat inside of Luca. They made passionate love to each other and she was going wild, chanting and moaning and begging for more of him. It was lovemaking at its best. The sounds of their heavy, wet, and fervent sex filled the room as he kept pounding into her. He was a man on a mission, and she was a woman on a mission too. She wanted to get pregnant again. She wanted his cum swimming around inside of her and his seed digging into her egg.

He fucked her harder.

She moaned louder.

He could feel the cum in his nuts boiling up like a volcano about ready to erupt. Luca pulled him down on top of her, their glistening bodies tightly entwined. "Come in me, baby . . . come in me, I wanna have your baby," she cried out fervently.

Squirrel thrust harder, which was followed by loud grunting. And then he came inside of her, giving Luca what she wanted. He couldn't hold out any longer, her pussy was just too good. He pulled out of her and looked down to see his big, black dick glistening with her juices, and then he rolled over and collapsed on his back. He stared up at her ceiling and looked dazed for a moment.

They cuddled together in her bed and Luca couldn't be any happier. She wanted him to make her a priority in his life. It was all she asked for—his time and his everlasting loving.

She wanted her life to become a fairytale.

14

She fell asleep in his arms and woke up with Squirrel still holding her as the morning sun percolated through the open windows in her bedroom. It was one of the most blissful nights that Luca had ever had. It was like a dream come true. For once, she didn't feel like his personal booty call, his cum collector, or some desperate sidepiece or jump-off. She wanted to be his woman—his queen.

Luca gently removed herself from his arms. Squirrel was passed out, looking dead to the world. He was a gorgeous looking man, even when he was sleeping. She was ready to cook him breakfast and serve him in bed. It was that type of love she felt for him. He looked too fine naked in her bed, his body wrapped up in her sheets and his various tattoos showing like an advertisement of his ghetto, violent, and prosperous lifestyle.

Luca went into the bathroom to shower, leaving her man to sleep comfortably in her bed. Her pussy had put the nigga to sleep, and she was proud of it. In the bathroom, she gazed at her naked reflection for a moment and smiled. Life was becoming good to her. Despite the setbacks that happened over time, finally, she was coming into her own and had blossomed into the loveliest flower in the room. Some might say she was poison, but Luca didn't care what they said, as long as they respected her and stayed out of her way.

She twisted the hot and cold shower knobs to bring her shower to life. She waited for the water to get steaming warm, then stepped in to cleanse herself. As the water cascaded down on her, Luca closed her eyes and thought about something pleasant, she and Squirrel making their millions of dollars in the drug business and then retiring from the game completely. They would have a family together, great-looking kids: a son, then a girl, then maybe another boy. New York City would become a memory to them and maybe they could live abroad— somewhere foreign and tropical. Maybe the Caribbean, she came up with. She always wanted to see the Caribbean—Barbados, Jamaica, St. Barts or the Virgin Islands: nothing but the sun, the warmth, the scenic beaches, and freedom.

The thought of it all made Luca smile like the Cheshire cat in Alice in Wonderland. It was where she wanted to be—in Wonderland. Yes, it was her time to shine and to be completely happy. When Squirrel woke up, she was about to make his morning, breakfast in bed, more sex, and just the two of them.

She was so happy, she felt like singing in the shower.

Squirrel woke up with the bright, morning sun shining in his face and heard the shower running in the bathroom coupled with the master bedroom. Luca wasn't by his side, so he figured she was in the shower. He stretched and yawned and was surprised that he'd actually spent the night with her. It was fun. She was fun, and the pussy made him ready for seconds in the early morning.

He removed himself from the bed and stood up, dick swinging and all. He scratched his balls, farted like the sound of thunder, and went to join Luca in the shower. He walked toward the bathroom, ready to join his side bitch in some morning glory, but hearing Luca's cell phone ringing and vibrating on the nightstand stopped him from entering the bathroom and curiosity got the better of him. He picked up her phone and the name on the caller ID was "Ryan." Who was this muthafucka and why was he calling her so early in the fuckin' morning? He was tempted to answer it, but he didn't.

The phone stopped ringing, but Squirrel didn't put it down. He was curious. A person's cell phone was their personal daybook—their life—and it said a lot about someone. What had Luca been up to since he had sexually and personally been out of her life? he thought. Squirrel wasn't shy about going through her phone while she was in the shower, only it wasn't going to be that easy because it was password protected. The first random four numbers he typed were incorrect. He thought long before he entered the second set—the four digits on her home address. When her iPhone vibrated because he'd entered the incorrect numbers, he increasingly grew frustrated. The last set of numbers were a long shot. He typed, 1-1-8-7 and—*bingo!*—he was in. All he could think was, *Damn, this bitch is on my dick*. Luca's pass code protected phone was his month and year of birth. Some queenpin techie she was.

The first thing he did was go through her call list, looking at her dialed and received calls. He came across the names, Rondo, Ryan, Dominic, Kool-Aid, Phaedra and a few others. He noticed that Luca had dialed Dominic, Ryan and Kool-Aid the most. He already knew who Phaedra was, but this Ryan and Kool-Aid seemed to be the ones she communicated with the most, back and forth in her phone. Next, he went through her text messages and saw some personal and steamy texts that she shared with some fool named Rondo.

WHEN YOU GONNA LET ME SLIDE UP INTO THAT PUSSY AND STROKE THAT PINK BOX, BOO? I'VE BEEN THINKING ABOUT YOU SINCE WE MET. HOLLA AT ME, BEAUTIFUL.

HEY, SO YOU'VE BEEN THINKIN' BOUT ME, HUH?

WHAT YOU BEEN THINKIN' ABOUT? TELL ME…

YOU KNOW WHAT I'VE BEEN THINKIN' ABOUT,
THAT TIME YOU JERKED MY BIG FAT DICK IN THE CAR
AND MADE ME CUM SO HARD, AND I PLAYED WIT' YA PUSSY,
THAT SHIT WAS SO PINK AND FEELING TIGHT LIKE CRAZY,
I WANNA FUCK YOU, LUV

LOL…YOU DO, HUH…

STOP BEING A TEASE AND LET'S DO THIS,
I SO BADLY WANT TO FUCK YOU, YOU ARE TRULY BEAUTIFUL
AND ONE SEXY FUCKIN' WOMAN, I KNOW YA PUSSY IS GOOD, MA…

Reading the text made Squirrel infuriated and jealous. He was seeing red for some reason. Luca wasn't his woman, but he still had some strong feelings for her and seeing that she was fucking with somebody else sent a wave of ambiguous emotions through him. He continued reading the sexual texts that she and Rondo sent back and forth, and they became steamier and more vulgar. Squirrel was ready to kill this muthafucka. The more he read, the angrier he became. He no longer cared about getting some of that morning glory.

The shower stopped running. He stood in her bedroom scowling. He put on his boxers and jeans and was ready to confront Luca about the texts he read. He heard her singing and whistling in the bathroom; she was obviously in a happy mood, but he was about to seriously change the flavor in the room.

Luca stepped out of the bathroom into the bedroom wrapped in a blue towel. When she saw Squirrel was awake, she smiled widely and said, "Good morning, baby. What do you want for breakfast?"

She walked toward him with open arms, expecting to hug him and love him some more, but unexpectedly, she received hell. Squirrel marched toward her and gave her a backhand smack so hard it sent her stumbling across the room.

"You whoring bitch!" he shouted.

Squirrel had a history of issuing out domestic abuse to every woman he dated. His jealousy and insecurity could sometimes be murderous, and Luca was no exception.

Luca found herself on the floor with blood in her mouth and Squirrel standing over her. She was dazed and dumbfounded. The sudden hit brought back terrible flashbacks of the night when Charter attacked her in the same bedroom. Was this a curse on her—was this house some kind of omen?

"Are you fuckin' crazy putting your hands on me?" Luca screamed. She wasn't about to go through the same ordeal with Squirrel like the one she went through with Charter. The nightmare wasn't about to repeat itself.

Squirrel still had her cell phone in his hand, and he started to read the steamy texts to her. "Text from Rondo, 'When you gonna let me slide up into that pussy and stroke that pink box, boo?' You fuckin' this nigga?" he shouted.

"No! Baby, I only love you and only you. He's nobody to me, just some clown-ass nigga I met in the club last week," Luca exclaimed.

"I'll kill this nigga for fuckin' wit' my bitch," he screamed.

Though he put hands on her, hearing Squirrel call her *his* bitch made her feel wanted by him, and the fact that he was jealous that she was fuckin' with another man expressed that he did care for her.

Luca wiped the blood from her mouth and glared at Squirrel. She loved him, but she wasn't about to take another beating from any man. She stood up, ready to confront him if necessary.

"I just want to be with you, baby. You're my king! *My KING*!!" she hollered with passion in her voice.

"And you want to be my queen when you fuckin' niggas?" he countered angrily. "Fuck outta here."

"I ain't fuckin' anybody. He doesn't mean shit to me! You and me, baby. I promise you; it's only you and me."

"Fuck that. How I'm supposed to trust you?"

"All that I do for you, the money I bring in, my loyalty and you doubt me. But you can trust that bitch, Angel!"

They locked eyes and argued heatedly. Squirrel went into a jealous rage and started destroying things in her bedroom. Luca picked up a baseball bat she kept near her closet and readied herself. If he came charging her way, though it was going to pain her, she was going to swing and knock his head off. She had to protect herself first.

During the midpoint of the chaos and arguing, Squirrel's cell phone rang. At first he wasn't going to answer it. Luca looked at him suspiciously when he stared at his ringing phone. Squirrel smirked.

"Hey baby, what you want now?" he greeted.

"Baby?" Luca uttered in disbelief. He had the audacity to accept his baby mama's phone call and call her "baby" after he told her he was done with Angel last night.

Squirrel shot Luca a dagger-like stare, and she wanted to take the baseball bat upside his head and crush his fucking skull in. She stood naked in a towel in front of the man she loved, her pussy still tingling, but her heart feeling like it was being crushed in a vise, squeezing and squeezing, with her emotions running high.

"You sorry . . . I know you're sorry," Squirrel said into the phone to Angel, showing sheer disrespect to Luca in her own place. "I told you, baby, you can trust me. I love you and I ain't tryin' to play the mother of my kids. But look, we gonna talk later. I gotta handle something real fast."

Squirrel smiled at his baby mama's comment and hung up. Luca stood in front of him in full-blown tears, her heart and feelings in chaos. "Are you fuckin' serious?!" she screamed out.

"Look, it's been fun, Luca. I had a great night with you, and I needed that nut, but I gotta go," he said to her like she was some prostitute.

"I thought you were done with that bitch," she exclaimed.

"Obviously, I'm not. She's the mother of my kids, and you think I'm supposed to forget about her and not deal wit' her ever again?"

"Yes!"

He chuckled. "You know, ya one of the smartest bitches I ever known, but when it comes to simple shit like this, a relationship and kids, you're a fool, Luca. When you have kids—"

"When I have kids!!" she screamed heatedly. "I was about to have a baby! Your baby! And it was stolen from me! And that wasn't the first time I lost a baby! You think this is easy for me?! I want kids, Squirrel! I want a family! I wanna have your babies inside of me! I want us to be together, Squirrel—just you and me!"

Her tears rained from her eyes and puddled on the floor. The wonderful morning she expected transformed into one of the most painful and worst days of her life.

Squirrel looked at her aloofly. "I don't know what to tell you. I'm sorry for your loss. Shit happens."

Luca shot her tear stained eyes at him and snapped. She swiftly charged at him with the bat raised over her head. She screamed and swung in a frenzy at his head, and missed striking him by inches.

"What the fuck is wrong wit' you?!" Squirrel screamed, ducking and moving out of the way of her wrath.

She smashed a lamp and the dresser mirror, leaving shards of glass on the floor trying to beat him with the bat. Squirrel bobbed and weaved out of the way, with Luca swinging the bat at him like Muhammad Ali in the boxing ring. When he saw his opportunity, he snatched the bat out of her hands and punched her squarely in her face, pushing her back into the dresser. She fell to the floor from the hard blow.

"You crazy fuckin' bitch," Squirrel growled standing over her.

"Fuck you! I'm tired of your shit, Squirrel. I'm fuckin' tired of you treating me like shit! I'm tired of all y'all niggas! Get the fuck out my house!!!"

"I should have never gotten involved wit' ya crazy ass and just kept it business between us. I should fuckin' kill you right now," he threatened through clenched teeth.

"Go ahead, I don't give a fuck! Kill me! Fuck you! Kill me!"

"Fuck me? No, fuck you!"

Squirrel dropped the bat and decided to let her live. Despite their fight, she was still valuable to him. With Luca defeated both physically and emotionally on the floor, her eyes overwhelmed with tears and pain, he pivoted on his heels, said, "I'm out," and walked out of her bedroom.

Luca sobbed for hours in her bedroom. She couldn't get up. She felt paralyzed by the pain and grief constantly coming into her life. Death seemed welcoming at the moment, and love; it seemed unreal and too agonizing to put up with.

✳✳✳

All day, hour after hour, Luca sat still in her bedroom, her tears perpetually falling because of the heartbreak. Her cell phone rang time after-time, and the majority of the calls came from Phaedra. Luca ignored every phone call. She wanted to be alone and swallow herself up in sorrow.

She finally picked herself up off the floor and gazed out her bedroom window. She wanted to free her mind from the pain. She had wasted her entire day crying over him. She wasted her time and energy for a man who didn't care anything about her. Ironically, after what he put her through, she still loved him and missed him already. What kind of power did Squirrel have over her? Was it the dick? Was it his clout? It was something about him that continually magnetized her to him.

Luca's cell phone rang for the umpteenth time in the fading day. It was Phaedra once again. She had left a half dozen voicemails and several texts. Her friend was worried about her. Luca decided to call her friend, road dog, and trusted lieutenant back.

The phone rang once and Phaedra quickly answered with a nippy, "Luca, you okay? I've been fuckin' calling you all day."

"Where are you?" Luca asked.

"Brooklyn," Phaedra said.

"Come pick me up. I need to get out this house."

"Okay, I'll be there within the hour," Phaedra replied.

Luca hung up.

She wanted to get away from a home she felt was cursed. And she felt that she was being haunted. Why was she being haunted? Or why was her life cursed?

✳✳✳

It didn't take long for Phaedra to show up and pick up her friend. She could tell by Luca's voice that something had happened, but Luca refused to say what it was. It bothered Phaedra that Luca would shut her out sometimes. Since the incident with Charter, Luca had become remote to everyone that cared about her. She was there, but there was a change inside of her. Phaedra had a hint of what made Luca highly upset and what was bothering her—it was always the same fiasco with her, Squirrel.

During the ride in Phaedra's Escalade from Rockaway Park to the city, Luca peered out the window for a moment, and then she closed her eyes and said nothing. She had a lot on her mind and couldn't shake the darkness dwelling inside of her. She also felt like she was being haunted. Naomi was becoming frequent in her dreams, and if it wasn't one thing then it was another. Despite dealing with Squirrel's shit, the streets, her cousin World stalking her, the murders, she was becoming one of the most influential females in the drug game. But it was taking a toll on her.

Driving west on 495, coming closer to the city, Luca turned to look at her friend and asked, "Do he haunt you?"

Phaedra was caught off guard by the question. She whipped her head around toward Luca and asked, "What? Who haunts me?"

"Your first kill. It was Abioye, right?"

"You were there. You know he was. And why would you bring that muthafucka up? I thought we would never speak about it ever again."

"Does he haunt you?"

"Him? No!"

"She does sometimes," Luca admitted.

"Who?" Phaedra asked with a raised eyebrow.

"Naomi."

"That bitch! Why the fuck you thinkin' about her?"

"She's in my fuckin' dreams."

"So get her out your head," Phaedra said, like it was so simple.

"How? I see this bitch all the time."

Phaedra didn't have a correct answer for her. Killing Abioye was so long ago that she had forgotten about it, and she wasn't haunted by his ghost like Luca insisted she was.

Luca continued expressing her feelings to her friend. Phaedra was the only one she could talk to and be honest with. She always knew that Phaedra was going to be real with her, no matter what, the good or bad. She wasn't about to sugarcoat anything.

"Look, you're my friend, and if ya having dreams about that bitch, I wonder why? You killed her a while back and you feeling guilty about it?"

"No," Luca answered.

"It happens to some people. I've heard that sometimes your first always comes back to haunt you, but then it'll go away. Fortunately for me, it ain't like that. That nigga meant nothing to me, and Naomi, you once considered her a friend. But she never was a friend to you, and you did what you had to do, plain and simple," Phaedra stated.

Luca nodded.

"Look, you seemed stressed 'bout other things, but I know you ain't 'bout telling people ya business like that. So let's go to this spot, have a few drinks, do us, and forget about the bullshit."

Luca managed to smile. "I'm down with that."

"I know you are, cuz ya wit' me and we sisters, and we gonna get tipsy and enjoy the night," Phaedra said.

Luca was ready to do that. She figured wherever Phaedra was taking her would be better than staying home alone and having a heart attack over Squirrel. She closed her eyes and rested her head back on the headrest. She felt everything was fixable, even the bitch haunting her in her dreams and the nigga that made her scream with madness.

15

Luca and Phaedra walked into the Paradise lounge in SoHo looking like a couple of divas. It was going to be girls' night out for them both, and they needed it. The tasteful lounge was the perfect welcoming place for anyone needing a drink, along with an inviting social setting and good music. Phaedra had been dying to bring Luca to the place. And there she was, willing to relax and have a few drinks with a friend.

Luca removed her mink coat, revealing a form-fitting black sweater dress by Gucci. It hugged her curves and caught the attention of the men inside. Recently, Luca had been wearing black. It had become her color—her routine. It became her soul. For a while, Luca felt she had no light in her life, inside her heart, or in her love life, and her world had always been dark.

Phaedra tried to compete with Luca's wardrobe with tight-fitting jeans that highlighted her young, luscious curves and showed off her fatty. Her black bandanna top hugged her breasts, and the makeup she had on made her look fresh and sophisticated. Luca rarely saw Phaedra dressed this way; she was usually a tomboy in baggy men's clothing. Now, she looked feminine and beautiful. It felt great to see her friend dolled up, looking like a sexy woman. They looked equal for once, and underneath the baggy attire she always wore, Phaedra had a body to die for.

Luca knew Phaedra hadn't gotten dressed up solely to have a drink with her; there had to be a reason. Luca quickly found her reason. She thought it was a woman who had caught her friend's attention, but as they sat at the bar sipping on Cirôc Peach and Sprite, Luca noticed Phaedra's eyes slyly going back and forth to a man dressed handsomely in a dark suit. He was talking to some men at a table, obviously looking important and distinguished.

The tall Panamanian man caught Luca's attention, too. His bright, white smile generated a radiance of liveliness, and his tall, lean build and full lips enclosed by his dark goatee made him a sex symbol.

"Who's he?" Luca asked Phaedra.

"What ya talkin' 'bout?" Phaedra responded, playing naïve.

"The man in the suit, by the table. The one you've been looking at since we walked into this place?"

"He's nobody. He's just a friend."

"Just a friend, huh? Well, your friend is looking over at us." Luca smiled.

Luca locked eyes with Clyde accidentally. He smiled their way and Luca averted her attention away from his, not wanting him to come over, not desiring any male company at the moment. But it was too late, Clyde excused himself from the table of men and walked their way.

"He's coming over," Luca said to Phaedra.

She noticed how uneasy Phaedra became. Luca never saw her friend look so nervous about a man coming their way. Phaedra supposedly hated men, but there she was, looking like a schoolgirl with a crush. It was cute to see.

Clyde approached with his charming smile. He looked at both women with the same esteem, but his focus was mainly on Luca. He wondered who this stunning, young beauty in the black dress was sitting next to Phaedra. The minute he turned and saw her, she inadvertently grabbed his attention. She was too alluring to ignore.

"Good evening, ladies," Clyde spoke cordially with a smile.

"Hey, Clyde," Phaedra greeted with a matching smile.

"I see you came with a new friend this evening, and a very beautiful one, too," said Clyde with his eyes fixed on Luca.

"I did. Clyde, Luca. Luca, this is Clyde," Phaedra introduced.

"It's nice to meet you, Luca." Clyde took her hand in his and smoothly kissed the back of it.

Luca was overwhelmed. He was even finer up close, and his masculine voice instantly talked to her pussy. *Who is he? What is he about?*

Taking his attention away from Luca for a moment, Clyde looked at Phaedra and asked, "Where is your male friend this evening?"

"He's around, but not tonight," Phaedra replied.

"He's quite an interesting fellow," said Clyde.

"He is," Phaedra agreed.

Clyde smiled. He was always smiling. His smile was radiant, catching the attention of many women in the room. His sex appeal was alluring. He had swag out of this world. He was a single man. He hoped Luca was a single woman.

Clyde continued talking to the ladies, but his agenda was getting to know Luca more. Her eyes were magnetic and her beauty breathtaking. What attracted him to her even more was when she pulled out a cigar from her small clutch to smoke. A woman of his own caliber.

"Can I smoke in here?" Luca asked.

"Smoke away; my place, my rules," Clyde said. "I see you favor Cubans too."

"I do."

"A woman with taste, nice," Clyde said. He applied the cigar cutter and lighter for Luca to light up. She took a long drag from the flavorsome cigar nestled between her glossy, full lips while locking eyes with the handsome Panamanian.

"I love the way you suck on a good cigar. You do it with style, and not too many woman smoke cigars," Clyde added, obviously flirting with her in front of Phaedra.

Phaedra remained quiet, realizing the inevitable was happening right in front of her eyes.

Luca smoked her cigar with grace, her sweet lips taking control over the manly cigar that was caressed between her fingers. Clyde seemed like he didn't want to leave her side. He positioned himself closer to Luca, smelling her feminine fragrance and admiring how well put together she was.

"Drinks are on me, ladies," he mentioned, wielding his authority and power for them to see. "And anything you want to dine on from our menu. I have an amazing chef who prepares the best Panamanian cuisine in the five boroughs."

His place, his rules.

Luca was impressed, but she wasn't about to show it. "I'm a big girl who can pay for my own tab."

"I know you can. But in here, we show beautiful women hospitality and ardor, and I personally would feel more enchanted if you allow for me to treat you to a lovely evening, on me," he said.

Enchanted? Smooth word, she thought.

"It's your place and your money. You can do whatever you want," Luca returned nonchalantly.

"Sometimes it's fun being the boss."

"I know it is."

The two engaged in a brilliant conversation that covered everything from business, to food, cigars, and humor. Their chemistry was visible to all eyes watching. His personality was domineering, but at the same time enticing and smooth like ice. Phaedra was kind of hurt by the two talking so closely, knowing Clyde had a thing for her boss. She kept quiet about it, refusing to say anything.

The night went on with Phaedra drinking and chilling, knowing she didn't have a chance with Clyde in the first place. Luca had an attractive personality. She was smart, more mature and business minded. She and Clyde shared big words in their conversation that Phaedra couldn't grasp the meaning of. It was like they were two poets on stage, in their own light, connecting through significant vocabulary that poured from their lips.

"Where you been all my life? Why haven't you come around?" Phaedra heard Clyde ask her boss.

It was painful to hear, and Phaedra decided to remove herself from the equation. "Luca, I'll be in the bathroom," she said.

She excused herself from the bar, giving Luca some privacy with the man she had a crush on. The night was about to end with them exchanging numbers and Luca seeing a man who was probably worth her time. He was suave and polished from head to toe, but behind the suit and tie, there was something unsettling about him. He knew the right things to say to Luca—the precise words that grabbed her attention and made her swivel her barstool in his direction, with her legs crossed and an engaging smile permanently planted on her face for the evening. Somehow, Clyde made her forget about her troubles with Squirrel, and other things. He seemed to work magic on her, wooing her with some type of potion from his eyes to his speech.

It was getting late, and Luca was ready to depart. It had been fun, but she had the urge to leave. Phaedra was engaged with some long-legged female at the other end of the bar. It appeared that she had forgotten about Clyde for the moment, downing shots and laughing it up with her newfound friend.

Clyde continued to entertain Luca and the customers in his place. He would excuse himself from their conversation for a moment and take care of his managerial duties, running the place as smoothly as he could.

Luca glanced at the time. It was nearing midnight. Time had flown by quickly—four hours had gone by, but she was having a good time. Her good time in the lounge came to an abrupt end when she saw his shadowy figure seated in the corner, alone at a table by the doorway. He had followed her there. But how? How was he finding her? Luca sat frozen on the barstool aghast at the sight of him. Was he crazy enough to try something there, in front of dozens of people, in public?

World gawked at her with his dark, cold eyes, clad in another dark hoodie draped over his head. He seemed to go unnoticed by everyone in the bar, like he didn't exist at all. He was like a shadow. It seemed like she was the only one seeing him. His deadly black eyes were fixed on her. His hands were in his front hoodie pocket. Was he concealing a weapon? His face was contorted with craziness.

Luca swallowed hard. For some reason, World put tremendous fear in her heart. She was a deadly woman with a vast fortune who ordered people killed, but whenever she saw World, it felt like she couldn't move; like she was helpless prey in the wilderness. She locked eyes with him. With a contemptuous gaze aimed at her, he slowly raised his index finger to his own throat and placed it against his skin like it was a sharp blade and implemented a throat cutting motion.

Phaedra walked over to Luca and tapped her on her shoulder from behind; Luca spun around, startled by the sudden touch and snapped at her, "What the fuck you doing?"

Phaedra was caught off guard by the harsh response. "I came to see if you were okay."

Luca turned back around to see if World was still there, but he was gone—vanished in thin air like some apparition. It spooked her. It was too much to handle. Luca collected herself and was definitely ready to go now.

Clyde came over to see if they were okay, and her coy attitude was now gone. She became brasher and cold. "I need to go," she said.

"Already?" Clyde replied.

"It's getting late, and I have business to take care of in the morning," she said.

"I understand."

Luca stood up in her six-inch heels and pivoted toward the exit. Phaedra was beside her. Clyde was willing to escort them out, but Luca made it obvious that she wanted to be alone. Clyde was thrown off by her impulsive aloofness. He wondered what had happened since he walked away from her. Luca wasn't willing to explain the situation.

"I'll call you," said Clyde.

She marched toward the exit with Phaedra following behind her. Luca couldn't get her cousin out of her mind. He was scaring her with his stalking. He could strike anytime, anywhere. First it was the hospital, and then he was in her bedroom, now he was in SoHo. She didn't want to wait around to find out where he would pop up next.

Luca cautiously approached her car. Phaedra knew something was wrong. She couldn't pinpoint it. Lately, her boss hasn't been herself and been acting weird. Phaedra wondered if Luca had seen Naomi again. Whatever it was, it had Luca truly spooked.

Luca quickly climbed into the passenger seat of the truck, and Phaedra dropped her ass down behind the wheel. She started the ignition and drove off. Luca sighed and then looked at her friend.

"I want you to call up everyone right now and tell them I want to meet with them. This is important."

Phaedra nodded. "When and where?"

"My place, in two hours."

While driving, Phaedra got on the horn and called up Kool-Aid first, then Egypt, and then Meeka. They agreed to stop what they were doing and drive to Luca's Rockaway Park home in the middle of the night. Everyone figured it was critical.

***

Luca and Phaedra were being keenly watched by World and one of his cronies. He was seated in an idling black Chrysler 300 right outside the door to the Paradise lounge. World leaned back in the passenger seat and took a pull from the burning weed sandwiched between his lips and observed Luca and Phaedra quickly exiting the place. He relished on seeing his cousin looking worried. He enjoyed the panic he brought onto her. He watched as she climbed into the high-end Escalade with her friend and sped away. He was going to get his fortune by any means necessary. He zeroed in on the license plate before the truck sped by him and took a mental photograph of it.

"Yo, World, why we always sittin' on this bitch and not making a move, huh?" his crony, Doc said.

Doc took a rich pull from the blunt that World passed him, exhaled the strong smoke, and continued with, "I'm fuckin' hungry, nigga, and this bitch got ends like that? Fuck that, let's call up some niggas and get this bitch, get this money, then body her and everything moving."

Doc was a firecracker that was always lit and ready to pop off and murder everything moving. Like World, his heart was as cold as ice, and murder, mayhem and stealing was the only thing he knew how to do. He was young, black, and didn't give a fuck about anything but getting money, and if bloodshed had to come-about, then so be it. He loved the shit and he was World's right hand man/enforcer. The two did time together in Sing-Sing prison upstate. Doc was a South Bronx native standing five-ten with a hawkish nose, a lean, muscular build from constantly working out while in prison, and a gleaming bald head with a scraggly beard—along with a devil-may-care outlook about life.

Watching the Escalade pull away and not following it disturbed Doc. What was World thinking? He couldn't sit around any longer and toy with this bitch. He was ready to get it in—put in that work and make this money.

"So we just gonna watch them drive by and ain't gonna do shit? C'mon nigga, I'm tired of this shit. For two months, we been stalkin' this fuckin' bitch. I'm fuckin' ready, World, I'm ready to do this shit. You ready, nigga? You ain't actin' like it," Doc complained.

"Yo, Doc, shut the fuck up!" World cried out. "She's my fuckin' cousin, and I'm gonna deal wit' this bitch my way, not yours! You understand?!" World was a lunatic and Doc knew it. Though they matched craziness, World was on a whole different playing field when it came to being psychotic. He was actually on medication for the longest and had been diagnosed with having psychosis—suffering abnormal conditions of the mind and sometimes losing contact with reality.

Doc remained silent, knowing not to push World. He was the one running things and he was the man with the plan. Doc pursed his lips into a frown, continuing smoking the blunt.

"Give me that shit," World said, snatching the blunt from Doc's hand, taking a quick puff and then throwing the lit blunt into his mouth. He seemed unfazed by it. He chewed it up like it was bubble gum and said, "She owe me, nigga. She owe me my Phantom. I want my shit. I want my shit."

"I want my shit, too," Doc repeated him.

"Fuck it, I know about her peoples. I know who she connected wit'. We gonna light this muthafuckin' town up crazy, my nigga. We are. Yeah, like the wild, wild west on this bitch," World proclaimed.

"My nigga, that's what I'm talkin' about," Doc replied excitedly. "Let's get this shit started."

***

It was 2 a.m., and Luca's Murder Inc. crew sat at the table exhausted, but ready to hear what the meeting was about.

"Look, I'm being stalked by my own cousin. His name is World and he needs to die, ASAP. He knows too much, and he's a threat to all of us."

Kool-Aid nodded. "I'm wit' it. You know how I do; just point and I'll fire."

"It's not that simple, Kool-Aid. He's really crazy, and he's difficult to track down in these streets."

"Anybody can get got. I don't care where they try to run or hide, I'ma see this nigga, Luca," Kool-Aid replied.

Luca hoped he was right. She was tired of World's harassment and wanted it to end. Deep down she knew all she had to do was honor their deal. Pay him off for the work he put in— buy World his Phantom, as she'd agreed. Each time the thought crept into her mind she would push it right back out. Somehow the thought of paying off World made her feel weak. It most likely had to do with the way he *demanded* payment. When he came out of prison Luca was a new woman. She wasn't the weak Luca who'd pleaded with her strong cousin to murder Nate. She was a boss bitch with a crew of triggerman, clout, and money. And the fact that World didn't see her as she now saw herself was going to cost him his life.

She removed an old picture of World that was taken several years ago from a folder and placed it on the table for her peoples to see. The picture was when he was a teenager; however, his features had not changed much since then. Kool-Aid was the first to snatch up the picture and study it. He was going to remember his face and whenever he saw him, it was shoot to kill.

"I'ma find this nigga for you, Luca. You got my word. You think he crazy, he ain't met me yet," Kool-Aid declared wholeheartedly.

16

Kendall and Poor Billy crossed the Connecticut state line, riding north on I-95 in their Dodge Intrepid, two hours away from their destination. They were headed toward two cities—first, New Haven and then Hartford to drop off fifteen kilos each in both cities. Connecticut was a goldmine for Bad Girl. A local hustler in New Haven named Dallas was one of their biggest clients, and a big shot in Hartford named Cheo was another profitable customer for Luca's organization. In estimate, both cities generated close to a quarter of a million dollars each in one month, paying fifteen thousand a ki.

Kendall and Poor Billy were two traffickers for Luca's organization. They were highly recommended by Kool-Aid. Both men were loyal to the gun-toting killer and were put on the payroll months ago. Connecticut became one of their frequent trips, where they established a somewhat trustworthy bond with Dallas and Cheo.

It was a chilly evening and Kendall was driving his prized car. He made sure to do the speed limit and both men had their seatbelts fastened, and everything was legit on the car. Kool-Aid warned them not to be stupid when transporting thirty kilos of heroin concealed in secret compartments in the car across state lines.

Kendall nodded his head to a Kanye West track and smoked a Newport. He was wide awake and focused on the road. However, Poor Billy had been falling asleep during the hours-long ride. His head was pressed against the glass window; he was snoring, wrapped up in his winter coat, arms folded across his chest, looking dead to the world. The traffic on I-95 was sparse and they hadn't seen a state trooper for miles. He wasn't complaining.

A few miles after passing Stamford, Kendall noticed he was low on gas and he needed to refuel. He turned off the next exit and navigated his car through a small town called Darien, a relatively small community on Connecticut's "Gold Coast" with a population of twenty thousand. The town was quiet and still and most businesses had closed hours ago.

Kendall searched for the nearest gas station. He soon found an Exxon in the heart of the town, five miles away from the highway. He pulled up to refuel and get some snacks to munch on. Stepping out of the car and slamming the door shut, he awakened Poor Billy. Poor Billy yawned and looked dazed for a minute, noticing that they had stopped to get some gas.

"Yo, where we at?" Poor Billy said. "Damn, you couldn't wake a nigga up?"

Kendall walked to the gas attendant to pay for the pump while Poor Billy got out of the car to stretch his legs. He hated stopping in small towns when they were transporting drugs. He had the fear of being stopped by some redneck cop somewhere and being lynched by some crackers. Poor Billy was as black as they come, looking like tar with cornrows, but his eyes were as white as snow. He was nicknamed Poor Billy because he had been homeless most of his life, always scraping for pennies and begging until he got down with Kool-Aid. Now he was draped in name-brand clothing and flashy kicks, and carried no less than a stack in his pocket. He had come up and he planned on staying up.

Kendall slowly walked back to the car. He was slightly overweight with brown-to-reddish skin, dark eyes and straight, frizzy hair. He saw Poor Billy standing by the car smoking a cigarette.

"You finally awake, nigga," Kendall said.

"Yeah, you ain't wake me up, slamming the door on a nigga…and damn, it's fuckin' cold as fuck out here," Poor Billy griped.

"Nigga, at least pump the gas that I already paid for."

"Oh, so you can get all warm and cozy in the car."

"Yup," Kendall replied, smiling.

"Fuck you, nigga," Poor Billy replied in good humor.

Kendall jumped into the passenger side and said, "Oh, and it's your turn to drive."

Poor Billy threw up his middle finger while he pumped gas into the car with his cigarette dangling from his lips. Five minutes later, Poor Billy climbed behind the wheel shivering from the cold weather. He rubbed his hands together for quick warmth and said, "Yo, Kool-Aid gonna have to start payin' us more for these cold-ass trips upstate and shit."

"You complain to that nigga, I'm good."

"Pussy."

"Yeah, whatever."

Poor Billy started the car and slowly exited the gas station. It was Kendall's turn to sleep. The duo only made it a mile away from the Exxon before they noticed flashing blue and red police lights in his rearview mirror.

"Fuck!" Poor Billy cried out with his attention absorbed in the mirror. The cop was approaching fast.

Maybe he would pass them by, Poor Billy hoped. He alerted Kendall. "I think we got company."

Kendall rose up and looked behind him. It was an unmarked Dodge Charger, apparently a police vehicle, and it wasn't passing them by. It was definitely pulling them over, lining up directly behind them indicating they needed to stop. Poor Billy thought about outrunning the police. However, the Charger was a much faster car, and he hoped it was only a routine stop.

"Just be cool, yo…we probably got a taillight out or sumthin'," said Kendall.

Poor Billy pulled to the side of the road. The area was isolated, dark and silent. The glaring police lights shone heavily on the street, and the nearest homes were on a vertical hill covered by thick shrubberies with a brick wall on one side and a lake on the other.

Poor Billy put the car in park, but left it running. He and Kendall remained cool. Their eyes stayed in the mirrors. They figured it was just a routine stop; they prayed it was and nothing else. Poor Billy knew he wasn't speeding, so maybe it was something minor wrong with the car. Plus, the thirty kis in the car were skillfully hidden, and it was going to take a miracle for some local, state cop to find the drugs.

Both doors to the Charger opened up and two cops got out. They were in plain clothes, but their badges were displayed outside of their clothing, their guns holstered on their hips. One was white with military cropped hair, the other black with a fade, and both had the same lean and tall physique. They approached with caution, the white cop positioned on the driver's side and the black cop watching the passenger.

The cop rapped on the window lightly. Poor Billy rolled the window down half-way and looked up at the cop.

"Is there a problem officer?" he asked coolly.

The white cop responded. "We need for y'all to step out of the vehicle."

"Why?" Poor Billy asked.

"Look, let's not make this a problem. You do as you're told and we can solve this problem easily. You start making a fuss about it, and I guarantee you, son, we will make this a very long night for you."

Poor Billy sighed out of frustration. He looked at Kendall and shrugged.

Neither was smart enough to know there was something suspicious about the officers. First, their badges read NYPD instead of Connecticut PD, which should have instantly raised suspicion as to why a NYPD cop, with no jurisdiction, was pulling them over in the state of Connecticut.

Poor Billy and Kendall were ushered to stand at the back of their car with their hands placed on the trunk and their heads down. The area was secluded to an extent, not a neighbor or any vehicle traffic around. The white cop looked at the black cop and he gave the head nod, indicating something crucial was about to go down.

"Look, officers, everything is legit on the car and we just riding to New Haven to see a friend," Poor Billy spoke.

The white cop smirked and replied, "Like I said, son, we're not trying to make this a long night for anyone."

Their Glock 17s were removed from their holsters and simultaneously pointed at both men's heads. The cops didn't hesitate to fire.

Boom…Boom! Boom! Boom! Boom! Boom!

The muzzle flash from the guns lit up the night around them. Kendall and Poor Bill were killed instantly with multiple gunshots to the back of their heads and back. Their lifeless bodies lay sprawled out on the side of the road. The third door to the Charger opened up and a third man stepped out. It was Xavier. He walked toward the bodies and looked down. The two corrupt cops looked at him and said, "Easy as one, two, three."

Xavier smiled. He was aware that the dead men were trafficking a large quantity of drugs, over twenty kis or more concealed somewhere in the car. Now, they were his drugs, and the two corrupt cops were his partners. Together, they planned on becoming rich. Together, they planned on taking over the lucrative pipeline that belonged to Luca and her organization.

Xavier climbed into the dead man's car and planned on continuing the trip into New Haven and meet with a different connect, a rival of Dallas.

The corrupt cops climbed back into their unmarked Charger and would be Xavier's police escort into the city. They had an order to fulfill fifteen kilos. This was only the beginning. Unbeknownst to Luca, a conflict with corrupt officials had ensued and things were about to heat up dramatically.

17

Luca pulled up to the sprawling Wagner Houses on the east side of Harlem in the early afternoon. It was a clear and gentler day, with the temperature reaching 45 degrees. The wind was calm and the sun was shining. She had yet to receive the news that two of her men were brutally murdered and thirty kilos were stolen from her. So far, her main focus was the hit on World, her business affairs with her attorney, and reaching out to Squirrel for another large re-up. Clyde also crossed her mind a few times.

She stepped out of Phaedra's Escalade with her cell phone glued to her ear. She had been calling Squirrel nonstop, trying to reach him about business, but to no avail. He wasn't answering her calls, and it was making her upset.

"He still ain't pickin' up?" Phaedra asked.

"No."

Luca decided to bravely walk into the projects and meet with Squirrel personally. If they had beef, then so be it. She was tired of being mistreated and taken advantage of by him. If only their personal relationship was as great as their business relationship, then she would have been the happiest woman on earth. But it was the opposite. Her personal life was hell, and Squirrel had a huge hand in that.

Phaedra watched her boss walk into the lion's den. She held onto a .9mm with a sawed-off shotgun in the backseat. She was ready for anything coming her way and not about to take any chances, especially when Luca was being stalked by her crazy cousin. Phaedra was willing to go into the projects with Luca, but her boss insisted she should go alone. Luca had developed the heart of a lion. She became fierce and ruthless, and had definitely changed since they first met in the college while taking courses to pass their GED exam. They'd come a long way together.

She remembered Luca having that innocence and inexperience inside of her. She was smart, but had no idea what she was doing in the game. They had both learned so much in such a short time.

Phaedra waited with her cell phone on the dashboard, remaining cautious, knowing there was no place for them in Harlem. In her mind, they did business with Squirrel, but they would always be in enemy territory. She didn't trust anyone. She lit a cigarette and watched the thugs move about on the streets and inside the projects. Her truck stood out like a sore thumb. She exhaled the smoke and waited. When her cell phone rang, she assumed it was Luca, but it was Kool-Aid calling. She answered immediately.

"What is it?"

"Phaedra, we got a fuckin' problem," Kool-Aid announced with a sense of trouble in his tone.

"What problem?"

"Kendall and Poor Billy are dead, and we out thirty kis," he informed her.

"What?"

"They found their bodies this morning in Connecticut, on the side of the road, shot multiple times. We don't know by who yet."

It was news Phaedra didn't want to hear, and it was something she didn't want to relay to Luca at the moment. Her boss already had enough troubles on her plate, but it wouldn't be wise to keep the news from Luca either.

"The boss wit' you?" Kool-Aid asked.

"No, I'ma call you back. Keep ya fuckin' phone on."

Phaedra hung up. Right away her mind was spinning with potential culprits that were capable of committing the robbery and homicide. She thought about World. Now she had to relay the bad news to Luca when she came back down. It was one thing after another, but that was the game—trouble and death lurking around every corner you turn.

The Wagner Houses were filled with 20 BLOCC and Flow Boyz loitering around the area, some hustling and some serving as look out for police or rival gangs. Luca strutted by them with ease but received heavy scowls from the thugs out front. Her face had become a regular in the hood, and every soul knew she was closely connected to Squirrel. She marched into the lobby and took the elevator to the eighth floor. Stepping out into the narrow hallway, she walked closer to his door and took a deep breath. She was so nervous that she found herself becoming nauseated. She was there on the pretense of business, but in actuality, she wanted to see Squirrel again and rekindle something with him.

But why? She would constantly ask herself. Since the day she got sexually and romantically involved with him, he had been treating her like shit, and she endured it—always being an alternative for his sexual pleasure whenever he and his baby mama weren't working out. She was something like a doormat to him, wiping his feet before he walked inside to his real home.

Luca stood outside the apartment door clad in something sexy for Squirrel to see her in once again—a black side-tie halter dress underneath a fifty-thousand-dollar, black-and-white chinchilla coat. She had every eye on her when she walked on by, and heads turned in awe at the young woman bold enough to wear something expensive in the Harlem projects.

Rap music blared inside the apartment. She knocked. It took a minute for someone to answer, but they did. It wasn't Squirrel, but one of his lieutenants. He grimaced at Luca in her nice attire and then smirked.

"Yeah, you lookin' for Squirrel, right?" He chuckled jarringly afterwards, like he knew something she didn't.

"Is he here?"

"Nah, that nigga ain't here right now. In fact, he ain't gonna be around for a while. So he told me to let you know from now on you gonna be doin' business wit' me."

"What you talking about?"

"What the fuck I'm tellin' you? I'm ya connect now, not him. The boss is away on some personal matter."

"What?"

"And you know, whatever business you had goin' wit' him, shit, you know you can start wit' me, you feel me, ma? I can treat you very different," he said, rubbing his hands together like a greedy fool with a lecherous grin aimed at Luca.

Luca was furious. Once again, Squirrel had put her on ice and separated himself from her, pawning her off to one of his lieutenants like she was nobody. Her heart sunk down into her stomach. She kept her cool and didn't show any emotion, though. She couldn't look weak, especially in front of this lieutenant.

"I'm sayin', I got you, ma, and I know you got me, comin' up this way lookin' all good in that nice fur coat. What you wearing underneath it?" He reached out his hand to open up her coat, and Luca reacted suddenly, stepping back and slapping him in the face so hard, her hand stung.

"Don't you ever fuckin' touch me again," Luca shouted.

"Bitch, you insane? You know who the fuck I am?" he exclaimed.

She knew. His name was Pug, and he was one of Squirrel's right-hand men. He was also a man who'd had a powerful crush on Luca since he laid eyes on her. Luca didn't care for him at all. His was a sleazeball, known for fucking crack whores and prostitutes, and was probably a disease-infested, dirty muthafucka.

Luca glared at Pug and dared him to put his filthy hands on her ever again.

"Where is he?" she demanded to know.

"Look, ma, I'm ya connect now, not Squirrel. He made that very clear to me before he took off."

"To where?"

"It ain't ya business to know."

Like hell it ain't, she thought. They were playing games with her, and she was sick and tired of it. It was obvious Pug wasn't going to give up Squirrel's location. He was pigheaded and loyal to his master. Luca was left to only wonder where he could have gone off to.

"Now look, this is how it's gonna be. I'ma call you wit' a new location, and . . ."

Luca pivoted on her six-hundred-dollar heels and stormed off before Pug could finish giving her the new arrangements. He stood in the hallway dumbfounded by her response. He knew from Squirrel that she was one stubborn bitch, but she was fine as hell. Luca's heels click-clacked against the floor, echoing in the hallway toward the elevator. She stood by the elevator and waited. She didn't turn to look at him once. When the elevator came to the floor, she hurried inside and pushed for the lobby. Words couldn't even describe how she felt. She clenched her fists and was ready to punch something. She should have punched him, but it would have been a grave mistake. Pug was also known to assault females and brutally beat them to a pulp. He didn't care. His reputation as a woman beater reigned profoundly through the projects and most of Harlem. Luca said to herself that if he came at her violently, then she wasn't going to falter in killing him. There was no way she was about to become victim to a man's abuse ever again.

Luca stormed out of the building lobby, steaming mad. The thugs lingering outside noticed her anger and were amused by it. They didn't like her. They thought she was out of her league and nothing but some uppity bitch playing in a position that was way too big for her shoes. She didn't belong in their world, and she never would.

Luca got on her cell phone and dialed Squirrel's number repeatedly, but only got his voicemail over and over. She left him a nasty message, saying, "You muthafucka! You leave town and don't let me know. I bet you with that bitch, right? I mean this seriously, fuck you, Squirrel! I do mean fuck you, and I hope you die, nigga! I fuckin' hate you! You and that bitch you with, can go and burn in hell. You ain't shit. Stay the fuck out of my life."

She marked the message urgent and hung up. She was on the brink of tears. Her calm and collected demeanor was collapsing under the pressure and stress. Luca hurried to the truck.

When Luca jumped into the passenger side, Phaedra looked at her with some more bad news to tell her.

✳✳✳

Flight 679 landed in Barbados and Squirrel and Angel stepped out into paradise. The tropical sun cascaded down on them like a diamond in the sky, and the humid heat made them want to strip off the clothing they arrived in. Stepping down the flight onto the tarmac, Squirrel was already in awe of the country's beauty. Grantley Adams International Airport located in Christ Church was nothing like Kennedy Airport in Queens. The place was more relaxed and welcoming with the locals ready to greet everyone the minute they stepped off the plane to enter the terminal. The terrain around the airport was relatively flat and quite suburban. The sky was as blue as the sea and the serenity of the place was heaven-sent. Squirrel already felt the difference in the quality of the air and the wind that gently blew in his face.

He needed a vacation, and coming to Barbados with Angel was definitely a good idea. It was his first time in the Caribbean, and he was going to take full advantage of it. For one week, he was going to be a different man. He was going to try and forget about business and his troubles in New York. He left Pug and Floyd in charge of all of his business affairs. He was able to trust them; they'd known each other since they were kids.

After going through customs and being screened, the couple exited the terminal onto the glorious-looking island. Outside the terminal were a chain of taxis lined up and waiting to pick up passengers. Squirrel flagged down the nearest one, and they climbed into a white, late model minivan which was clean and comfortable.

The driver smiled at his passengers, not knowing that one of them was a murderous drug kingpin from Harlem. It didn't matter, though; Squirrel didn't appear to be a threat to anyone. He actually smiled and was in a good mood. He placed his arm around Angel.

"Where to?" the Bajan driver asked in his patois accent.

"Take us to the Butterfly Beach hotel," said Squirrel.

"Ah, good choice, my friend…good hotel and good service," the cab driver said. "And welcome to Barbados."

"I'm glad to be here."

He was professional and courteous, and looked like he was a man who truly enjoyed his job.

Angel cuddled up next to her man in the backseat and peered out the window, smiling overwhelmingly as the cab drove through Christ Church parish, one of eleven historical political divisions of Barbados. It appeared that she had forgotten about their latest spat and chose to forgive him once again. She was ready for a week of bliss and joy. She could never leave Squirrel, no matter how many times he cheated on her and how many times he beat her. She felt rooted to him with his wild love and his treacherous ways. It was like he had put a spell on her.

The hotel was only five minutes away from the airport. When the cab pulled up to the beachfront hotel with direct access to two beaches, Squirrel and Angel couldn't contain their excitement. They both were ready to leap from the cab and burst inside to experience what the place had to offer.

Squirrel and Angel paraded inside with *American* written all over them. Their clothes, their speech, and their awe of being in paradise caught the staff's attention.

"You come from foreign?" one of the hotel staff asked them.

Squirrel nodded. "Yeah, we do. Why?"

"Welcome to Butterfly Beach hotel. We are glad to have you," the staff member greeted in his Bajan accent.

"Thank you," Squirrel replied happily.

He and Angel looked around the lobby and courtyard. It was magnificent. Its pristine opulence drew their attention. Surrounded by palm trees, the hotel featured a unique separate terrace with three whirlpool bathtubs, tables, and chairs. There was also an extensive sun terrace with lounge chairs and sunshades. Also, the hotel had a seaside restaurant-bar that served Caribbean cuisine and a common lounge area with a large-screen TV for daily entertainment and happy hours.

Squirrel hurried to check in and get to his room. The skinny, smiley faced bellhop in his vintage attire was happy to carry the guests' bags to their room. They took the glass elevator to their floor and searched for ecstasy. The bright apartment room with colonial furniture and

Caribbean-influenced décor presented a panoramic ocean view and an outdoor pool—in addition to a four-poster bed. The room had free Wi-Fi, cable television, and the latest amenities.

Squirrel tipped the bellhop fifty American dollars and the young boy smiled widely before going on his way to give the couple their privacy.

"Ohmygod Squirrel, this is so fuckin' beautiful. I can't believe something like this actually exists," Angel said.

"It is, right?"

Angel ran from room to room, genuinely overjoyed that she was finally out of Harlem and out of New York. It had taken some time for them to get their passports right, as well as some financial doing, since they both had criminal records. Squirrel paid off the right guy at the right time and bingo; he and she had the privilege of traveling aboard.

They stepped out onto the terrace with the panoramic ocean view and gazed at the rich blue sea as it glistened under the dazzling sun, making the water look like there were diamonds hidden beneath it. Angel fell into Squirrel's arms and felt right at home.

"This is so beautiful, baby. I love it," she said.

"I do too."

"And I love you," she added.

"I love you," he replied.

He held Angel's thick and plump body in his arms. His baby mama wasn't as curvy and soft as Luca, but she had her plusses. In her tight jeans, Angel rubbed her nicely ample booty against his pelvis, slowly creating some arousal in her man. The picturesque surroundings were making her horny, and she wanted to fuck now. She turned around in his arms and gazed into his eyes. Her man was so damn fine; it should be a crime to let him out at any time.

Squirrel pressed his lips against hers. He tasted the softness of her lips and his tongue explored further. He could feel the underside of his tongue gently graze her bottom teeth; he inhaled her breath as his own. He used his entire mouth and lips on her, driving Angel insane. It was like she was a sensual fruit and he was savoring every inch of her with his mouth, his lips, his tongue.

With the sultry heat of Barbados on them, the couple started to undress on the terrace. Angel shimmed out of her tight jeans to reveal the pink thong underneath. Squirrel pulled his T-shirt over his head, exposing his chiseled body and six-pack that glistened in the sunlight. They wrapped into each other's arms again. He kissed her body, her neck, her shoulders and her stomach. He was hungry for her. Angel felt consumed by his lust. The way Squirrel touched her body, making love to her with his hands—it was out of this world.

"Fuck me, Squirrel," Angel cried out between her quivering lips.

The inside of her pounded with lust and desire. Her body seemed to melt in his grip. His masculinity besieged her in the luxurious setting. She removed her pink thong and tossed it to the side, her throbbing pussy exposed for him to take. Her round, ample ass was like two bouncing basketballs in his hands. She pushed herself forward from his grasp and curved her body over the railing to the terrace. Her legs spread eagle style with her pussy lips spread as an invitation, her luscious, full ass cheeks before Squirrel to enjoy.

"Damn, girl, you is so fuckin' sexy," Squirrel said.

"Take this pussy, my nigga."

Squirrel undid his jeans and dropped them around his ankles. As he stepped out of them, he removed his boxers and stood butt-naked with his dick rising to attention. Angel's juices were flowing freely. She was wet and ready for him to enjoy the inside of her. He positioned himself behind her and between her legs, and she grabbed his dick and placed the head at the entrance to her pussy.

"Put it in me, my nigga . . . right here. I want you inside of me so badly," she cooed.

He slid his erection inside of her and cried out, "Ooooh shit. You feel so fuckin' good, baby. Ooooh, hells yeah…damn," feeling the sensation of her wet pussy surround him. He felt his heart racing as waves of pleasure consumed him to the highest degree.

It was the perfect atmosphere for a sexual rendezvous; the island of Barbados surrounding them as they lay eyes on the ocean lightly splashing against the white-sand beaches. They both were in a zone. Angel gripped the railing and backed her ass up into his dick thrusting inside of her. Between her thighs was another ocean. If there was one thing Squirrel knew how to do, it was make her pussy cream and squirt. He started stroking and Angel's eyes were rolling back in her head.

Angel was in need to change up the position. With him hitting it from the back, she came numerous times, and she was greedy for several more orgasms. She threw herself onto Squirrel with her legs wrapped around him. His strength secured her and he carried her into the room.

He pushed her down onto the four-poster bed and climbed between her warm, thick thighs. Once again, Angel wrapped her legs around him and she grabbed his hips and pulled him to her. She yearned for more. They weren't done yet. In missionary, he fucked her deep, slow, and hard.

"Take this good fuckin', nigga. Take it, baby, it's yours," she hollered, ghetto fabulous.

He could feel her pussy grab him and start throbbing with Angel grasping for air. She felt full but was desperate for more. Squirrel pushed her legs back to her chest, and drove his dick inside of her until his cream coated her insides.

"I'm coming," he cried out. "I'm gonna cum in that pussy. Oh shit! Ooooh, baby! Ooooh, shit!"

Panting and breathing, Squirrel was at the point of no return. He couldn't hold his man liquid back any longer. She screamed into the air as Squirrel grabbed her hips and distributed his creamy essence inside of her while they exploding together.

It was the perfect beginning to a beautiful day in paradise.

18

"Vengeance is mine," said Luca. And she meant every word of it. Everywhere she turned, there was chaos and deception. It seemed like the world was coming against her, but she was willing to fight back with everything she had. Luca had to deal with what seemed like a boatload of issues. She was furious that Squirrel was plainly ignoring all of her calls, sending them to voicemail. And it was upsetting that once again he allowed one of his soldiers or lieutenants to make the drug transactions for him. She was about to go crazy, continually searching for him at any known residences. She was becoming a stalker, and it wasn't cute. Despite her tireless efforts, he was nowhere to be found.

Second, the news of Kendall and Poor Billy being gunned down in Connecticut and her organization missing thirty kilos was a huge blow. Now wasn't the time for any more surprises, but they were popping out of nowhere. Luca was out close to half a million dollars. And worse, her supply was running low and Squirrel was nowhere to be found. She needed to re-up, but dealing with Pug was her worst nightmare and she was doing her best to avoid it. He was a pussy-craving lunatic who wanted to fuck Luca in so many ways. The way he would stare her down when she was with Squirrel, like she was a piece of meat, was unsettling.

Third, her cousin World was still out there somewhere in the big city, continuing to stalk her, and definitely plotting against her somehow. He was an unpredictable, constant threat. Seeing him at Paradise lounge proved she needed armed security around her, twenty-four-seven. When he struck, she wanted to be ready.

Fourth, the NYPD were a great nuisance in her life. Luca and anyone associated with her had a red target on their backs. If they couldn't indict her with a felony, then she felt it wouldn't be long until they took matters into their own hands. It was the reason she felt she had to strike first, the way she already had with the two detectives' deaths. Everyone said it was crazy to war with police, but Luca didn't give a fuck. Vengeance was hers.

She woke up one morning and decided to retrace her steps the night she killed Charter. Since she couldn't find Squirrel, she took her frustration out on the people she believed had robbed her. There were two ambulance workers on the scene and all of them had to die. Guilty or not, she didn't care.

Luca spent the day going over the police report with a fine comb and analyzing everything about it. She was going to go through page after page and leave nothing unturned.

The police report she had gotten stated that there was a call from her next-door neighbors, the Ramseys, of "shots fired" at 1:34 a.m. However, the police and ambulance mistakenly went to the wrong location. At 3:14 a.m., there was an anonymous call to send an ambulance. The caller was a male who refused to leave his name. She found that suspicious. Who was the anonymous caller? Where did the calls come from? It was eating away at Luca to find out.

She used her technical skills to pull up her landline phone records and also Charter's phone records, and after about ten minutes of scrolling through the calls, bingo! She found something. The last call Charter made was right before Luca shot him dead. It was made at 1:10 a.m. The call had lasted nine minutes, and had been to his partner, Quincy. In all the chaos, murders, and drug deals, Luca had forgotten about Quincy. He and Charter were like brothers. They spent many years on the force together and were loyal to each other.

Why hadn't Quincy reached out to her? Luca asked herself. She was responsible for killing his partner after he tried to kill her and the baby, but Quincy didn't come to her with his own investigation or any condolences. She found that odd. It appeared that he fell off the planet and into oblivion.

Luca knew in her right mind that if any bitch killed a good friend of yours, despite the jurisdiction issues, you would have questions and want answers to what actually happened on the night in question. That person would make themselves visible in the suspect's life, especially if they were a cop. Quincy did no such thing. He didn't come around at all. He didn't call. He was a Brooklyn detective and this happened in Rockaway Park, but what did that mean? Luca felt she had found another potential suspect, but she needed to dig further.

Meanwhile, she refused to call off the hits on the two ambulance workers. In her cold blooded mind, a violent and bloody statement still needed to be sent out. Kool-Aid and Phaedra were on the hunt for the unfortunate civil workers who had no clue they were being hunted.

***

Victim number one: Her name was Ramona Payton, and she was twenty-six years old and had been an EMS worker for the FDNY for the past two years. She was a woman who loved her job. She loved helping people, taking care of others and saving lives. She lived alone, had no kids and loved to read during her free time. She was a single white female and lived an introverted lifestyle outside of her job. She had a Bachelor's degree in forensic psychology and planned on attainting her Master's degree from NYU in a few years. She planned on becoming successful in her field, and becoming an EMS worker was a start.

Unfortunately for Ramona, the call she and her partner received that chilly night in the lavish Rockaway Park home would be a fatal one. She was only doing her job, trying to revive one of the two victims in critical condition.

It was her evening off, and she chose to spend it in the house reading, cooking and watching her favorite Wednesday-night programs, as she always did on her day off. Her routine was predictable, which made her easy to locate and plot against. She lived on the third floor of a three-story clapboard house with wood plank floors and pale green shutters in Mount Vernon. The neighborhood was a still, sparsely settled, working-class suburban outpost of the city, near the railroad.

The cold winter wind blew fiercely outside her living room window. The TV was on CBS, showing *CSI*. Ramona settled in her cushioned chair, in her blue house robe, a good book in her hands and tea brewing on the stove. She was an attractive young woman: slim, with flaxen hair and a freckled face. Her blue eyes were astonishing. As she sat and read, she was unaware that her home was being stalked and an intruder was lurking in the darkness, watching and waiting to strike because he had his orders to kill.

Kool-Aid slowly crept up the stairway in the quiet building. He was clad in all black, wearing latex gloves with his Glock 17 stuffed in his waistband. He moved toward the doorway and pressed his ear to the door. He heard the TV and some movement. He already knew the woman's routine and the layout of her home. It was his job to prepare ahead of time. He made that one mistake with detective Cannon, and he wasn't about to be surprised again. This time, he watched her movements for several days, memorizing her comings and goings, knowing she lived alone. She was a simpler target.

Luca commanded that she only wanted them dead, not tortured, but seeing Ramona moving about, looking like a precious snow bunny in her pale white skin, Kool-Aid's sick and twisted mind decided he would have some fun with her before he did his deed.

He hated white people. In his eyes, they were the devil. And white women, they were nothing but cockteases and destruction to the black man. They all deserved to be brutally murdered. His father was set up by a white, blonde-haired, blue-eyed bitch many years ago. He had fallen in love with her, and she destroyed his life. She accused him of rape, because she was committing adultery on her husband. He was a powerful man in the city back then, a mafia captain for the Gambino crime family. When news of her infidelity spread, the white woman lied on Kool-Aid's father and told her husband she had been raped and could never be with a "nigger!"

He had been arrested, but his crime never made it to trial. Three days after being held without bail on Riker's Island, Kool-Aid's old man was murdered—stabbed in the face, neck, chest, groin area, and back seventy-six times by another inmate, who was clearly paid to do the hit.

Kool-Aid was a young lad when his father was murdered, but it changed him into someone dark—a young black man with a grudge against society, a chip on his shoulder and an appetite for destruction.

Kool-Aid took a deep breath and slowly and skillfully began picking the lock to the apartment door. It was a simple task for him, one he'd been doing since he was a kid. He became a master at entering homes. Slowly, he pushed the door open and made his way inside. He crept into the unlit foyer with the Glock in his hand. Instantly, his eyes darted around the place, making sure he was in the clear; so far, he had entered undetected.

Kool-Aid made his way farther into the apartment. The whistling sound of a teapot going off indicated she might be in the kitchen. He proceeded that way, moving like a shadow. He couldn't wait to lay his hands on this one. They would be alone for hours, he made sure of that when he chose her date of death.

Kool-Aid rounded the hallway into the kitchen area and saw her standing over the stove with the teapot in her hand. Her house robe was loosely undone, revealing bits of her pale flesh scantily dressed in panties and a bra. She was about to pour her tea into a mug, but then, he came out of nowhere, frightfully startling her. Ramona shrieked loudly. The mug fell from her hand and smashed against the floor. The stranger in her home wasn't there to have tea with her. His dark, cold eyes glared at her. She instantly panicked and tried to run. Kool-Aid took off after her. Her small, comfortable apartment had without warning turned into a snare of entrapment. She tripped over the rug and crashed into the coffee table. Kool-Aid pointed the gun at her and smiled wickedly.

"Now bitch, we gonna have some fun tonight," he said. "This is for my fuckin' father."

Raping, torturing, and killing her would be his indirect revenge for the woman who did his daddy wrong.

She was hurt and dazed. Kool-Aid struck her repeatedly in the head with his gun, spewing blood, blackening her eyes, busting her lip, and nearly knocking her unconscious. Then he undid her robe completely and tore away her panties. Her pink walls of soft tissue became exposed to him. Quickly, he undid his jeans, put on a condom, wrapped his hand around her neck roughly, forced himself between her legs, and pierced himself inside of her. Ramona jerked from the aggressive entry inside of her pussy, her pink lips being spread open like the Grand Canyon. Kool-Aid choked her while he fucked her with brute force, panting and huffing against her, ready to explode inside of her. His victim gasped for air and pleaded for him to stop, to have mercy on her. Tears of agony and soreness flooded her eyes.

"Ugh! Huh . . . ugh, mmmm . . . ugh," he grunted and moaned on top of his victim.

He soon reached the point of no return. She had been violated in so many ways, her innocence snatched away from her, and she felt paralyzed by the pain. Her body ached from her pussy to her face. She wanted to scream, but her voice, her soul had been tarnished by his violent abuse and tremendous fear. Kool-Aid stood up and smiled. She thought the worst was over, but he was far from done with her.

He fastened his jeans and said, "Yeah, now the real fun begins."

He placed his gun in the chair and cracked his knuckles loudly. He didn't need a weapon to destroy her. He had his imagination, and it was about to become medieval in her cozy, two-bedroom apartment.

It was uncanny; she was so far removed from the troubles of the ghetto, the urban war between rival gangs and drugs that plagued the residences and the killers that inundated their fear on everyone. And yet, she ended up being the target of one of the deadliest and most feared men of the hood—like Snow White coming across the Terminator—two different movies, two different lifestyles, one innocent and pure, and the other, hell on earth.

It was after midnight, and Kool-Aid sweated profusely. His vicious work was finally done. His latex gloves were covered in blood. Ramona Payton's death would make major headlines across the city. It was a masterpiece in his eyes, but it would become a ghastly nightmare for anyone else to see.

Her face was literally ripped into shreds with flaps of her skin hanging from her cheeks and forehead. Her lips had been cut away but left to dangle. Her tongue was protruding and it had been sliced into two. Blood was splattered over her throat and her naked body was an ugly mess. He had cut off her nipples and devastated her vagina.

Ramona Payton was desecrated.

Kool-Aid was a monster, and Luca didn't know what kind of monster she had working for her. He was the perfect killing machine. He was out to spill blood, because he loved murder and chaos.

Kool-Aid collected himself from a magnificent torturing and killing, and went into the kitchen to wash his face and removed the bloody gloves from his hands. He loved his job and was going to die doing it. He gathered his things and exited the apartment, also making sure to not leave behind any prints.

"That was fun," he said to himself.

Shit, he thought. He had gotten so carried away with his job, that he'd forgotten to ask her where the money or drugs were.

***

Next on his list was Melvin Anderson, of Yonkers. This one, he would do simple and fast, maybe a little torture. This Melvin character was a loudmouthed playboy who lived with a male roommate. Kool-Aid wondered if he would have to kill the roommate too.

Melvin Anderson woke up naked and wet with his feet and hands bound to a chair in a cold, barren, concrete room. He was dazed and scared. The last thing he remembered was having a good time in the bar with a few beautiful ladies and some male friends, and then walking to his E-Class Benz with a beautiful woman under his arm, laughing and talking, and anticipating a pleasurable night of sex. From there, his memory was blank. He couldn't remember what happened next. He couldn't remember how he'd gotten to the strange room or how he'd been kidnapped so suddenly and made a prisoner.

Melvin noticed an aluminum galvanized large tub filled with water. Aside from that, the room was empty, dimmed and silent. Melvin spun his head around frantically and desperately. He tried to free himself from his restraints by madly jerking back and forth, tugging and trying to be Superman in the chair, but to no avail. His restraints were chains wrapped around him tightly. He was cemented to the chair, going nowhere.

"Help, somebody help me! Help! Help me!" he cried out frantically. "What the fuck! Why am I here? Whyyyyy?"

He received no answer. He thought he was alone, but from behind, in the shadows of the basement room, Kool-Aid watched him struggle and scream out for help that never would come.

"Help me, please! Somebody please help me! Get me out of here!"

"No one is coming to help you," Kool-Aid said.

Melvin heard the voice come from behind him. He hastily tried to swivel his head in the direction of the voice, but he couldn't. His heart beat rapidly and he panicked. "What do you want from me? What did I do to you?" he asked.

"Unfortunately for you, you committed no crime against me, but I'm sad to inform you, you simply received the wrong 911 call on a certain day and now my boss has accused you of theft," Kool-Aid straightforwardly replied.

"Theft?!" he replied angrily. "I'm no damn thief! I didn't take a got-damn thing from anyone."

"Well, I'm here to see if ya tellin' the truth or lying to me."

"I'm not lying to you!"

"We'll see," Kool-Aid replied calmly.

Kool-Aid walked over to him and positioned the tub near his feet. Inside, the water was full of lye. He stood behind Melvin and the chair, gripped the back of it, and tilted Melvin off his feet. Kool-Aid hovered Melvin's bare feet over the tub, slowly placing his feet into the lye-filled water. Little by little he immersed the man's feet in the water, and the horrifying scream that followed echoed like a banshee in the room.

Kool-Aid did the interrogation his way and it was very painful, methodical. Each time he removed Melvin's feet from the tub, they became more corroded and his toes kept melting and melting—dissolving away the skin into bones.

"Tell me sumthin'."

"I don't know anything! Please stop! PLEASE!!!" Melvin screamed in agony, and tears trickled down his face as the pain pierced through his entire body.

His pleading fell on deaf ears. Kool-Aid was going to torture him until there was nothing left for him to hurt and peel away. His howling sounded like a wounded animal, and the agonizing pain he endured was about to make him pass out.

For an hour, Kool-Aid tortured poor Melvin until there was nothing else to hurt and destroy. His victim looked like pieces needing to be put back together. When it first started, Melvin didn't want to die, now, he was begging for Kool-Aid to kill him and put an end to his suffering.

Kool-Aid decided to do him that favor. He pulled out a pistol, pressed it to Melvin's forehead, and squeezed, blowing the man's brains out the back of his head. With no regret, Kool-Aid stared at his handiwork. He figured, job well done.

19

Luca read about it in the papers and saw it on the news, what he had done to her, how she was raped and murdered. She was shocked that Kool-Aid could carry out such a brutal and sadistic act. He had disobeyed her and tortured that woman so madly, the media dubbed the gruesome crime: *Real-Life Horror, Blood and Carnage: Woman Found Brutally Murdered.* There was a citywide manhunt for her killer. Ramona Payton's name became famous throughout the city and in other states. One officer stated it was one of the most horrendous crime scenes he has ever seen in his twenty-two years on the police force. Even the mayor of the city mentioned Ramona Payton and the bloody murder during one of his press conferences.

Luca couldn't believe what she was hearing. She already had enough problems, and now one of her skilled killers was probably going to be on the run for the crime. Luca was furious with Kool-Aid. Just kill the workers, she'd said, no torture at all—but Kool-Aid took his job to the extreme. Now she had to worry if he left any incriminating evidence at the crime scene—DNA, fingerprints. She needed Kool-Aid and couldn't afford to lose him in a critical time like right now.

Kool-Aid and Phaedra walked into the private backroom of one of Luca's private establishments in Brooklyn, and the minute Luca saw him, she tore into him with anger. Her right hand slammed against his face and she hollered, "Are you fuckin' crazy?! You do this shit? This!"

Kool-Aid didn't seem fazed by the slap to his face. He remained cool.

She tossed the newspaper at him. It had his handiwork displayed as the headline—front-page news.

"What the fuck is wrong with you, Kool-Aid?" she scolded.

"I was doin' my job," he spat.

"This! This isn't your fuckin' job, to bring more heat toward this organization. I already have enough on my plate. Now the mayor's talking about a citywide manhunt for her killer and possibly bringing in the feds. I don't need this shit right now!" Luca screamed out heatedly. "What kind of monster are you!"

"The kind that gets the job done by any means necessary," Kool-Aid replied.

"This fuckin' chaos you committed, it wasn't fuckin' necessary, nigga! I said I wanted them dead, not fuckin' raped and tortured and making the front-page news. You know what type of negative attention this brings, and the downfall it could stir up for all of us? These white people aren't about to let this white woman's death go unsolved. They gonna have every agency on this shit!"

Kool-Aid and Phaedra stood silently at their boss's scolding. Luca paced the room, fidgeting. She locked eyes with her two trusted lieutenants and had to think. But it was too late; the floodgates had already opened. Luca sighed, and then she softened her attitude and said, "You're my best killer, Kool-Aid, and I respect that. But I can't afford to lose you now. I would say lay low for a while and leave for somewhere far away from here, but there's too much going on right now that needs your expertise."

"I'm ride or die, boss. I'm here to stay," Kool-Aid replied convincingly.

"I know. But from now on, no more gruesome shit like this."

He nodded.

Luca looked at Phaedra next. She needed answers from her about the problem they faced. "You have any word or information on the muthafuckas that jacked my shit in Connecticut?"

"Nah, not yet," Phaedra frankly replied.

The news of not knowing who took thirty kilos from her and killed two of her soldiers was maddening. She picked up a chair and flung it across the room, smashing the wall mirror into shards of glass on the floor. Nothing was going right for her at all. Squirrel was still MIA, and she was losing money left and right.

She walked over to her personal bar and poured a much-needed drink. Being a boss bitch had its advantages, but it also had disadvantages. It was a stressful, demanding role, and there were so many haters on the bottom vying to knock her out to sit on the throne. She wasn't about to allow that to happen.

With her Cirôc Peach in a Strauss double old-fashioned glass, she took a seat in her high-backed leather chair behind her desk and reclined. She gazed at her two lieutenants and commanded, "Leave my office. I need to be alone for a minute."

"No problem," Phaedra said.

She and Kool-Aid spun toward the exit and walked out, closing the door behind them. Luca downed her drink and closed her eyes. She was too smart to be played like this. She thought about enemies who yearned to see her downfall, and there were quite a few. She heaved a sigh of frustration and closed her eyes. Her cell phone ringing and vibrating in front of her on her desk made her reopen them to see who was calling. She looked at a number she didn't recognize and hesitated to answer. The last thing she needed was some more bad news to put the icing on a fucked up day.

She answered the anonymous call.

"Who's this?" she asked in a stern tone.

"Hey, beautiful. It's me, Clyde."

Hearing his voice didn't change her mood. She remained cold, not really in the mood to socialize with anyone, especially anyone new in her life.

"And you calling me for what reason?" she asked in a snappish voice.

"Okay, I see I probably caught you at a very bad time. I was just thinking about you, seeing if you were okay. You did leave my place kind of abruptly the other night," he said.

"I did." She was very terse.

She heard him chuckle lightly at her cold reply, but it didn't deter him from his next question. "Listen, I want to take you out to dinner, if that's okay with you. You sound like you need a break from something."

She did, but she wasn't about to tell him what it was.

He continued with, "It's just dinner, you and I. We both need to eat, right? So why not do it together?"

"It's just dinner, that's it, right?"

"Luca, I'm not trying to rock the boat. It's just dinner."

"Okay, I'll have dinner with you."

"Great. Say tomorrow evening at eight? I'll pick you up."

"No. I'll meet you somewhere." She had to be cautious. She didn't know this man and wasn't too trusting with anyone.

"I'm fine with that."

"You have no choice but to be fine with that," she returned with finality.

He chuckled. "I see this is going to be a challenge. You're going to have a good time with me. I promise you that."

"We'll see."

Clyde gave her the information she needed for their dinner date tomorrow night, and she jotted it down. When she hung up from his call, she immediately called one of her soldiers into her office. Little Roc was a henchman under Kool-Aid's Murder Inc. crew. He was their young errand boy. She instructed Little Roc to survey the restaurant in midtown Manhattan and see what it was about. He was ready to do so. Luca wasn't about to walk into anything blind. Now with Little Roc doing his part, she got on her computer and did her part—a thorough background check of Clyde. She was able to hack into police files and other confidential sites and look up anyone. She soon found some very interesting stuff on Clyde Kant Lorenzo.

20

The silver Nissan Quest minivan, the suburban soccer-mom vehicle with tinted windows, wasn't about to transport any screaming adolescents to any soccer games on this day. Inside the minivan were five armed, homicidal thugs ready to carry out a dauntless crime. Thick weed smoke lingered in the minivan as it circled the Wagner housing projects once, surveying the area, the layout, and the hustlers that loitered everywhere from the street to the front lobby of the main stash building.

The minivan sat discreetly parked on 124th Street, across from a residential parking lot and the towering brick building the drug shipment was supposed to be delivered to. The sun was fading, and there were hordes of people out and about in the breezy evening. World and his crew had tediously planned for this day. It was payout time for them. Squirrel's organization completely took over the heroin trade in and around Harlem with sales estimated at about a hundred thousand dollars a day. They wanted a percentage of that large profit and were going to take it by deadly force.

World, the homicidal thug in charge of the daring heist about to take place, remembered the last time he was there—a while back, when he and Doc gunned down Nate and Cheez in the night, not knowing it would be the start to Luca's rise in the drug game. He had created a monster, and now it was time to destroy that monster.

World, dressed in black fatigues and combat boots with a ski mask perched on his head, took a pull from the burning weed being passed around, ready to get the fireworks started. His bloodlust-filled eyes keenly watched everything around him as he sat in the backseat holding a Tec-DC9 with a 32-round magazine. Doc sat beside him holding a Tec-22. John-John, who literally came straight out of the psycho ward, clutched a sawed-off shot gun. The two other passengers in the van—part of World's lunatic crew, were the driver, James, and Sing, a gun-toting, towering, dreadlocked black male lunatic who was HIV positive with nothing to lose.

They knew the right building to strike, and thanks to a snitch in the Wagner projects, they knew the right time. A large re-up was coming into the building—at least seventy kilos of pure heroin from the Dominicans from South Beach, Florida.

Two hours passed, the sun fading more and more into oblivion, and the men patiently waited for their payday to arrive. They knew the drop-off was coming soon because of the activity happening around the project building. They noticed more muscle lingering around and watching the block keenly and armed with pistols concealed underneath their coats and in their waistbands.

"Yeah, it's 'bout to go down," World said to his crew.

They grinned and were filled with anticipation. With time passing, it was time for World to tactically place his men around the drop-off point, with them looking unsuspicious. Sing stepped out of the vehicle in a large overcoat, black shoes, and a collared shirt, looking like a working man coming home from a long day. Underneath his overcoat was an Uzi ready to be used. He walked to the corner of 124th Street and Second Avenue, and smoked a cigarette, then walked south on Second Avenue and came through the other side of the building. Moments later, John-John exited the vehicle disguised as a crack fiend in ragged clothing and a tattered coat concealing the sawed-off shotgun. He went the opposite way of Sing and walked toward First Avenue.

Half an hour later, a dark colored, full-size Chevy Tahoe pulled into the residential parking lot. Three men stepped out of the truck, two Dominican and the third an aging black male. They were dressed in urban attire and were quickly greeted by one of Squirrel's lieutenants. One of the Dominicans went to the back of the truck and pulled up the lift, removing two large duffel bags quickly. World's eyes lit up. He was ready.

World and Doc exited the minivan and took a quick breather, their firepower cocked back and ready to spray. They had to be quick and accurate. The Dominicans and Squirrel's street lieutenants didn't think anyone would be bold or stupid enough to strike at them in broad daylight, but they were about to be wrong.

World was about to do what the projects thought was unthinkable: rob Squirrel.

As the working-class residents in Wagner moved in and out of the side walkway and lobby, Sing moved with them, cloaked as a civilian, walking toward the Tahoe slowly reaching into his overcoat with a keen eye focused on who he was going to hit first. The duffel bags were making their way into the building carried by dangerous men, but before they could reach the side maintenance doorway, Sing sprang upon them with the Uzi outstretched in his hands and opened fire.

Tat! Tat! Tat! Tat! Tat! Tat! Tat!

He dropped two, killing them quickly as bullets tore into their skulls and blood splattered like raindrops. At the sound of loud gunfire, panic ensued among the residents, and civilians nearby hastily fled from the encroaching danger. Several of Squirrel's men immediately went into action, pulling out pistols and automatic weapons thinking it was one man. They were misled. John-John pounced into action, firing the sawed-off shot gun and opening the chest cavity of one poor victim. The shotgun blast lifted him off his feet and sent him flying several feet into the air. He was dead before he hit the ground. An intense shootout ensued.

Boom! Boom! Boom!

Bak! Bak! Bak! Bak! Bak...

"Fuck y'all muthafuckas! This our shit!" Sing screamed out.

Gunfire erupted, and people were screaming and running everywhere, hiding behind cars, trees, scampering in an undignified haste into the buildings, and plunging to the ground to shield themselves from the heavy barrage of bullets. World and Doc's assault weapons were a game-changer. They burst onto the hectic scene with a hail of bullets laying every man down to the concrete, sounding like World War III had started in the projects. Several bodies were spread across the blood-splattered ground with spent ammunition all about.

World snatched up one duffel bag, and Doc grabbed the second one. They took off running back to the vehicle. Soldiers hearing the gunfire started to come from everywhere. They were under attack and being robbed. They hurried to hold down the fort and protect the product. But it was too late.

"C'mon! C'mon!" World screamed out.

His crew ran toward the vehicle, mowing everything down that got in their way. James sat behind the wheel anxiously ready to speed away. World and Doc threw themselves into the minivan, breathing and sweating heavily; Sing and John-John were trying to keep up. Bullets whizzed by their heads, and a crescendo of police sirens got louder in the distance as they approached. Sing flew into the van headfirst, but as John-John tried to follow, several slugs tore into his back and legs and he stumbled from the painful blow.

"Aaaah!" he cried out. "Shit!"

Doc and Sing hurriedly pulled John-John into the van, slammed the sliding door shut. James pressed his foot into the accelerator as the Nissan

Quest went careening down the street. It slammed around the corner toward the Triborough Bridge.

After the smoke cleared, every last one of Squirrel's men who were left standing stood dumbfounded. They had no idea who had robbed them, but they knew one thing for sure, Squirrel was going to be really pissed the fuck off. They'd lost seventy kilos, and heads were about to roll because of carelessness. Someone was going to have to call and cut the boss man's vacation short.

21

Three days into their Barbados vacation, Squirrel and Angel were having the time of their lives. They took an island tour and experienced the very best that the tropical island had to offer. They rode through Barbados' bustling capital, Bridgetown, the island's only city and situated on its natural harbor, where they were drawn into the old colonial buildings. On the side streets of the main drags they discovered residential neighborhoods scattered with rum shops and chattel houses. Later that evening, they were off to the western coast with its white-sand beaches, calm turquoise water, spectacular colorful reefs, and perfect snorkel locations.

"I never wanna go back to New York," said Angel with a smile. "This is like a dream come true."

Squirrel wished he could lose himself completely in the blissful seventh heaven, but he knew he had business to take care of. This was only temporary, but it was a much-needed escape from home. He relaxed somewhat, but he was always thinking about business in the back of his mind. The last time he'd spoken to Pug, which was two days ago, everything was fine.

The small island that was only twenty-one miles long had some of the most breathtaking places they've ever seen. They took in Saint Thomas and the famous Harrison's cave, St. Lucy with its River Bay, Christ Church with its Miami Beach, St. John with its landmark Ashford Bird Park, and St. Andrews with its rolling green hills.

During the day, they shopped along Board Street and on pedestrian-only Swam Street, which buzzed with the rhythm of the local culture. In the evening, they enjoyed fine Caribbean cuisine at the cafes and snack stands along the south bank of the Constitution River.

Then at night, when an astonishing dusk spread over the island and their day drew to a close, the yellow sunset reminded them that yet another day was about to pass. It gave them the opportunity to reflect on the day and be thankful for everything they've experienced.

The island sunset was the most romantic and inspiring sight nature had to offer them. Squirrel and Angel sat on the terrace, enjoying rum punch and transfixed at how the beauty of dusk was like God painting the sky.

The exquisiteness of the night led them into the bedroom, where Angel was sprawled out butt-naked across the four-post bed and was ready to sex her man down once again. The island made her so horny that it was inevitable she was going to end up pregnant before they left.

Squirrel lay on his back, and his woman hovered over him and licked his sensitive nipples. She had her man whimpering like a baby. His dick was so hard and ready to be satisfied by her wet pussy.

As Angel grinded her hips like a porn star, Squirrel's phone started to ring and vibrate loudly. He wanted to ignore it, but his instincts told him it might be something important. Angel paused her action and said, "Don't answer it, baby."

Squirrel didn't have any intention of interrupting their moment. He urged Angel to give him head. She wrapped her full, sensual lips around his big dick and bobbed her head up and down while jerking him off. Squirrel moaned.

A minute later, his cell phone rang again. Now he knew it was something important. Only one lieutenant had access to him while he was in Barbados. He pushed Angel's face away from his dick and rose up. "I need to answer this." He walked over butt-naked to answer his phone. It was Pug.

"Yo, why the fuck you callin' me? This better be important."

Pug swallowed hard, hating to be the bearer of bad news, but his boss needed to know what had gone down just a few hours ago. "We got hit, Squirrel."

"What? What the fuck you talkin' about, Pug?"

"I'm sayin' we got jacked for the re-up, seventy kis gone. Niggas came in wit' guns fuckin' blazing, killed four of our men, put another three in critical condition."

"What?! Who?" Squirrel screamed furiously.

"I don't know who."

"You tellin' me I'm out seventy kilos and you ain't got a fuckin' name?"

"I'll find out."

"Yeah, you better fuckin' find out, and I want them dead by dawn."

"I got you."

"No, Pug, this is on you. I left you in charge and you fuck up like this? Matter fact, I'll be on the next fuckin' plane back to New York. And when I arrive, I better have some answers!"

Squirrel hung up. His blood was boiling so much, he was ready to explode. Suddenly, paradise in Barbados turned into a living hell, and he couldn't wait to get back home. He irately paced around the room naked with his fist clenched. He had the urge to destroy something. He cursed and ranted so loudly, even other hotel guests heard him through the walls. Angel plunked on her knees on the bed and gazed at her baby's father, hating that their sexual charge had been cut short. She heard everything and knew this would be their last day there.

She didn't want to leave so soon, but Squirrel already had it in his mind that he couldn't afford to stay any longer.

He turned to her and, as predicted, he exclaimed, "Pack ya shit. We off this fuckin' island first thing tomorrow morning."

It was the life they lived.

22

The customized pearl-white CLS Benz with custom pink interior and white rims came to a stop in front of the Fogo de Chao, an authentic Brazilian steakhouse a short walk from Times Square. Luca climbed out of the car underneath a rapidly graying sky and made her way inside. The night's wind chill was below zero, and the freezing air was blowing hard enough to cut bitterly through even her black-and-white chinchilla coat. It was the frostbite weather that New York was sometimes known for.

The place had valet parking, but Luca came with her new security. She wasn't too trusting of having strangers park her car. Her six-foot-three, three-hundred-pound private bodyguard, Morocco, escorted her inside.

She felt ambivalent about her dinner date with Clyde. He seemed to be legitimate. He had passed the background check, and his easygoing attitude was probably something she needed to be around. However, with so much shit going on in her world, new faces became a problem.

Luca walked into the classy establishment where a blazing fire visible to passersby welcomed guests, and an interior consisting of dark woods, custom-blown glass chandeliers, and intricate murals set the stage for an elegant and memorable dining experience.

Clyde was on time and waiting at the table he'd reserved, enjoying a cocktail in comfort amidst the hues of southern Brazilian soil and slate.

When he spotted Luca approaching, he stood to greet her with a warm smile, being the gentleman that he was. It was great to see she wasn't going to have him waiting too long. They both were punctual. He loved her already.

Clyde was in awe at her beauty. She peeled away her fur coat to reveal her sexy curves.

"You look beautiful this evening," said Clyde.

"Thank you. And you look good yourself." She gazed at Clyde in a gray pinstripe Armani looking like he belonged on the cover of GQ magazine. His eyes dazzled.

Clyde moved toward her to relieve her of her coat and pulled out her chair. He helped seat her at the table. He sat opposite of her and said, "I noticed you didn't come alone." He motioned his head toward the hulk of a man standing near the exit looking like he was the black Terminator.

"A lady can never be too cautious."

He chuckled. "We didn't meet on Craigslist."

"That's true. But you never know, you could be a closet rapist," she joked.

"Well, I'm only here for dinner and conversation. Seems you might have had other wishes . . ."

Luca feigned embarrassment. "Why, I've never been so insulted."

Once again, Clyde chuckled. "We both know you have."

Luca laughed, then asked, "So what's good here?"

"Mostly everything. This is one of my favorite places to eat."

"Why don't you like to eat at your own place? I assume the food is good there too."

"It is, but sometimes a man likes to have something different in his life—change up his diet, try something new."

"Am I something new to you, since you came from Baltimore and survived being shot multiple times and left for dead? You found a way to bounce back."

"So you know a little something about my past," he replied, somewhat surprised. "You did your homework on me, I see."

"Don't be offended. I vet everyone. I'm not too trusting of people lately, especially new faces coming into my life."

"I'm not offended. I'm slightly annoyed, but not offended."

The blonde waitress in her white shirt, black tie, and black apron brought over a bottle of pricey white wine to the table. Clyde had pre-ordered it before Luca arrived. She popped the cork and poured them both a glass.

He raised his glass to toast and said, "To success."

"To success," she repeated.

They clinked glasses and Luca downed hers easily. So far the evening was starting off fine. Both of them ordered the steak and some Brazilian side dishes and treated themselves to the gourmet salad bar.

"So, tell me something about yourself," Clyde said.

"What is it that you need to know?"

"What makes you smile? What makes you enjoy life? What makes Luca the woman she is today?"

"What are you, my date or some reporter?"

He chuckled. Her sense of humor was golden like her beauty. "I think in a different life, I might have been a really great journalist. I have a knack for getting information from people and finding out what I need to know."

"Well, where I'm from people that talk too much usually end up in too much drama, and maybe labeled as a snitch."

"It's just you and I talking, nobody else. Just two people trying to get to know each other. And how can we get to know each other if we can't talk about our lives, our likes and dislikes?"

His vocabulary was proper, and his posture was aristocratic, giving him the appearance of being born into money. His eyes told Luca he definitely had a story to tell—one that contradicted the persona he wanted people to buy into.

Luca wanted to hear the real story come from his mouth. The computer told her one story; maybe he was going to tell her something different.

"You're smooth with words," she said.

"And you like to beat around the bush."

She smiled. "What I like is loyalty. And what I dislike are liars and stupidity."

"Well I'm no liar. And as far as stupidity, well, I'll let you be the judge of that."

Clyde took a sip of wine. He was enjoying her time. She was intriguing and intelligent. There was an air of mystery about her; something he wanted to see for himself. He was no fool though, it didn't take a rocket scientist to know what she was into—the taste in fine, high-priced clothing, the money, the cars, the harrowing man watching her back like she was the president. It reflected the life he once lived in which he felt was many lifetimes ago.

He poured her another glass of wine and they dined on a lovely meal.

"So your background check of me, what did it turn up?" he asked like a schoolgirl waiting to hear the latest gossip.

"A few interesting things."

He took a few sips of wine and gazed at Luca, like he was waiting to hear his criminal profile from some special agent in the FBI.

Luca wasn't timid. "A few arrests in '99 and 2000 for possession, assault, petit larceny, unlawful possession of a firearm, and burglary."

"Rough year for me. And my lawyer was supposed to have that expunged," he said warmly. "What else?"

"You find this amusing, don't you?"

"I find you very interesting . . . and beautiful."

"Well, there's more to me than meets the eye," she replied.

"I know that."

"And you look at me like you really know me."

"Maybe I do. You can tell a lot about a person by their eyes and how they stare at you. You ever heard the saying that the eyes are the window to the soul?"

"Yes, and according to scientists, patterns in the iris can give an indication of whether we are warm and trusting or neurotic and impulsive," she countered.

"From my knowledge, the saying stems from a passage in the bible, Matthew 6:22, and a form of that quote has been traced back to Cicero, who lived from 106 to 43 B.C. Many different poets have used the proverb, including William Shakespeare. It is basically stating that by looking deeply into a person's eyes, you can tell who they truly are on the inside."

"Guess I have to brush up on my Bible, huh?"

He laughed.

They looked at each other with minor admiration, matching wit and cleverness. Each sized the other up.

"Since you're so smart, then tell me something about myself, you looking into my eyes and all. Surprise me," Luca said.

"Surprise you?" He laughed quietly.

"Yes, surprise me," she repeated.

Clyde placed his elbows on the table and leaned closer to her face. He fixed his eyes on hers and looked deeply. Right then and there, he became a mind reader. He was quiet for a moment, gazing at her, calculating the right answer.

"You come from a hard life," he started.

"Anyone that meets me can tell you that. You have to come with something better."

"You didn't let me finish."

"It's your domain for now."

Clyde continued with his analysis of her. "Right now, you seem troubled about something, maybe more than one issue, and it's of grave concern to you. Your grizzly looking bodyguard is a clear indication of that. Also, by the expensive and extravagant clothes you wear, you came up poor, but not just poor, but mistreated, made fun of, bullied, and taken for granted. So now your wardrobe is a strong statement to everyone, shouting out loud and proudly, *'Look at me now.'* You spent most of your time alone, so you read a lot, studied anything that interested you, and a lot of things interest you, and because of that, you became an introvert . . . that became your only comfort."

Luca sat quietly, inwardly aghast at what she was hearing about herself. So far, he was dead on about her life—almost like he had a personal window into her soul and was continually looking in.

"You have no kids, but you want some. I can tell the way your eyes constantly look behind me at the couple seated at the next table with the twin girls."

Who was this guy? Luca couldn't believe her ears. She sat straight-faced, still as a statue, feeling her privacy torn away by some man she barely knew.

"Shall I continue?" he asked smugly.

"Please do," she said coolly.

"And most important, you yearn to have love in your life. You're so reserved, but at the same time willing to have dinner with me. You don't want to come off desperate with a man, but somehow, you always do. You can love hard, but don't get the same love in return," Clyde said nonchalantly.

Luca was dumbfounded by his analysis of her. She couldn't believe he knew and understood so much about her. It was like he put the pieces of her life together and remembered how the puzzle fit. So he could scramble them apart and always put it back together again.

"Who the fuck are you?" she snapped.

"Just a man who knows how to pay attention to certain details."

"No, how do you know so fuckin' much about me—my life?" she asked with a flare in her eyes.

"The world I come from, paying attention to the littlest details about a person or situation can save your life. And the day I saw you, I paid you attention because I really liked what I saw."

"Despite what you say or think about me, you don't fuckin' know me."

"Give me that chance."

Clyde leaned toward her again and looked at her with high regard. He wasn't intimidated by her brashness. In his mind, it was all a defense mechanism because she had been hurt too many times and came from a troubled past.

"Excuse me for a minute, I need to use the ladies' room," she said, pushing her chair back and walking in the direction of the bathrooms at the far end of the restaurant.

Clyde gawked at her, hoping he hadn't offended her too much. He was a persistent man and wasn't about to give up on something that he really liked. Women like Luca were the best in his book: smart, educated, beautiful, and a little feisty. She was a dream come true.

Luca walked into the bathroom with her emotions running high. She had to excuse herself because she was about to burst into tears or throw her drink in his face. Either way, she didn't want to draw any attention to herself. Clyde's words hit home, and regardless of her being a coldhearted, murderous gangstress, she was still a woman; flesh and blood, emotional from time to time, and yearning to be with a man who truly loved her.

She stared at her reflection and took a deep breath. She was a beautiful woman—the ugly duckling who transformed into a beautiful swan. Now everyone wanted to swim in her pond. As she lingered in the bathroom, her cell phone rang. When she looked at the caller ID and saw who was calling, Luca got the shock of her life. It was Squirrel suddenly hitting her up. But why now? The phone rang in her hand and all she could do was stare at it, letting it ring and ring. Her heart pounded inside her chest like a boxer thrashing the punching bag. Every womanly inch of her mind, body, and soul wanted to answer his call, but she hesitated. Unexpectedly, he uprooted himself out of her life, going off somewhere with his baby mama, and now when he was done having his fun, he wanted to call her and slide himself back inside of her like she was some blow-up doll.

Luca took another deep breath and placed the phone on the countertop, allowing his call to go to voicemail. It was hard for her to do, but she needed to do it. It stopped ringing. Seconds later, he was calling her again. She didn't answer. It rang a third time, then a fourth. Why was he blowing up her phone like this? She refused to answer any of his calls. Luca fought the urge to hear his voice, to feel his presence, to taste him, to go see him and allow his foulness back into her life. She had a fine-ass man in the restaurant waiting for her to return, and from the look in his eyes, he was ready to make her his priority.

Finally, she turned off her phone. Ignoring Squirrel when he called her and not trying to think about him was a first for her, and a huge step forward. She tossed the phone in her purse, gazed at her lovely image again, and decided to give Clyde a chance. She needed to phase Squirrel out of her head, and there was only one way to do so—being with another man, especially one as fine as Clyde.

She spun around on her shoes and marched out of the bathroom with a different attitude. She was going to stop playing hard to get and maybe try someone new in her life.

Clyde sat at the table, patiently waiting for her. When Luca came back to the table, he stood, gazed awkwardly at her and said, "I'm sorry if

I offended you with my psychoanalysis. Sometimes I can take things too far."

Luca was no longer concerned about it. In fact, she smiled, and replied, "It's already forgotten. I'm ready to get out of here, though. You down?"

He smiled. "Where you want to go?"

"Someplace fun, someplace different. Tonight, I want to become someone else," she said.

Clyde's smile implied he had the perfect idea. He reached into his Armani pocket and pulled out a wad of hundreds, dropping two crisp hundred-dollar bills onto the table, tip included, and left the restaurant with Luca. They both jumped into her customized Benz and sped away. Morocco was right behind them, keeping a keen eye out for any trouble.

23

The American Airlines flight couldn't land fast enough at JFK Airport in Queens for Squirrel. He was impatient to arrive back home to handle his business. After a five-hour flight, and another hour going through security and customs, he hurried out of the bustling terminal with Angel trying to keep up with him. He scowled the entire duration, from departure to arrival. His mind was plagued with being robbed of seventy kilos of pure heroin. Whoever committed the act was about to be dead.

Squirrel tried to think of potential suspects, and the first person who came to his mind was Luca. Did she plot the robbery out of revenge? He remembered she had taken a great loss not too long ago, plus she was probably pissed at him for messing with her feelings. If she was involved, then he was going to kill her. Period.

Seventy kis was just too much work and too great of a loss. Squirrel needed answers. He needed someone to kill.

Pug parked his black-on-black Infiniti QX56 outside waiting for Squirrel to exit, nervously smoking his cigarette while keeping an eye out for his boss. Pug knew he was going to have to give his boss some kind of explanation, and Squirrel wanted to snap his lieutenant's neck for being so stupid and careless.

Traffic outside the terminals was hectic, people and cars flooding the area, greeting loved ones and friends, and airport security was trying their best to keep the traffic flowing while cops commanded double-parked cars that were clogging up the roadway to move immediately.

Pug stood clad in his winter coat and ski hat braving the cold and his boss's return. Every so often, he would turn his head in the authorities' direction and see the cops slowly approaching with their blaring lights and loud horns, instructing those cars that didn't belong to clear the way. Finally, he spotted Squirrel exiting the terminal carrying his duffel bag and wearing a nasty frown. Pug took one final pull from his cigarette and flung it away. He quickly went toward Squirrel to help with his belongings. Angel followed right behind him, carrying her belongings with the help of airport baggage handlers.

Squirrel looked fiercely at his lieutenant. He had no words for him at the moment. There were too many people around, and too much security, cops, and personnel bustling about. Pug removed the duffel bag from Squirrel's hand and carried it to the truck. There was no "Welcome back," or "How was your trip?" Nah, it was just apprehension and concern. Squirrel went from tropical bliss to the frostbite cold of New York City.

After everything was loaded and secured into the truck, everyone climbed inside. Pug got behind the wheel and started to navigate his way out of the crushing airport traffic toward the nearest exit.

"You got a cigarette?" Squirrel asked coolly.

While stopped at a red light, Pug took out his pack of Newports and passed one to Squirrel and lit it for him. While still waiting for the light to change green, Squirrel took a few drags and looked cool. He exhaled the smoke and gazed out the windshield, looking somewhat aloof. Angel was in the backseat, quiet as a mouse. All of a sudden, Squirrel snapped. He gritted his fist and squarely punched Pug in the left side of his face.

"You stupid muthafucka!" Squirrel screamed heatedly. "What the fuck! Seventy fuckin' kilos? Seventy, Pug? How the fuck we out seventy kilos!"

Pug had no answers. He was taken aback having a bruised cheek.

"Answer me, nigga!" Squirrel shouted.

"I don't know man," Pug replied submissively.

"What the fuck you mean you don't know?"

"Niggas just ran up in broad daylight while the shit was being dropped off and started gunning niggas down like some Rambo shit," Pug explained.

"How did they know when the shipment was being delivered, Pug? Did you ever ask yourself that?"

Pug was quiet. His boss was right.

"You think we gotta snitch in our crew?" Pug replied.

"What the fuck you think, nigga! We always tight wit' our shit, never any losses, now this."

"So what you thinkin'?"

The light changed green, and Pug started to drive off while massaging his hurt cheek. He knew he wasn't out of hot water yet. Squirrel smoked his cigarette some more and looked pensive. Angel stayed quiet, out of her man's business. Barbados was still in her mind, and it pained her greatly that they had to cut their trip short to come back to this shit.

"I tried to call that bitch, but she ain't answering," said Squirrel.

"You mean Luca? You think she involved?"

"If she is, I'ma personally cut and carve that bitch's pussy out."

Hearing that cruel declaration from her man made Angel smile. She couldn't stand Luca. She'd wished her dead so long ago. Squirrel always insisted it was only business between the two of them, but she wasn't stupid or naïve.

"When she came by lookin' for you a few days ago, she wasn't too happy wit' the new arrangement," Pug let Squirrel know.

"She ain't never happy wit' any arrangement unless it's wit' me directly," Squirrel replied.

Angel sucked her teeth in the backseat. Squirrel heard it and turned around. Scowling, he cursed to her, "What the fuck you suckin' your teeth for?"

Angel couldn't hold in her resentment. "You need to be done wit' that bitch."

"Angel, I ain't in the mood for your shit right now. I'm warning you," he replied through clenched teeth. "I will toss you out this fuckin' truck right now."

Squirrel stared angrily at his baby mama for a moment, and she got the hint. She coiled her head away from his angry stare with an attitude and looked out the window. Things were going from bad to worse.

Pug drove toward the Van Wyck Expressway and headed north toward the bridge leading into Harlem. Squirrel was smoking his third cigarette when they arrived in Harlem at the Wagner Houses. There was still a heavy police presence at the crime scene. Yellow crime-scene tape looped around where the bodies had been sprawled out. The excessive shootout happened yesterday evening, and police swarmed the area like ants at a picnic. There were news cameras and reporters everywhere, and bystanders looked on in awe at something that was straight out of a movie.

"Fuck," Squirrel cursed with his attention fixed on police and detectives roaming everywhere. "This shit here, it's bad for business. It's gonna slow us down to a crawl, Pug."

Pug had nothing to say. He stopped the truck on Second Avenue, across the street from the fiasco of cops and reporters. Squirrel gazed from a distance at the chaos, and just seeing the confusion made him angrier. He felt like striking Pug again, but he didn't. It was going to be impossible now to continue operating from that building while so many eyes were watching and authorities lurking. The shootout made the front page of every city paper, and the media covered it like it was the presidential election. All eyes were on Wagner Houses.

"Just get me the fuck outta here, Pug," said Squirrel with distaste in his tone.

Pug drove away. Squirrel had to regroup and come up with some solution. He smoked another cigarette and said to Pug, "I want everyone on the hunt for some fuckin' answers, Pug, and I mean every fuckin' one. You better find me sumthin' on these muthafuckas."

Pug nodded. "I'm on it."

"You better be."

He drove Squirrel to an undisclosed location in the Bronx that only Pug and Angel knew about. From there, Squirrel would lay down another foundation to his organization, smoke out those who took from him, and plan to war with whoever was responsible. He continued calling Luca, but she wasn't picking up her phone, which he felt was indicative of her involvement. Luca was so obsessed with him that she would never reject any of his phone calls.

***

On the outskirts of Newark, New Jersey, the fire department had been alerted about a blazing fire in an empty lot. Two fire trucks hurried to the scene and saw it was a vehicle on fire. The heat was immense and the raging fire engulfed the entire vehicle. Firefighters hurried to put it out and did so immediately. After the fire had been put out, they found a charred body inside. They were shocked by the discovery, and homicide detectives were called to investigate the murder scene.

The charred vehicle was at the shootout at the Wagner Houses—and the body discovered was John-John. He didn't make it. He died during their escape, so World dumped the car along with his body and set it ablaze, destroying all evidence that might point toward himself or the crew.

24

Surprisingly, Luca was having a golden time with Clyde. She smiled as they toured the aquarium in Coney Island, Brooklyn—the oldest continually operating aquarium in the United States. It was their second day together since having dinner, and already she didn't want to leave his side. Clyde had a unique love for fish. She found it quite interesting, him and the fish. He was intelligent with a lot of culture in him. They walked around fourteen acres of aquarium looking at over three hundred and fifty species of aquatic wildlife. Clyde educated her on a few species, and she was listening attentively.

"How come you love fish so much?" she asked.

"I just do. Since I was a kid, my mother bought me my first small aquarium since she couldn't afford to buy me any pets, especially not a dog. So that one goldfish I had in my room, he became my best friend. I used to talk to him every day, hour after hour, and watch him swim around that tiny little bowl without a care in the world," Clyde said.

"So cute," said Luca with a smile.

"I mean, look at them," Clyde said, pointing to giant grouper fish swimming among schools of other fish. "The ocean is a wonder within itself."

"And what kind of fish is that?"

"It's called a giant grouper. They come from Australia, and are the largest bony fish found in coral reefs," he said.

"They're so ugly."

He laughed.

The giant grouper had a large mouth and a rounded tail with faint green-grey to grey-brown mottling and numerous small black spots on the fins. It swam toward the thick glass looking like it took a personal interest in Luca.

"I think he likes you," Clyde joked.

Luca laughed. "He's too ugly for me."

"Am I too ugly for you?"

"No, you're very handsome."

"Why thank you, beautiful."

The two continued walking throughout the aquarium looking at the fishes. Luca was captivated by the dolphins. They were her favorite species.

"I love dolphins," she announced.

"You do, huh? Well this is the bottlenose dolphin, and they are well-known members of the family Delphinidae, the family of oceanic dolphins. And they typically live in groups of ten to thirty members called pods. And their diets consist mainly of forage fish."

"You know, if the lounge-and-restaurant business doesn't work out for you, then you can get a job as a tour guide. You would be great at it."

"Growing up, I wanted to become a marine biologist."

"So what happened?"

"The streets, life happened, and then I changed my mind," he said.

Luca was curious about his past. It seemed he knew a lot about her, broke her down in the restaurant like she was transparent, but there was a mystery about Clyde that intrigued her.

They exited the aquarium onto the boardwalk of Coney Island. From there, they had a view of the beach and the ocean. It was too cold to tread any farther, so they paused up by the railing and gazed at nature.

"You ever wonder what's really out there, I mean what lies at the bottom of the ocean? Mermaids, an aquatic city, vast treasures or species, or creatures of enormous size," said Luca.

"The ocean is a phenomenal place. I don't ever get tired of looking at it. It brings me peace."

"It does."

He added, "And it's stated that only five percent of the world's ocean has been explored."

"Oh, really?"

"Yes. There are so many undiscovered things out in the sea, it makes you think about what could possibly be out there," he said.

Luca thought to herself that she could never have a discussion like this with Squirrel. He was a brute, but intelligent in his own way. The afternoon gradually went by with them walking, lunching, and forgetting about their outside troubles. In Luca's world, no matter how far she tried to escape the problems at home, they always came looking for her.

As she walked side-by-side with Clyde on the boardwalk, her cell phone rang. When she saw who was calling, a deep contemptuous feeling swirled inside of her.

"I need to take this," she said, excusing herself from Clyde's side.

She walked away a few feet from him to answer her phone. Her heart started to beat swiftly again. Seeing that Squirrel was trying to contact her repeatedly made her feel in some way . . . *wanted*. He was too much drama, and it was rude to accept his phone call when she was out on a date with Clyde. Her mind screamed at her to answer it, see what he wanted. He was going to keep on calling.

"What?" Luca answered with attitude.

"What the fuck you mean, what? Bitch, I've been muthafuckin' callin' you and now you fuckin' pick up," he barked.

"I've been busy, Squirrel."

"Busy, now all of a sudden you fuckin' busy when my shit gets taken."

"What are you talking about?"

"You dumb bitch, don't play stupid wit' me. Seventy kilos was taken from my peoples and four of my men chalked up. Niggas came into the projects blazing and disrespecting my organization. I want names, bitch."

"Squirrel, I have no fuckin' idea what you're talking about. I had nothing to do with that."

"You are fuckin' lying!"

"Squirrel, I wouldn't disrespect you like that and be crazy enough to pull some shit like that off, especially kill your peoples. It wasn't me!" she screamed, shocked and hurt that he would think that way about her.

"Then who?"

"I don't know!"

Clyde stood aside at a short distance observing Luca scream into her phone. It wasn't his business, but deep inside, Clyde wanted to make it his business. He hadn't known her long, but he strongly felt something for her, and if she was in trouble then he would have been able to help.

"I promise you, Luca, you better not be lying to me, cuz I fuckin' swear to you, I'm gonna track every last muthafuckin' soul responsible behind this and kill 'em so slowly, they gonna be begging to die."

"It wasn't me," Luca strongly repeated.

"It better not be."

Squirrel hung up. Luca was flared up with her argument with Squirrel. *Fuck him!* she thought. He had the audacity to blame her when he should have been home handling his business instead of going off somewhere with his baby mama and leaving her out to dry. It wasn't her problem.

"Is everything okay?" Clyde asked, walking over.

Everything wasn't okay. She looked at Clyde and replied, "Just business, nothing serious," she lied.

"It looked serious to me."

"Well it fuckin' wasn't," she snapped.

"I didn't mean to intrude."

"Then fuckin' don't!"

That one phone call had changed her mood and she abruptly took it out on Clyde.

"Listen, I'm not the enemy," he replied in a stern tone. "I'm just concerned, and if I can, I'll help you out."

Luca exhaled. "I'm sorry. I just have a lot on my mind lately."

"Well, I'm here to relax you. And don't let whoever that was get to you. I know you're better than that."

"I'm trying to be," she replied cordially, changing her mood over back from the dark side.

"C'mon, I have somewhere else I want to take you. You need to smile and have some fun." He put his hand in hers and led the way. She followed easily.

They ended up at his lounge in SoHo. It was closed for the moment, giving them the privacy they needed. Clyde guided her into the kitchen and he removed his jacket and tie and started removing cooking items from the cabinet and shelves.

"What are you doing?" she asked.

"Making you a nice meal," he said.

"You cook?"

"What? I'm the best," he replied jovially with a smile.

She smiled too, and then observed Clyde work his way around the kitchen, putting together something delicious for them both to dine on. He sat her up on the countertop like she was a young girl watching the master chef at work. He danced around the kitchen whistling and mixing together a recipe that already started to smell so good.

"Today, I'm gonna make you fall in love with me," he joked.

Luca gazed at Clyde with wide admiration and said to herself, *I think I already am.*

Maybe he was meant to come into her life. Maybe he was a new chapter for her. It was time, because Squirrel was getting on her damn nerves. She watched him cook and he made her laugh. Food and laughter—they were the two perfect ingredients to cure a wounded heart.

25

World took a drag from the Newport burning and looked around his surroundings. It was dark, cold, and after midnight. He and Doc were parked near a baseball field not too far from City Island in the Bronx. The parking lot was thin with cars and no people around. The field was closed for the night, and the parking lot was secluded with trees and vagueness engulfing the vicinity. The area where World and Doc lingered was almost a stone's throw away from Turtle Cove. World felt it was the perfect place to meet.

He felt sad about John-John's demise, and how they'd had to discard the body the way they had, abandoned and burned with the car. It wasn't personal; John-John was just unfortunate to get hit several times, and he would have slowed them down. Hospitals were out of the question and dumping him somewhere in public was too risky. New Jersey was the perfect place to cover their crime. World didn't feel too much regret. Life went on.

With seventy kilos in their possession, World felt like a rich man. The shooting made every TV station. It was the talk of the town, and even the mayor addressed it on the steps of City Hall.

"We will capture these animals and they will be prosecuted to the fullest extent of the law," the mayor stated robustly in front of droves of reporters.

World wasn't worried about repercussions; his mind wasn't programmed to worry about anything. His insanity was bliss. In fact, he couldn't wait to strike again. This wasn't going to be the last time the city would see his work—his art of death was about to be displayed everywhere with the gun as his paintbrush and the city his personal canvas. He liked the media attention. He yearned for it. They hit a major kingpin and the streets were buzzing with who could have done the brazen robbery in Harlem.

"Damn, where this nigga at?" Doc asked.

"He comin'," World replied.

"He better hurry the fuck up. I hate sitting out here in the cold and open like this."

"Just relax, Doc. He coming," World said, looking cool and unperturbed about anything.

Both men were heavily armed with several automatic weapons on their person and in the backseat, and half of the seventy kilos were in the back of the gold Volvo XC70 they sat in. World continued smoking and waited. Not long after, bright headlights were seen approaching. World and Doc perked up and stared at the black Range Rover driving their way. It parked parallel to them, but left some distance.

"This is it," World said.

"These muthafuckas better be real," Doc said.

He and Doc stepped out of their vehicle. The two front doors to the Range Rover opened up and two men stepped out. They greeted each other at the back of their vehicles. World stared at both men; one of them boasted a gold NYPD badge around his neck and outside of his clothing. The other man wasn't a cop; he was the smarts of the group.

"Y'all did good—really good. I see y'all definitely took advantage of my snitch and made some heavy noise out there," Xavier said.

"You keep giving us the information we need, and we gonna hit that muthafucka all the time," World stated.

Xavier smiled.

Xavier and the corrupt cops had an inside man in Squirrel's crew, and with the surveillance they implemented on his top lieutenants, it wasn't hard to come up with the time and date that another large drug shipment from Florida was going to be delivered into the projects. Xavier reached out to World, a man he'd met a few years back when they both did time on Riker's Island. They connected, becoming something like friends, and many years later, became of some use to each other.

"So where's my cut?" Xavier asked.

World nodded to Doc. Doc walked over to the Volvo and lifted the back. He removed a shopping bag filled with thirty kilos of raw uncut heroin and placed it in Xavier's hands. He was having the month of his life. First he took thirty kis from Luca's people, and now he had another thirty kis from Squirrel's organization. His master plan was coming along perfectly.

Xavier looked into the bag and smiled.

Why get his hands dirty when he could always pay some fool like World to do it for him? It was a genius plan. Get rich and not die trying. World loved the action, and he loved the money and power. He had put together a crazy crew of maniacs that thought just like him, and now Xavier had released the beast into the streets to hunt with the protection of corrupt cops in their corner. Xavier and the dangerous men he worked for, rogue cops who called themselves "The Untouchables," executed a plan to create a war between Squirrel and Luca. With the competition out of the way on both ends, they could take over the market and make millions for themselves.

Xavier handed the bag of drugs to the towering white officer with the bald head. He then handed World a slip of paper with an address and time. World glanced at it, hearing Xavier say, "You know what to do with that," and World nodded.

"We gonna take over this city once everyone is out the way," said Xavier.

"No doubt, my nigga," World replied.

Xavier turned and walked back to the Range Rover with his cop escort. The meeting was brief—a few words and a quick exchange. World and Doc watched the two men get into their truck and drive away. Doc looked over at World and asked, "You trust these niggas?"

World replied, "If they get out of pocket, we rock them to sleep. But for now, they dependable."

"Yeah, but cops, man. I never trusted pigs."

"Yeah, pork is always bad for ya health. But I ain't Muslim, and if the five-0 and Xavier fuck us over, best believe I'm on a strictly pork diet and we gonna slaughter every last pig."

"Yeah, I like that . . . I like that," Doc said with a menacing grin.

✳✳✳

Bad Boy, the potent heroin flooded the west side of Harlem, Washington Heights, areas of the Bronx and parts of east Harlem like a new plague, and the fiends were running to the new brand of heroin like a sneaker-head lining up outside the shoe store for hours, craving the next new Jordans. The fiends were oblivious that it was the same shit they were already pumping into their veins. Slap a new name on a product, and it becomes the talk of the town.

The young hustlers pushed Bad Boy like candy and were making serious money daily. A few local crews from the Amsterdam houses on the Upper West Side and the Grant houses set up shop under the guidance of World and Doc. Soon word had traveled to rival drug crews. Squirrel was convinced that Bad Boy was *his* stolen product, and it didn't take long for word to reach Luca—and she became convinced that Bad Boy heroin was *her* stolen product. They both wanted payback, and neither would hesitate to dish out extreme violence to those responsible for taking from them.

It was one of the warmer days from the brutal winter the city was having, and most of the community took advantage of the bright sun and 55-degree temperature. People went for walks, ran errands, lingered in the parks or just enjoyed some much-needed sun and warmth for once.

A shady hustler named Spooky stood on the corner of Amsterdam and 133rd Street, clad in an oversized dark hoodie, sagging black jeans, and a red bandana tied around his head. Spooky lingered out in front of the corner bodega, leaning against a broken payphone. He watched the block and people passing and going in and out of the bodega while he smoked his cigarette. He obscured several glassine bags of Bad Boy in his boxer shorts and sold drugs from sun up to sun down. Hustling and the streets were his life. Harlem was all he knew.

He worked for World. He was making money. He was a menace to society.

Spooky took a pull from his cancer stick and gazed at one of his cronies approaching. Soon, a man named Fever gave dap to Spooky and joined him on the corner.

"It's good out here?" Fever asked.

"It's butter, my nigga. Makin' that paper and whatnot," Spooky replied. As he talked, he looked past his friend and noticed a young fiend coming their way. Her name was Brenda, and she was hooked on heroin and had become one of his favorite customers. The woman lazily swaggered up the block toward her dealer. She was dressed in a pair of dirty black sweatpants, a tattered and soiled windbreaker, and house shoes in the winter. Her hair was matted and uncombed, her lips were dry and terribly chapped, and her eyes were sunken deeply into her head. She was grotesquely skinny and looked to weigh no more than one hundred pounds. It was the side effect of being hooked on drugs.

Brenda didn't care anything about her gross appearance. Her main concern was getting high, all day and every day. Her sunken eyes were fixed on Spooky, and she flashed him a toothless smile as she walked closer.

"Hey, Spooky, you know I'm sick, right?" Brenda said.

"What you need?" Spooky asked.

"I need two."

Spooky nodded.

It was too risky to make the transaction on the avenue, so Spooky directed her to go down a side street. Before either could take a step forward, a dark blue van burst onto the scene and came to a halting stop in front of everyone like they were police making a raid. The sliding door hastily slammed back and several dangerous men carrying baseball bats poured out from the vehicle and rushed Spooky, Fever, and Brenda.

Everyone was caught off guard and found themselves besieged by a rival drug crew.

"Muthafucka!" one of the masked attackers shouted, swinging the baseball bat at Spooky and walloping him across the chest so hard it took the breath out of him and had him doubling over in pain and stumbling. The second goon swung and struck Fever in the face with a powerful blow, breaking his nose along with several bones in his face. He dropped to the concrete rapidly, in severe pain, and was beaten severely until he was unconscious.

The men even attacked drug-addict Brenda, giving her no mercy even though she was a woman and a fiend. Her fragile body was broken in two by numerous baseball bats slamming into her and beating her into a bloody pulp. The brutal scene unfolded in front of over a dozen witnesses looking on in awe at the attack.

"Grab that muthafucka!" one of the masked attackers shouted.

With brute force they snatched Spooky from off the ground, forced him into the van, and sped away. He was in awful pain. His breathing was labored and his bones felt like they were crushed.

Spooky soon found a revolver in his face and one of his kidnappers shouting, "The building and apartment number of the stash house. Tell us where, or I'll blow ya fuckin' brains out right now."

The butt of the revolver angrily crashed against his skull several times, spewing blood and almost knocking him out cold.

"Talk nigga!"

"Yo, he ain't talkin'."

"He gonna talk."

The armed man thrust the revolver into his crotch area and pulled back the hammer. "I'll blow ya fuckin' dick off, muthafucka!"

Spooky could barely keep his eyes open and hold himself together. Every inch of him was on fire and it felt like he was about to fall apart. He was surrounded by four masked men and driven around randomly.

"You got till five. One, two, three, four—"

"Building 5," Spooky puffed out. "Off of Broadway, ninth floor, apartment 918."

"You better not be lying, nigga."

"I'm not."

The driver of the van hurried toward the location. He pulled into the residential parking lot and parked. The masked men replaced baseball bats with pistols, Uzis and sawed-off shotguns. They duct-taped Spooky's wrists and feet and left him in the van for dead, then exited the vehicle and hurried toward the building. Five armed goons walked briskly into the lobby concealing their weapons underneath large winter coats. They piled into the elevator and pushed for the ninth floor. Soon, the elevator carried them up.

They exited the elevator into the walls of the narrow hallway, which was covered in graffiti and smelled of Purple Haze. The men made their way to the apartment with their weapons drawn—locked, loaded and ready. They had their own key—the sawed-off shot gun aimed at the lock—and soon it was about to become a rude awakening for everyone inside. The carrier of the sawed-off looked at the man in charge of the assault and he nodded, giving his green light.

Chk-Chk—Boom!

The apartment door nearly flew off the hinges from the shotgun blast, and all five men charged inside ready to create havoc. The Uzi was the first to light up the room with gunfire. The two male occupants seated on the couch playing Xbox in the living room were immediately caught off-guard and viciously mowed down by machine-gun fire. Quickly, the gunmen spread throughout the apartment, killing everything moving inside. A poor young soul suffered the brutal fate of having his head blown off by the shotgun blast at point-blank range. Another victim was cut down by gunfire in the hallway as he tried to scurry for safety in the two-bedroom apartment. The final victim was trapped in the second bedroom. He was wide-eyed with fear, panicky, and found himself peeing in his pants.

"No, please! I ain't gonna say shit, I promise," he pleaded in a quivering tone.

Boom!

The shotgun blast to his chest sent his body flying across the room and slamming into the wall. His blood splattered everywhere. The gunman smirked and said to the dead soul, "Yeah, I know you ain't gonna say shit now."

Two shooters pumped a few more rounds into his body, desecrating him even more just for the fun of it. Then, everyone left without taking a thing; no money, no drugs. It was a death crew sent out from Squirrel to demonstrate a gruesome message to anyone selling Bad Boy. Whoever had a hand in taking from him and then profiting from his product were dead men. Squirrel put his most lethal hit men on the streets to kill 'em all.

26

Having a good time with Clyde didn't mean Luca's troubles had stopped, or had been put on hiatus. She still was on a vendetta and had not forgotten about Quincy, the soon to be dead detective. She continuously investigated everything about him. When word got back to her that there was heroin being sold on the streets under the name Bad Boy, it angered her more, but she had to take care of one thing at a time.

Her research on Quincy soon hit pay dirt, and she dug up substantial evidence that he'd just paid cash for a vacation home in Barbados and was laundering a great deal of money through securities frauds via a stockbroker friend. She had the muthafucka red-handed, documentation of all his transactions that he tried to cover up. It could have been easy for her to leak his illegal money trail to the IRS and the NYPD, have him investigated and incarcerated, but that was just too easy. Luca had better plans for Mr. Quincy. She was ready to sic her dogs out on him and show that her bite was much fiercer than her bark.

Luca sat behind her desk in her home office, puffing on a cigar with her laptop on and thinking about a few things. She was clad in a black silk robe with a matching sash. It was another warm evening with spring a few weeks away. She had something different on her mind. She was thinking about Clyde. For the past three weeks, they had become an item and things were heating up. Luca was going over Quincy's transaction when she heard the doorbell downstairs. She was alone in the home, but was expecting company. She rose from behind her desk and removed a .38 revolver from inside her desk. The gun was for precaution. She proceeded toward the door. Her security footage showed that it was Clyde standing outside and patiently waiting. She smiled. He was alone and waiting for her. Tonight, it was going to be their special night.

She opened the double front doors with the revolver still in her hand and Clyde stepped into her beautiful home with an engaging smile. When he noticed the gun in her hand, he said, "Now that's a unique greeting."

"Oh, I'm sorry. You know a bitch can never be too careful," she explained.

"I understand."

Luca smiled seeing Clyde finally inside her home. He looked ravishing in his charcoal grey suit with blue windowpane and a peak lapel. He had a white shirt underneath with lavender stripes running up it. His tie was deep purple, solid and sleek. It tied with an impeccable, effortless dimple, and his pocket square was vibrant, yet tasteful.

The man loved his suits. He looked remarkably good in everything he wore, standing out quite elegantly, like he could play a James Bond character.

Luca looked at him, hypnotized by his sex appeal.

"You look beautiful in that robe," Clyde said.

"And you look very stunning in that suit. You do have taste in fashion," she replied.

"I try my best."

"You don't need to try anymore."

Clyde smiled.

They walked into her chic living room where the aromas of amazing food filled the air. Luca had prepared a wonderful dinner with a candlelight setting and champagne displayed on the table ready to be opened up and for them both to enjoy. He'd cooked for her; now it was her turn to cook for him. She made beef bourguignon, which was melt-in-your-mouth yummy, whitefish in tomato and black olive sauce, smashed red baby potatoes, and saffron rice. She'd gotten the recipe from her grandmother. And it was good! Tonight, it wasn't about the streets, drugs, revenge, or murders. It was an intimate setting with the man she was attracted too.

With soulful R&B music playing in the dimmed milieu, Luca and Clyde dined on a wonderful meal and talked the night away. They couldn't take their eyes off each other. His words were captivating; her eyes were mesmerizing—a wonderful mixture of equal romance. How could a man this fine be single and real? His boldness, along with his bass voice and gregarious personality were a big part of his alluring character. His spicy aroma was appealing. When he spoke, his voice was gentle, but commanding.

"Who are you, really?" Luca asked out of the blue.

"My story, it belongs in a book."

"Read it to me."

Clyde inhaled deeply and began. "My mother was a whore and my father was killed during the U.S. invasion of Panama in 1989, during Noriega's capture. I came to the States right after my father's death. My father was a career soldier for Noriega and he died for what he believed in, his country. I came to the States with my mother a very poor child, first it was Philadelphia where I was made fun of and ridiculed because I was different, I had a thick accent and because I was poor. And then it was Baltimore. I became a U.S. citizen as a child. When I turned ten, my mother was murdered by her boyfriend and I was sent to live in a group home in Philadelphia. Since I was a kid, I've had to protect myself and fight bullies and adults. I became tough, ruthless, and by the time I was fourteen, I was a seasoned criminal.

"At fifteen, I ran off to Baltimore with some friends and joined a gang called the Warriors. We robbed, terrorized, fought, and sold drugs. I soon became an enforcer because I was good at hurting people. It was my forte, distributing pain. At seventeen, I became a murderer, and by the time I was twenty, I was running my own multimillion-dollar drug empire with over fifty loyal soldiers at my beck and call and making close to thirty million a year.

"I had more money than I could spend, more power than I could control. I ran East Baltimore with an iron fist. I was feared, connected, and respected. And then it all changed because of disloyalty. A trusted friend, my right-hand lieutenant, he became greedy, and jealous of my position and jealous of my love for a once-beautiful woman," Clyde said.

He had Luca's undivided attention. She was like a youthful camper sitting by a camp fire and listening to a good ghost story.

"So what happened?" she asked.

"I should have seen it coming, but I didn't. My friend, he resented me for keeping my connect's identity a secret and pressured me to reveal my connections. We were supposed to be brothers. He was fucking my woman and plotting my downfall. He had me followed, figured out my connections, struck a deal with them with lies about me, and tried to have me killed. He almost succeeded. I got hit outside my own home. Two assassins were waiting, came at me and shot me several times. I was fortunate to survive the hit on my life. As I lay in that hospital room for over a month, I did a lot of thinking. I was done. I was finished. I couldn't do it anymore. I had made some smart investments and they were paying off. I decided to leave the streets alone, because there's no love, no loyalty, and no honor in the game—just lies, deceit and betrayal."

Clyde paused for a moment, gazing into Luca's eyes. He could almost predict her future. He knew what eventually would lie ahead for her. He understood her flow and knew she was mixed up deeply in the drug game.

He saw some of himself in her.

He took a sip of champagne and said to Luca, "I know what you do, Luca, but I love you regardless, and I'm not judging you and I'm gonna always be there for you. But this game, I've been there and I'm fortunate not to have done any lengthy time and survived. I advise you to leave the streets alone before they turn on you. And best believe one day, it will, and those you trust are going to be the ones to stab you in the back."

Luca looked at him without expression. She wasn't worried. And she was in too deep now to turn her back on it.

"You really love me?" she asked.

"I do."

"How? You barely know me."

"I believe in love at first sight. And the day I saw you, I knew I just had to have you. And these past three weeks have been some of the best days of my life."

She smiled.

They veered off the subject and talked intimately. He was humbled by her beauty and grace. They romantically leaned toward each other and locked lips. He knew without a doubt that he was created for her and she for him. Clyde kissed his way down her neck, causing her to throw her head back and revel in the sensation. His hands found her breasts. He cupped and massaged them through the sensual material of her silk robe. He slowly undid the ties that held up her top and exposed her soft, enticing body. He began massaging her nipples and stroking them, sucking on them, loving them, and gently pulling them.

They kissed again. This time her hands explored him. She methodically undid the buttons on his shirt—one button at a time, revealing his flesh—and admired his chiseled physique, and placed gentle kisses on his neck. Her gentle touch stroked him to hardness as her mouth enveloped him and the softness of her lips painted pleasures.

Clyde stood and let his pants fall to the ground. He stepped out of them. The stage was set for some serious lovemaking. He pushed Luca on her back and fell to his knees, and then he positioned himself between her legs to make a feast of her pussy. Luca gasped at his strong but alluring touch. His lips started from the top of her knees to the center of her desire. Pushing her legs back, Clyde softly licked and sucked her clit. He buried his tongue inside of her as she grabbed the back of his head and held him there.

Her breathing became labored, her moaning danced across the candlelit room. Her breathing was like harmony to his ears aware that it was his sex that sent her to drift off to such a heavenly place. Her pussy couldn't stop throbbing. It was constantly wet and aroused. He sucked and licked on her clit. Her taste drove him insane with lust.

"Mmmm, ooooh, yes," she moaned. "I wanna feel you inside of me."

Her legs quivered. Her eyes were closed while she squirmed against the floor, aching to feel his penetration inside of her. Clyde gazed upon her nakedness and fondled the soft, round curve of her ass. He yearned to feel her magnificent insides. Her hard nipples were like magnets to his mouth, and he began to leak precum.

"You got condoms?" she asked.

Clyde produced a Magnum in his hand. He tore it open and rolled it back onto his thick, long erection.

"Fuck me," Luca said.

Hearing those two words, Clyde surrendered to the feeling of ecstasy and pleasure. He climbed between her inviting legs and drove himself into her and moaned loudly. Their mouths met again. Their breath became one. Their bodies collided with an erotic purpose with her slippery, sticky, sweet juices intoxicating him to the fullest.

She turned around and mounted her man, placing Clyde's throbbing erection at her core and descended. He grabbed her hips and she placed her hands on his strong thighs and they bumped together. She levitated and plunged on his dick, riding and enjoying the wave of pleasure that filled her. Her sweet juices were evident on his shaft, and her moans were louder, more urgent.

Luca wanted to make him cum and cum hard.

He flipped her over and pushed her legs back, pumping his length and thickness inside her, enveloping her pussy with pleasure. Then soon, they both exploded like fireworks in the room. Their orgasm was strong, and they were winded. He collapsed beside her, their faces full of satisfaction. Clyde could definitely give Squirrel a run for his money. His dick was good—too good.

Luca had another surprise waiting for him. She stood up to walk into the next room and Clyde hypnotically gazed at her naked, round ass and craved for a round two with her immediately. She came back into the room right after with two Cuban cigars for them to smoke. She nestled against him, satisfied, and they sparked up the cigars and enjoyed the blissful feeling and each other.

"My kind of woman," Clyde said.

"I better be."

They both giggled like little kids.

27

Reclined behind the steering wheel of a Lincoln MKZ, Kool-Aid smoked his Newport, exhaled, and glanced at Phaedra. "You should have said sumthin' before it got too far, yo. Fo' real."

"Say what, Kool-Aid?" Phaedra replied.

"I don't know, if you really liked that nigga, then you should have took ya shot. I mean, what you scared of?"

"I ain't scared of shit."

"Well, you should have pushed up on that fool. I don't know why—he ain't nobody to me—but you should have let Luca know how you really felt about him. Maybe she would have backed off."

"She wouldn't," Phaedra said.

"How you know? You ain't even brought it up."

"It's spilled milk now."

"You can always lick it up," he joked. "I thought you like to lick things."

"Fuck you."

"Hey, since you back to liking dick now . . ." he teased again.

"Fuck you fo' real, Kool-Aid."

"Don't get mad at me because the boss cockblocked you from that dick down. I'm sayin', what happened to you liking pussy? When then you started switch hittin' and playing for the other team again?"

"My sex life is none of ya business," Phaedra replied dryly.

Kool-Aid laughed.

"What's so funny?"

"You, tryin' to see you back wit' some dick in ya life. You gotta wipe the cobwebs from the pussy first."

Phaedra flipped him the middle finger. It was all fun and jokes while they sat inside the Lincoln, passing time by as they surveyed their target. They were parked outside of Quincy's modest three bedroom home in Far Rockaway, Queens. So far everything was quiet. The block was quaint and near the bay.

Kool-Aid took a few more pulls from the cigarette and gazed out the window. Since Phaedra had come back into his life and looked out for him, he'd come a long way. He had high regards for her as a best friend, and hearing her talk about another man made him think.

"We go back a long time, don't we Phaedra?" he asked, looking somewhat nostalgic.

"Too long."

"Yeah. But honestly, when I first seen you, I wanted to fuck you."

"Eww!" Phaedra replied with her face twisted up in shame like it was her biological brother talking about sexing her down. Kool-Aid was a great friend, nothing more.

"I remember you being wit' my cousin and I knew how much he loved you and how much you loved him. Y'all made a great couple, always holdin' each other down and together. No lie, I used to hate on my cousin when he used to be wit' you," Kool-Aid confessed. "Man, I wanted a bitch just like you. You know, help me out, slow my ass down and shit."

"I always had respect for you. You one of a few niggas I like and respect in these streets. You know it will never go there between you and me."

"Yeah, I know. I always had respect for you, too. You know me; I don't violate anybody's relationship. I keep it real. You and my cousin were tight, and you family to me. Yo, fo' real. I love you, Phaedra, and I ain't talkin' 'bout that mushy, in-love love. Nah, you a sister to me, and I gotta thank you for puttin' me on. A nigga was dying out there, yo, struggling and just surviving. The day you pulled me off of the street when I was 'bout to rob that bodega, you saved my life. Cuz I ain't give a fuck anymore."

"You welcome," Phaedra replied, smiling. "So, I'm ya guardian angel now, huh?"

"Yeah, kind of."

"What you mean kind of?"

"I mean kind of, cuz I looked out for you and Luca more times wit' the murder game I put down out here."

"That's true."

"I do what I do best, pop the fuck off. What would y'all do wit'out me?"

"Not make the headlines," Phaedra quipped. "What you did to that ambulance worker, what the fuck were you thinkin'?"

"I was doin' my job, and tryin' to get mines, too," he replied with a cocksure smile.

"You always been a lunatic, Kool-Aid."

"I always been feared out here."

"True that," replied Phaedra.

"Real talk, what would you do wit'out me? You know I'm ya knight in shining armor, swingin' my sword out there on the battlefield, protecting the castle and killing all our enemies that approach. Fuck King Arthur, I'm the real knight. Ya heard?"

Phaedra laughed. "You crazy. Why you be buggin', Kool-Aid?"

"Cuz I just do, that's why. I do what I do."

Phaedra continued to laugh. He made her forget about her minor heartbreak with Clyde and Luca hooking up. Kool-Aid had always been able to do that, make her laugh and take her mind off of troubling things.

He was a reckless spirit—a killer when he wanted to be and a lovable jokester when he was in the mood. Even when she was with his cousin and they would get into it, Kool-Aid would come around and make her smile and laugh. She truly loved him like a brother.

Kool-Aid lit another cigarette and stared at the cop's house. It was becoming a long night. "This nigga ain't like the others, Phaedra. I got a funny feelin' 'bout this one."

"Like what?"

"I don't know. But we been watchin' this nigga for a week now, and he ain't got a routine. He ain't predictable."

"Well, he needs to get got."

"Yeah, I know, and he gonna get got. Killing cops is what I do, and since Luca got that concrete evidence on this muthafucka, oh, I'm 'bout to give him the special treatment, fo' real," Kool-Aid proclaimed, shaking his head.

Kool-Aid gazed at the cop's picturesque place near the beach. It was rigged with motion sensor lights all around, and there were two vicious Rottweilers roaming freely about in the backyard. The iron gates were always locked and so was everything bordering the place. The detective was a military man, a veteran who had done two tours with the Marines. He also had a black belt in martial arts, was a gun nut with a large collection, and was a crack shot with pristine accuracy. He wasn't supposed to be a New York City cop; he was supposed to be a fuckin' mercenary.

Kool-Aid knew he had his hands full with this one. He lived alone, moved alone, and was always armed and cautious. The one vulnerability the detective had was his nineteen-year-old baby mama and his one-year-old son. He liked his women really young.

"What you thinkin'?" Phaedra asked.

"Just plotting. We might have to come at this nigga directly from the front."

"That's risky," said Phaedra.

"I know, but this muthafucka is all over the place."

Kool-Aid smoked his cigarette and fixed his eyes on the house. He couldn't help but to have a bad feeling about this one. He wasn't scared, but this Quincy character wasn't like his partner or the other detectives. There was something not right about him. Kool-Aid had a job to do, and funny feeling or not, he was still determined to complete his mission. This was the one who'd stolen from the organization and was spending Luca's money like he'd won the Lotto. There had to be serious repercussions. Kool-Aid couldn't wait to murder this muthafucka in his own special way.

***

The location was supposed to be Squirrel's private and secret reserve, but it wasn't private or a secret anymore, and it was no longer reserved— shit was getting taken. World and his lunatic crew held six of Squirrel's soldiers at gunpoint. The men were on their knees with their bleeding fingers locked behind their heads and in fear for their lives. They remained completely still, and their breathing was unnatural. It was inevitable that they would die today.

The million-dollar question on everyone's mind was, how did they know about this stash house? It was across the Hudson in New Jersey, rarely talked about, and only a handful of people knew of the location. Maybe that was a handful too many.

The place was supposed to be heavily fortified with steel doors, locked windows, 360-degree camera surveillance everywhere, alarm systems, soldiers and lots of guns, yet World was able to place it under siege. World and his goons ran up in the spot with their guns blazing, quickly taking control of the room and striking gold. The New Jersey stash house contained fifty kilos of heroin, another fifteen kilos of cocaine, several automatic weapons, and five hundred thousand dollars in cash. World was a very happy man.

"Now this is what I'm talkin' about," Doc hollered excitedly. "Yeah, this is payday right here."

Everyone in World's crew smiled. The only gloomy faces in the room were Squirrel's men.

The goons ransacked the entire place from top to bottom, starting from the three bedrooms, then the living room, and so on, and right away they found product hidden in the cupboards, the stove, underneath the sink, inside the light fixtures, behind the walls, and concealed in the kitchen floor. World and his men took their time tearing the house apart. For now, they kept everyone alive to witness the destruction of something they were paid to protect and also for information. They tortured the men; pistol-whipped them and beat them severely. Their faces were encrusted with blood and bruises; their teeth had been knocked out, and some fingers were cut off. World took his job seriously, and the streets were going to know his name.

World looked at his captives and said, "Y'all thought we weren't gonna find this fuckin' place, huh? Nigga, Squirrel can't hide shit from me. You know who the fuck I am?"

Squirrel's men stayed quiet, scared and angry.

"I'm everywhere, muthafucka. I'ma be the head nigga running shit in Harlem. Nah, fuck that, I'ma be the one controlling shit in New York! Y'all niggas fuckin' hear me? Me, nigga!" World exclaimed to the captive men. "Y'all workin' for a fuckin' dead man."

"That's right," Doc cosigned with a nasty smile.

It was the third place World and his goons had hit this month. The second place was in the Bronx. It was an easy hit, an easy score—two dead, ten kilos snatched along with fifty thousand dollars cash.

Squirrel didn't have a clue who was robbing his stash houses, or how they were finding out about them. He was vexed, completely disturbed and going fuckin' crazy. He no longer suspected Luca was behind it, this was a different entity—a darker and more sinister force. The streets were running red with blood; his men were being killed off. He had to hire more soldiers to keep him and his family safe. Angel had around-the-clock armed protection with her and his two kids. Every last one of Squirrel's vehicles were tricked out with armored plating, run-flat tires, and bulletproof windows. He wasn't taking any chances.

World was going to apply perpetual pressure to his rival's empire until it cracked open like a walnut. In addition to their first takedown of seventy kilos at the Wagner Houses, this was their second biggest score. He was pleased with the outcome. His crew of disciples, who were extremely thorough dudes—G building crazy, damn psychos, and lunatics—were becoming a deadly force not to be fucked with.

They dumped the drugs and cash into several garbage bags, stashed the guns in a few duffel bags, and were ready to make their exit. Before their departure, they had to leave their bloody calling card. World had gotten extremely upset when he heard about the massacre at one of his drug depots off of Amsterdam Avenue. He was fond of Spooky. And what they did to him, cut him up so badly and left him to rot in a dumpster for the rats to feed on, it was tragic—and then they brutally killed five of his men inside the apartment. The massacre was front-page news and had cops everywhere in the area. The city was alerted to a drug war happening in Harlem. The gruesome murders were happening in insane numbers. Harlem and the Bronx had police departments putting together a task force to combat the crime wave, and they were also ready to ask for help from the FBI.

World continued to insanely preach to his bloody captives. They already had what they came for, but he lingered behind, flanked by Doc. He taunted them with his bizarre and intense stare. His dark, black eyes were cold like ice. He was stoic and shifty.

"Y'all muthafuckas, y'all killed Spooky. Spooky was my friend. He was a good friend. And y'all slaughtered him and left him for the rats. Spooky was good peoples. He was my nigga. He ain't do shit to y'all. Why y'all do that to Spooky, huh?" he ranted with his eyes brimming with anger.

No one answered him. They weren't the ones that murdered Spooky. They looked at World like he was crazy, which he was.

"Y'all killed Spooky," he continued to accuse them.

"It wasn't us," one of the captives spoke out.

"What?"

"We ain't had shit to do wit' that," the voice said in a sniping tone.

World shot back an incredulous stare, and blasted back, "Y'all niggas lying!"

World had a .9mm in one hand and a large bowie knife gripped in the other hand. The blade had a large, upswept ricasso to allow the user to shorten his grip on the knife for more control. He paced back and forth in front of the men still on their knees with their fingers locked behind their heads and wearing uneasy and fearful gazes.

"World, we ain't got all day, man. Do these niggas like how we do and let's get the fuck outta here," Doc said.

"Don't fuckin' rush me, nigga! I'm talkin' here," World retorted.

Doc sighed, knowing World was in one of his crazy and pugnacious moods.

World fixed his attention back on Squirrel's soldier. "You know, I'm a nice guy. I'm reasonable, so I'ma give y'all niggas a choice." He smirked.

The room was quiet. Squirrel's soldiers were breathing apprehensively and so frightened, that one began to pee in his pants.

"You nasty muthafucka," Doc ridiculed.

"Hey, when you gotta go, you gotta go," World joked.

No one laughed.

"But as I was sayin', I'm a reasonable dude, so I'm gonna give y'all niggas a choice how to die—by the gun, or by the knife," he said.

There was silence, no answers.

"If y'all niggas don't choose soon, then I'm gonna choose for y'all," he announced.

The men glared at World, wishing they could rip him apart, but they were all helpless and beaten. He paced back and forth in front of them, taunting them with both weapons in his hands.

"C'mon now, somebody must got the balls to say sumthin'."

"Fuck you!" one brave soul chided.

World laughed. "There we go, finally some nigga wit' some balls in this place."

He approached the antagonistic-looking man and glared at him. World and the man locked eyes intensely. "So fuck me, huh?" said World.

"Squirrel, he gonna fuck you up badly when he finds you," the man growled through his clenched teeth.

"You think so?" World chuckled.

"I know so, muthafucka!"

"You know so. Okay," World replied coolly. He looked at Doc. "It looks like we got a shit talker here, Doc."

"Yeah, it looks like we do."

"Maybe I need to shut this nigga up."

"Yeah, I think you do."

World situated himself behind the man, and then strongly placed him into a crushing chokehold and raised the blade to his neck. His victim struggled, but he was no match for World and his insane strength. World's biceps protruded and he yanked the man's head back and quickly carved the knife into his throat. A struggle for life or death ensued, but World continued to cut deeply enough to sever the carotid arteries, as well as the jugular vein. His blood spurted out like a fountain. He fidgeted violently in World's deadly grasps; there was still breath in him, but it sounded like a rubber bag releasing air. It was quite loud. Blood coated World's hand, the knife, and the victim. The other captives looked on in horror as World cut into the man's neck so deeply, it looked like he was about to sever off his head.

The man finally dropped dead, face first onto the ground, thick crimson blood pooling underneath the body. World turned to the other men and asked, "Who's next?"

"World, we ain't got time to do these niggas the same way," Doc spoke out.

"Damn, that's just too bad," replied World.

Quickly, he stepped toward each man and shot them in the head point blank range. For World, it was a blissful thing to see. They came at him, he came back harder. They killed five of his men; he'd try and kill six or ten of theirs in a heinous way.

World was going to continue using Squirrel's business like a grocery store when his product got low. And with Xavier tipping him off with locations of his rival's stash houses, and corrupt cops backing him, it was a win-win situation for him.

28

It was the first 60-degree, spring-like day in months, and Luca decided to spend it cruising with Phaedra in her pearl-white Benz. She was dressed to the nines in a sexy black jumpsuit with a plunging neckline, her wrists and neck bejeweled in 18-karat white gold and flawless diamonds. She sat in the backseat and puffed on her cigar like a boss bitch.

She had just come from an hour-long meeting with Dominic Sirocco to go over some real estate she owned, perform some smurfing tactics, secure her money-laundering procedure, and also see about liquidating some of her assets. Luca still felt a little distrust with her attorney since that bullshit he pulled when she was in financial trouble. Once he had managed to free up some of her money from her investments and send her a few more checks, her apprehension began to slowly dissipate. For now, he was still useful and valuable to her organization. He was still the best at his job.

Together in his lavish downtown office, the two of them scrutinized the majority of her assets, establishing the liquidation value of some of her possessions that were becoming too much of a burden on her. With a war brewing on the streets and a crazy cousin stalking her, she needed to administrate an emergency fund and her rainy day funds just in case things heated up too much and she had to leave town, or maybe leave the country. Luca had passports in different names made up, cash buried in certain locations, and had several overseas accounts, especially in the Cayman Islands. She was ready for the worst, but hoped for the best.

Dominic had reclined in his high-back leather chair, clasped his fingers together while looking at Luca and said, "You know, you're one of my most complicated clients."

"But I'm also your best-paying client," she had replied.

He had chuckled.

"Is there trouble in paradise?" he had asked.

"No, not yet. I'm just taking necessary precautions just in case. You're connected—any word from your political friends?"

"On your end, things have been kind of quiet."

"Okay."

"But liquefying the majority of your assets, it will take some time. And sometimes the liquidation value is how much you make in a forced-sale situation, and it's generally at least twenty percent less than the retail value. I have a few qualified appraisers that I trust and can work with, and they can establish the liquidation value of your assets, and also at a reasonable cost on their end. You understand?"

"Yeah, everything costs around here," Luca had replied.

"It's the price of doing business and expediting the paperwork."

Luca had stood up and replied, "I'll call you."

"You always do."

Luca's meeting with her attorney was productive, but what wasn't productive was the hunt for World. He was still out there, still a threat to her, and she had very good reasons to believe that he was pushing Bad Girl which was now renamed Bad Boy. It was a slap in the face. It was bad for business. He was an extreme threat to her life and her organization. With Bad Boy on her turf, her money was slowing up and her clientele drying out. The war between the rival crews was bad for business for everyone.

People were scared and straying away from any organization that was trouble.

Also, what was happening to Squirrel's organization, the constant robberies, and the murders, trickled down to affect her. Squirrel was still her major connect, and if his supply was dwindling, then hers was too. Money was being lost on both ends.

Luca and Phaedra cruised around Harlem during the sun-drenched day. Her mind was spinning with worries and business. The day may have been warm and springlike, but her life was still cold and icy. The only good thing in her life was Clyde. She was still seeing him and loving every minute of his time.

Phaedra eyed Luca via the rearview mirror. Her boss has stolen the man she really liked from under her nose and she felt she couldn't say anything about it. It was ironic, because deep inside, Phaedra still had a deep crush on her boss. Now, she couldn't have either one of them. It was a weird and vile feeling for Phaedra, being around the two people she liked with them now fucking each other. Talking with Kool-Aid about it helped her some, but there was still this void she was feeling.

Phaedra navigated the Benz through the Harlem streets in silence. The warm day seemed to have brought everyone outside. There were droves of peoples everywhere, and 125th Street was bustling with shoppers and traffic that stretched two blocks long. Luca eyed the activity from the comfort of her Benz. She noticed a few mothers with their families, pushing baby strollers and walking with their young children, and that feeling of loss percolated inside of her. She placed her hand against her stomach and felt snubbed. She had been robbed of motherhood twice.

Maybe it's for the best, she thought. In her predicament, being pregnant would make her vulnerable. And with enemies plotting against her, motherhood had to be put on hold.

"You okay?" Phaedra asked.

"Yeah, I'm okay," Luca replied. "I just have some issues on my mind."

"You still being haunted by that bitch?" Phaedra asked.

Come to think of it, Luca hadn't seen Naomi's ghost in a while. Was she finally gone from her dreams—her life?

"It's been a while."

"I told you it will go away."

The conversation was sparse. Luca wasn't in too much of a mood to talk, especially about her issues. Phaedra continued to drive. She made a left turn on Amsterdam Avenue and drove north. While they were passing a corner bodega, Luca noticed a black-on-black Rolls Royce Phantom parked on the street. The car stood out like a sore thumb. It was a pretty piece of machinery sitting on black rims. It was the type of car World requested.

Luca gazed at the vehicle that sat on the urban city street like a chariot, and then she caught the shock of her life. There was World, exiting the bodega with some cronies. She couldn't believe it, her worst nightmare was just a mere distance away. He was dressed like some rap star, decorated with jewelry and new kicks. Luca was transfixed by the scenery and aghast. She watched World climb into the driver's side of the Phantom and saw her opportunity.

"Phaedra, that's him!" she screamed. "World, he's driving the Phantom!"

Phaedra quickly shifted into aggressive mode and she spun the Benz into a sharp U-turn in the middle of the street, cutting off traffic abruptly. The Phantom sped southbound and the Benz gave chase. Luca removed a pistol from the console and cocked it back. She was sick of his shit. She didn't care where he was, she was ready to fuck up his world.

The Phantom sped through a yellow light, and Phaedra gunned it and ran through the red light. The car was fast, especially with World behind the wheel, driving like a madman. Phaedra tried to keep up, with Luca shouting out, "Don't lose 'em! Don't fuckin' lose 'em!"

The Phantom made a sharp right onto 125th Street and headed toward the Parkway on the west side. Phaedra was three cars behind the Phantom as it raced down Riverside toward the on-ramp of the Hudson Parkway. Phaedra was in and out of local traffic following behind them. Luca screamed, "Go! Go!"

Phaedra careened left and onto the on-ramp, but by the time she got onto the highway, World was almost twenty cars away and fading fast. Phaedra was no match for the Phantom's horsepower and World's maniac NASCAR driving. She lost him on the highway.

"Fuck!" Luca shouted.

"I'm sorry, Luca."

Luca couldn't believe she'd had her shot and lost it, but what she couldn't believe even more, was that World had gotten his Rolls Royce Phantom. It was a very pricey car. How the fuck was this happening? Her broke cousin in a chariot like that? Her cousin was a psychopath and a fuckin' idiot, but he was becoming a threat in Harlem and the drug game.

Luca's mind reverted back to when he showed up at her house without her ever telling him where she lived: Then it dawned on her—did World take her money and drugs? Was he somehow in cahoots with Quincy?

She was determined to find answers and fast.

29

The lyrics to Drake's "Crew Love" blared throughout the crowded 2,500-square-foot nightclub in the Downtown Brooklyn area. Club Money's full-size bar was crammed with drinkers, and the dance floor was lively with a mixture of people.

Looking out at it all in his Versace suit while perched above everyone in the VIP section was World. He and his goons took enjoyment in the party scene and drank Moët that was so expensive that the waiter had to wipe dust off the bottles. They all were in a celebratory mood, eight of them drinking, being garish, and taking advantage of the lovely female company with them. World had crowned himself the "king of New York." Everyone popped bottles and talked recklessly with prying ears around with their jewelry on display and their thuggish attitudes intimidating those nearby. Tonight it wasn't about killing anyone or stealing; it was about having fun, showing off, and getting some pussy.

Doc stood up on the small table in the center of the section to grab everyone's attention. He gripped a half-empty bottle of Moët, clad in a velour sweat suit and a rose-gold chain so big he replicated eighties' jewelry, especially the gold rope chains of the time. His diamond-encrusted earrings and diamond pinky ring caught the females' attention. It was obvious he had money. And it was apparent he was a drug dealer and most likely a dangerous man.

"Yo, I gotta give a toast," Doc shouted out. He looked over at World who looked like the don of Harlem in his fine suit with two beautiful, scantily clad females under his arms, and continued, "To my nigga World, for making all this happen. Yo, I always believed in you, my nigga, and you ain't let us down. We comin' up big time, gettin' that paper and runnin' shit. I love you, my nigga. Cheers to World. Crew love!"

"To World, Crew love," the other hoodlums simultaneously shouted out, raising their bottles and glasses into the air to toast to the new don.

The lovely females joined in on the festivities, also shouting out, "Crew love," while drinking and allowing the men to fondle any part of their anatomy. World and his crew were the center of attention. They tossed money around like it was nothing, and ordered expensive bottle after bottle like they were only spending pennies. Eager eyes wanted in on the wild madness of drinking and bitches, but as they partied like it was New Year's Eve 1999, they also caught foul looks and rivals' eyes.

Several men gazed at World and his hoodlums having the time of their lives, and there was no doubt in their minds the clowns partying out in the open and throwing money around so freely were the niggas Squirrel had been searching for. A solo goon went into the bathroom and dialed a lieutenant close to Squirrel. The man immediately answered and the news was spread.

"They still there?" the lieutenant asked via phone.

"Yeah, they up in VIP doin' it up big time. I know it's these niggas we lookin' for, and they got the audacity to crown this nigga named World the 'don of Harlem,'" the soldier informed.

"A'ight, stay there and keep an eye on them niggas, I'm 'bout to hit up Squirrel now and we gonna send some killers over within the half-hour."

"A'ight, bet."

The soldier coolly walked back into the party and observed World and his men. It was obvious that they weren't ready to leave anytime soon, which was perfect. It was about to be Armageddon inside of Club Money.

At a quarter past 1 a.m., and the nightclub was still jumping. It seemed like the place was overfilling and the music became louder, extremely loud. As World enjoyed the fruits of his hard and deadly labor, unbeknownst to him, a plot on his life was brewing. The young soldier who'd made the call stepped outside to smoke a cigarette and kept an eye out for the reinforcements. As he smoked, he spotted two black Yukons pulling up on the block and double-parking across the street. Over a dozen men exited the trucks. The soldier smiled and walked over. One of Squirrel's most deadly enforcers, Goggles, was leading the charge. He was a towering death threat with a passion for trouble. This harrowing creature was about to give World a run for his money and a world of trouble.

"They still inside?" Goggles asked.

"Yeah, in VIP," he answered.

Goggles nodded and turned to his goons. They all were ready to cause havoc and spill blood. The club was too crowded, but they didn't care; it was their chance to strike. Going through the front was risky, so it was the back for them. Goggles and four of his men walked toward the alleyway, to the back entrance of the club. They were clothed in all black and masked up, gripping Uzi machine guns.

Goggles banged on the back entrance intensely hoping to catch the attention of a guard or staff member. He banged the steel door with the bottom of his fist and waited. Some fool would open up soon. A half minute later, the back door to the club swung open and a towering, beefy security guard stepped out with a scowl. He was quickly met with an Uzi thrust into his face and a word of warning.

"Chill, nigga, chill. Our beef ain't wit' you, so don't let it be," Goggles warned him coolly.

The man nodded nervously.

He was pushed off to the side and held captive by one of the goons while the others entered the club heavily armed. They moved through the concrete corridor seeing the dancing strobe lights close at hand and hearing the blaring bass that made the room shake. They entered the scene of dancing bodies tangled together on the dance floor. The young soldier was leading the way and he pointed at the activity.

"Right there," he said.

Goggles flared up. He hooked his attention on them and seethed with anger. Because of these fools, a lot of their men had been chalked up, and product and money lost. Goggles pushed forward through the tight crowd, not giving a fuck who he knocked over. They were hoodie and masked up, and their Uzi machine guns seemed to be out of everyone's view so far, but that was only temporary. A woman froze in front of the threat, and when she saw the machine gun in Goggles's hands, she shrieked and took off running. Goggles aimed and opened fire unexpectedly at World and his men.

Tat! Tat! Tat! Tat! Tat! Tat! Tat! Tat! Tat! Tat!

Chaos ensued instantly. The first few rounds tore into Doc's chest, and he fell over violently. World erratically pushed the bitches off his lap and reached for his gun. He found himself overwhelmed with a hail of bullets ripping into the VIP area. Two of his men had been already gunned down. Screaming was everywhere and blood had gotten on his suit.

"Muthafuckas!" World shouted. He outstretched his arm and opened fire wildly into the crowd of people, not know who he was striking.

The party life had turned into the gunfight at the O.K. Corral. Dozens of people desperately tried to flee for the exit were pushed and knocked over, trampled and injured. Goggles's men tried to kill everything in the VIP area and caught a waitress in the crossfire.

World decided he wasn't going to die tonight. He was no match for the Uzis lighting up the club. He busted his gun repeatedly and then took his chance. He looked around crazily for his escape route and decided to leap from off the VIP area and fell into the panicking crowd. Goggles frowned. He aimed and tried to shoot World down, but there were too many bystanders blocking his line of sight.

World shot back while fleeing for the exit. He pushed several people out of his way, screaming out, "Fuckin' move!"

Bak! Bak! Bak! Bak!

Pop! Pop! Pop!

Security was outmatched and overwhelmed; they were no match for Goggles's killers. They called 911, frantically, and fearful people spilled out into the streets, screaming and crying echoing everywhere. Goggles and his men roughly pushed their way through the fleeing crowd chasing after World. He had made it outside, blending in with the escaping clubgoers. He was breathing hard, his suit stained with blood and ruined. He didn't know how many of his men had survived.

"Move! Get the fuck out the way! Move!" World heard his foes shout.

He scowled heavily and outstretched his arm with the gun aimed at the sound of his enemies approaching. His insanity wasn't about to allow him to run off like some chicken, not yet anyway, and at first sight at the enemy in black, he opened fire into the crowd.

Boom! Boom! Boom!

He twisted one of Goggles's henchmen's wig back; the bullet tore into the man's eye and spun him violently around to the ground. World shot until his clip was empty, and then he took off running.

"Get that muthafucka!" Goggles shouted.

It was too late. World ran from the chaos like a track star. He faded into the darkness with the sound of police sirens approaching.

30

Squirrel stared at Manhattan from the floor-to-ceiling windows of his penthouse apartment in Midtown, gazing down at the active commotion thirty stories below his place. He was alone and temporarily away from Uptown's chaos, and behind him was a whirlwind of damage done to the luxurious fortress he resided in. The penthouse looked like it had been raided by police with everything smashed to pieces, furniture turned over, the flat screen tossed across the room, shards of glass on the floor, and the walls smashed in.

Squirrel ignored the damage behind him. His mind was swamped with trouble after trouble. Goggles hit him with the bad news a few hours ago. They'd missed their shot. Their suspect had gotten away. Squirrel had cursed and fumed, thrown a violent fit, and destroyed his own home because of the news. He had gotten more bad news when Ike called and had said, "Yo, Squirrel, we been hit."

"By the fuck who?" he had shouted.

"Cops kicked in the door, yo, and raided the place, snatched some work and locked niggas up."

It was news that drove Squirrel mad. Not only he had to worry about a rival stick-up crew, now the cops were up his ass too. He was taking too many losses, and his empire was crumbling. He owed the Colombian cartel two million for the bricks he kept getting robbed for. His life was on the line, and if he couldn't make up for the losses and fix his continuing problem, then he was living on borrowed time.

Also, earlier, he and Angel had gotten into a huge argument and fight again, this time, he went too far. He beat her badly and pulled a gun out on her. He threatened to shoot her. She threatened to leave him for good. Her face was severely battered and she was sick of his shit. She hurried away from his wrath, leaving Squirrel to ponder his future.

As he stood by the window, he had no idea why he suddenly thought about Luca. He vowed to leave her alone, but like a tumor, she kept coming back into his head. He needed her help and he also needed her comfort. She was the only one smart enough to maybe drag him out of the mess that he was sinking in. Squirrel remembered her saying, "I need you now, but one day, you're going to need me."

He chuckled at the thought. It was like she had predicted his future, which was odd. He did need her right now. He needed her political connections—the men she had blackmailed. The men she had serious dirt on. He couldn't remember their names, but he had the information written down in a safe in his Harlem stash house. It was too risky to retrieve anything from there, between the cops swarming around the place like it was a hive and his enemies lurking. It would be a stupid move.

Squirrel stepped away from the window and picked up his cell phone. He searched for Luca's number and dialed, knowing she had to pick up. This time, he needed her more than she needed him, but he wasn't going to let it be known.

✳✳✳

Luca didn't know the exact day when she fell in love with Clyde, but she was in love with him—head over heels. It just happened. Clyde became her life, her giant love. And everything about him was genuine and fun. She could talk to him about anything. Whenever he came around, or she was around him, it felt like she was able escape from any danger. He was the man able to protect her—maybe this was the one. He came into her life like a knight in shining armor. Yes, she was the gangstress, the bad girl, and the queenpin, but overall, she was still a woman who wanted love.

Luca sat at her kitchen table puffing her cigar with the TV playing. She looked at the newspaper headlines. She read about the shooting at Club Money the other night—six dead, dozens of people injured, and complete chaos. The article highlighted gangland shooting spilling over into the Brooklyn nightclub. Dozens of witnesses gave their statements of what had happened. They explained it was something out of a gangster movie, how several armed men exploded into the club and chased this one man into the streets and there was gunfire everywhere.

Luca couldn't help but have a funny feeling that her cousin was involved in the chaotic gun battle.

When her cell phone rang, she assumed it was Clyde calling, but she got the surprise of her life hearing Squirrel on the other end. He sounded civilized. She didn't know what to expect.

"You busy, baby?" he asked calmly, like there was no rough history between them.

"What?"

"What you doin' right now? You not busy, right? I need you."

The audacity of him, she thought.

"You need me?" she asked rhetorically.

"Yes. I was thinkin' you should come to the city and meet me at my penthouse suite so we can talk," he suggested. "I really do miss you."

Luca was flabbergasted. She held the phone to her ear in silence, not knowing how to respond to what he'd said. She knew one thing for sure: She was no longer interested in Squirrel. She was no longer in love with him. She had been through enough with him. She was fed up.

"Baby, you listening to me?" Squirrel uttered.

Now it was "baby," but not too long ago it was "bitch," and "dumb bitch." Luca wasn't a fool and she knew something was wrong.

"Yes, I'm listening, and you know what Squirrel? I am busy," she nonchalantly shot back.

"What? What you mean busy? You too busy to come and see me now?"

"Yes, I am."

"What you talkin' about? You found somebody else? You fuckin' some other nigga?"

"Actually, yes, I am, and I love him so much right now."

"What, bitch?"

Now there was the Squirrel she knew.

Luca smirked and she wished Squirrel could see her expression and she could see his, but her voice was going to let him know that he should have known this day would come, and that she would find somebody else.

"You know once, I felt we could have been something good together, Squirrel. I felt we could have been that power couple. I loved you. I truly fuckin' loved you. You had my heart till the day I died. Now, it's not like that anymore," she said simply.

"What are you talkin' about?"

What she was talking about? She would always remember the past because she was a woman scorned.

"I don't want you anymore, nigga," she frankly told him. "I'm a good woman gone."

She hung up on him. She was tired, and that felt so good.

Squirrel didn't believe it. His pride was bruised and he wasn't the one to be disrespected by anyone. If she thought because she had someone new in her life that she would be done with him, Luca had another thing coming. After all the months of telling Luca to get lost, fuck her, cursing her out, and that he was done with her, the tide had turned and he could tell by her voice that she was really done with him. He didn't like the feeling. So, if he couldn't have her on his terms, then she was now enemy number one.

***

Parked across the street, World stared at Luca's silhouetted figure through the living-room window. He watched her move around her home while talking to someone on the phone. In the shadows, he lit a cigarette and plotted his revenge. He didn't know what had happened the other night in the club. It just happened so quickly. He got sloppy and fucked up. The shooters came out of nowhere. Doc was dead and two of his goons were also chalked up. He was ready to attack Squirrel on full force, kill every last one of his men brutally and maybe slice up his bitch and eat his kids. He was insane. He was ready to carry out some biblical shit against his foes.

Kill 'em all and let 'em burn in hell.

For Luca, he had a different agenda. If he wanted her dead, he could have done so on dozens of occasions. He aimed his pistol at the window and could have opened fire from where he sat, or enter the premises and tortured his own cousin. However, for some reason he couldn't kill his own family and go to her funeral. She was still his cousin.

She needed to die, but not by his hands. He felt she made a deal with him, and a deal was a deal, crazy or not. When Luca brushed him off like he was dirt and looked at him with accusatory eyes, he wanted his revenge. Bit by bit, he was tearing her world and her boyfriend's world apart, too.

He was the one who'd come to her aid when she needed him. When she wanted Nate dead, he carried out the hit for family with no questions asked. And now there wasn't any gratitude for his services. Because of him, Luca got to live a life of opulence while he had to wait and get his due payment. So now, he was going to taunt her like she never has been taunted before and hunt those she loved and trusted. It was only the beginning—the beginning of the end for Luca, Squirrel, and everyone else in their organizations.

31

Luca nestled against Clyde's strapping bare chest, lying naked in his arms in his bed, entangled in his satin sheets, in his affectionate presence and away from the madness she was experiencing. It had been over two weeks since Luca had been home. It had been over two weeks of unadulterated sex with him and feeling like no one would find her. The nightmares had started back again. Naomi was haunting her with a vengeance. She would wake up screaming in the middle of the night in a cold sweat. It felt like Naomi was trying to drag her into the depths of hell. It felt like Naomi was attacking her while she slept. She wanted Naomi gone from her dreams—from inside her head.

If being haunted by Naomi wasn't enough, Luca was experiencing trickery inside her home. She was being taunted by World. First, she would come home to see food out on her countertops that she knew she didn't take out. The TV would be on, blaring. And then there was a .45 caliber bullet placed on the coffee table in her living room. Her alarm system would still be activated, and her video footage didn't capture any images—no intruders, not a single soul. It spooked her. It was like World was a ghost. What would freak her out the most was when she would go to bed that night in one outfit and wake up the next morning in something completely different.

Luca started to question her sanity. She couldn't be tripping. How was World able to undress her and dress her without her waking up? The ultimate scary moment for Luca came when she woke up one morning in blood. It was all over her skin, on her panties and bra. When she turned to her left, there was Egypt, dead, her throat cut open and her naked body cold.

"What the fuck!" Luca had screamed out.

She had leaped from the bed, shocked by the horror. Egypt had been brutally murdered, and it was obvious who the culprit was. Luca panted heavily and felt her chest crushing in, feeling like she was about to have a panic attack. In some odd, twisted way, she was angered but relieved at the same time. Angered that World killed her friend, but relieved that it wasn't her and she wasn't losing her fucking mind. It was time to get out. She called Phaedra and Kool-Aid to dispose of Egypt's body while she cleaned up the crime scene. Everyone was angered, and Kool-Aid swore on his father's grave that he would find, torture, and murder World before the month ended.

Luca hated to admit it, but she was truly afraid of her cousin. He was no ordinary man. He was some demon spawn from the bottom of hell coming to earth to terrorize her. He was taking over Harlem by force, but he still had time to mock her, like it was some game he was playing.

Squirrel became an issue too. With the tables turning on him, Squirrel couldn't leave well enough alone, and out of the blue, he was the one stalking her, showing up at her door unannounced, and trying to mend his mistake.

"Baby, let's just talk about this and make us right again," Squirrel had pleaded.

"Get the fuck away from my door," Luca would curse, holding a gun in her hand, ready to shoot. "Go back to your baby mama, that bitch Angel, let her deal with your shit."

"I ain't goin' no fuckin' where," he would shoot back. "I'm yours to the end. You fuckin' hear me?"

"I have somebody that loves me, and I don't love you. This isn't your pussy anymore. It got someone else's name on it."

Luca's response would infuriate Squirrel greatly. Squirrel wouldn't come alone; his goons would linger by the car parked on the street while he tried to convince Luca to let him inside.

Luca wouldn't allow him inside at all. She was safe behind her door. She didn't want to fuck him. She didn't want to see him. She didn't want anything to do with him. Squirrel couldn't get it through his thick, fuckin' skull. He was cocky and his pride was at stake.

"You better get the fuck away from my door before my neighbors call 911," she had warned him. "This is the suburbs, Squirrel, and my neighbors don't think too kindly of niggas like you yelling and hollering outside my door."

"I'll be back, bitch. I ain't goin' no fuckin' where. We gonna talk," he had stated through his clenched teeth.

Luca knew he was right. He wasn't going to go anywhere, and it was going to become an issue with him.

Unbeknownst to Luca, Squirrel had followed her to SoHo and watched her go into a place called Paradise Lounge. From where he sat, Squirrel continued watching Luca with Clyde. She hugged and kissed him passionately. She was a happy woman around him. She was in love. Squirrel felt disrespected and betrayed. He fumed with anger and wanted to tear her and her newfound lover apart.

"What you want me to do wit' that bitch?" Goggles asked.

"I'ma deal wit' her in my own fuckin' way," Squirrel replied.

However, Squirrel was also being stalked and watched from afar. From a distance, World keenly watched his every move, trying to be deep in the nigga's head. World sat in an inconspicuous SUV with a carload of crazy muthafuckas and was ready to strike. He was ready to avenge Doc's death.

Xavier gave World critical information about a meeting Squirrel was going to have in a few days with some important peoples. His product was extremely low, the Colombians were displeased with him, and he was desperate to find some high-grade product from a different ethnic group at a reasonable price. It was a meeting Squirrel wasn't supposed to come back from. Everything had been arranged and set into play.

***

Squirrel and his cronies pulled into the large factory warehouse in Yonkers. It was another cold evening, and Squirrel had a meeting with some Haitians. He needed a new drug connect, and regardless of his dislike toward the Haitians, they were the only group in town with product that almost competed with the Colombians. His deal with the Colombians was falling apart, and he owed a lot of money to some heavy hitters in the drug game. The Haitians agreed to link up and talk about business. Squirrel's reputation was infamous, but the war with World was taking a toll on everyone. Even the Haitians were skeptical with meeting with Squirrel. But business was business.

Squirrel and four of his goons entered the warehouse. The roll-down metal gate lifted up, and Pug slowly drove the Denali SUV into the unoccupied warehouse with dozens of empty pallets spread out everywhere and the smell of sawdust permeating the area. The Haitians were already present and waiting for Squirrel to show up. It was an uneasy situation, but it needed to be faced. Pug stopped the vehicle, and all four doors to the Denali opened up. Squirrel was the first one to step out, followed by his henchmen.

Clint, the main Haitian Squirrel was to talk business with, was a skinny and dreadlocked man who was black as coal and fierce as a gladiator warrior.

He was flanked by several scowling Haitians anticipating the worst. It was always clear the Haitians didn't like the African Americans and vice versa. This evening, there was a pause in the decade-long animosity between both ethnic groups.

Every last one of Squirrel's men was armed, but Squirrel found it strange that none of Clint's men were carrying any weapons, not even a pistol on hand. They didn't even attempt to search him or his goons. Clint just stood there by his truck, looking aloof from everything. It was supposed to be quick—show me yours and I'll show you mine. Squirrel came to the meeting with fifty thousand dollars to purchase several needed kilos to keep the streets happy.

"I'm here, Clint, so let's talk business," Squirrel said.

Flanked by Pug and his men, Squirrel felt an unexpected, uneasy feeling swim around in his stomach. He looked around the place. Everything seemed normal, but something wasn't. The Haitians were acting strange. Clint could never be caught when it came to business without a pistol in his hand. The Haitians loved their guns more than they loved their women.

"What's good, Clint? What the fuck is wrong wit' you?" Squirrel sharply asked.

"Sumthin' ain't right, Squirrel," Pug spoke out.

Squirrel agreed.

Clint frowned. "This ain't on me, Squirrel. We fucked up," he finally said, incoherently.

"What?" he uttered with a raised eyebrow. "What the fuck you talkin' about?"

Then abruptly, it happened. Gunshots erupted out of nowhere, and two of Squirrel's men were dead. More gunshots exploded and the Haitians were gunned down in cold blood. They had been waiting, anticipating the meeting. Squirrel was aghast, and before he could react, he and whoever was left standing found themselves completely surrounded by World and his crew. His and his members' guns were taken and Squirrel was finally staring face-to-face with World, his number one nemesis.

Squirrel grimaced at being outsmarted and defenseless. Pug was ready to react; he refused to go out like some bitch.

"Fuck y'all, niggas!" he screamed out heatedly.

"You killed Doc, muthafucka? Was it you gunning for me inside the club?" World asked.

"Yeah, I bodied that nigga," Pug lied with a violent scowl, "And I wish I murdered ya ass too. Fuck ya man. Let that nigga burn in hell. He died like a bitch-ass nigga."

"You feel like that nigga," World replied.

Pug boldly spit in World's face. Phlegm trickled down World's cheek. World surprisingly kept his cool. He calmly wiped his face free of spit and remained stoic. He moved closer to Pug. Pug glared at him and spat, "Do what you want, muthafucka. I ain't scared to die."

World smirked. Then the strike came swiftly. World thrust the large knife that was in his hand into Pug's jaw and impaled his chin with the six-inch blade. Pug's body jerked like a fish out of water. World held him in place, admiring his handiwork, gazed into Pug's eyes with no remorse, and gladly watched the life fade from his eyes. Squirrel was horrified by what he saw. He couldn't help but wonder what his fate would be.

World yanked the knife free from Pug's chin, and the body dropped like a sack of potatoes. The ground around him was pooling with thick, crimson blood, and the warehouse was tainted with many deaths. Squirrel was the last man standing.

"Now you," World said, turning his attention to Squirrel.

Squirrel found himself encircled by several lunatics. He clenched his fist and stood silent and expressionless.

World looked at one of his men. "T.T., get the money and the heroin."

T.T. ran off to snatch the product, leaving World to deal with Squirrel. The two men glared at each other, their hate for each other manifested through their eyes. World dropped the knife and kept the gun.

"What the fuck you lookin' at, muthafucka!" World growled at Squirrel.

"Fuck you," Squirrel uttered. "You're a dead man anyway."

World laughed. "This is just too much fun."

All of a sudden Squirrel was severely pistol whipped with the butt of the gun by World. His blood spewed out everywhere, and he collapsed down on his knees, feeling crippled from head to toe. World continued to go ham on his face until the man was nearly beaten unconscious.

He looked down at a bloody and beaten Squirrel and said, "Nigga, I ain't gonna kill you, not yet anyway. Cuz you know why, it's just too much fuckin' fun taking from you. And plus, you got a thing for my cousin, huh? You know my cousin? Yeah, you do. I see you watching her all the time, stalking that bitch like I do. Yeah, Luca's family, bitch. And she owes me, nigga; owes me a lot. So blame her for this shit. And until I get what's fuckin' owed to me, I'm gonna keep taking from you. Understand? I'ma ruin you and her, nigga. This is my game, my fuckin' rules. I'm a muthafuckin' don, nigga."

Squirrel looked up at World with his closed eye and bloody face. He could barely get up. He was hurting. He could barely breathe.

World stood over him and continued to ridicule him. The king of Harlem, this was who he'd been defeated by. World needed to take a picture of this shit and post it on Facebook.

After everything was taken, World left Squirrel to be the only survivor in the place. With Squirrel beaten and rigorously handicapped from so many losses of product, money, and men, he would soon realize that World has suddenly become the most powerful man in all five boroughs. He seemed untouchable and he was everywhere, knowing almost everything.

He had enough product and power to put a hit out on every one of Squirrel's soldiers and still have money left to spare.

Left crushed and close to dead, Squirrel had a lot to think about. He was still alive, but why? To suffer? To get murked at a later date? Or to regroup? He was fuming. This wasn't going to be the end of him. Once and for all, he knew Luca had to go. First it was the detective harassing him and now it was her cousin. She was bad news. There wasn't going to be any more hesitation on his part. Once he was back on his feet and fully healed, he was going to murder that bitch.

She was dead.

32

World stood alone on the pier of City Island overlooking the freezing waters on a chilly night. He smoked his cigarette while waiting. The place was sparse with activity. The surrounding seafood restaurants were closed, some for the night and some closed until warmer weather prevailed. Clad in a leather jacket and ski hat with a .9mm tucked snugly in his waistband, he waited for Xavier to arrive. It was their designated meeting spot. It was isolated and far away from trouble.

World puffed out the smoke from his mouth and then flicked his cigarette into the waters. Doc was heavily on his mind. One of his peoples chalked up again. The night of his friend's death played over and over again in his mind. He felt responsible. Xavier had contacted him, told World that it was urgent for them to meet up. World agreed. Xavier was getting antsy. The body count in the city with a drug war escalating was rising to unprecedented numbers, and Xavier wanted it to end. The constant media attention on the hood was bad for business. Yes, he wanted murders to happen, but now everything was being blown out of proportion, and the people over him weren't too happy about it. The shootout and bloodshed at Club Money tipped the scales for everyone.

The mayor was pissed. NYPD was on the hunt.

Xavier wanted Squirrel dead. He wanted Luca dead. He wanted to take over the city and make World his enforcer and employee. He would supply World information and take over the areas Squirrel used to own and run. Xavier thought he was the one calling the shots, but Xavier didn't realize that he had opened Pandora's Box, and once the evil was out, it was going to be nearly impossible to place it back inside.

World wasn't done with his victims. He had one more surprise for Luca, and it was going to be a doozy. He got off on seeing her go out of her mind, wondering how he was doing what he was doing to her as he sneaked in and out of her home without a trace of evidence or footage. He got off on seeing her sweat. He knew she feared him. And with Squirrel, it was the same thing. He saw how Squirrel was now stalking Luca at her home. It was just too good to be true. The man was an idiot, and World could have easily killed two birds with one stone, but he hesitated in seizing the opportunity.

Bright headlights shone his way, and this time Xavier arrived in a burgundy Chevrolet Impala. He was driving with two other passengers with him, possible corrupt cops. He always traveled with corrupt NYPD officers; they were contract killers with badges.

Xavier exited the car alone. He approached World with a cold look. When he came close, he said to World, "What the fuck is going on in Harlem? Why isn't this muthafucka Squirrel dead yet? Why isn't his organization done with? I gave you exact locations of all his places due to accurate police surveillance. This is as easy as one, two, three, World. You could have killed him when you had the chance. You left him alive!"

"Don't fuckin' rush me, nigga," World chided.

"What you mean don't rush you?! I'm handing you over a fuckin' empire—money, power, pussy, anything and everything at your control, and you playing around with this nigga. This ain't something you play with."

World glared at Xavier. He was itching to hit the muthafucka, crazy enough to shoot him dead right there, but he kept his composure and listened.

"Next time you have that muthafucka dead to rights, you pull the trigger and end his fuckin' life. Do you understand me?" Xavier barked.

World didn't answer him right away.

"Do you fuckin' understand me?" Xavier exclaimed again.

"Yeah, I do," World reluctantly replied.

"And the same goes with that bitch cousin of yours. No more taunting her or anyone in her crew. You end this shit and the world is ours."

World nodded.

"Don't fuck with me on this, World. I gave you everything. I gave you life on these streets, and I can take it away just as fast. My superiors and me, we aren't anything to fuckin' take for granted or take lightly. If they are displeased with you, then they will make you disappear. They will fuckin' end you!" he shouted.

World stood there listening and fuming.

"Do not fuck this up for you and me," Xavier warned.

He pivoted on his heels and walked back to his car, leaving World standing alone again. For now, Xavier had the upper hand, but not for too long. World was about to change all the rules to the game. He grinned wickedly and said to himself, "Yeah, I understand, I damn sure do. They call me World for a reason."

33

Detective Quincy pulled into the driveway of his Far Rockaway home and climbed out of his pricey BMW 760Li. It was late and cold and he had the Caribbean on his mind. He couldn't wait to leave, but before his departure, he had to finish packing up things in his modest home. He had already put in his resignation with the police force. At forty-five years old, with over twenty years on the police force, he would receive his full twenty-year pension—not that he felt he needed it. He was a rich man.

Detective Quincy made arrangements to leave the States with his nineteen-year-old baby mama and their infant son and live in Barbados—warm weather twenty-four-seven, beautiful white sand beaches, cocktails on the terrace, and fun. And all of this pleasure and wealth was because of Charter's phone call to him a few months back.

Charter had called him in hysterics saying he'd beaten Luca to death and needed his help. Quincy told him to stay calm and he would be there within the hour. When he had arrived, he walked into a bloody mess. Charter and Luca were both clinging to life. He was about to call for an ambulance when he saw the treasure trove of goodies in the concealed room. He was staring at his retirement. All that money and drugs had him stunned. In a split second he made the choice to set the tone of life and think of himself rather than save his partner and Luca.

Quickly, he packed up all the money, drugs, and guns into his Nissan Pathfinder and never looked back. He was looking at millions of dollars between the cash and the drugs. It was the most beautiful thing he ever saw. Finishing what his partner started, he grabbed the duffel bag of electronics and DVR and erased any trace of evidence that he was there. He wiped away his fingerprints and left his partner and Luca for dead.

However, before he got onto the highway, which was an hour later, he called for help from a disposable phone he always carried on him. He was determined to separate himself from the incident. When he found out that his partner was dead, when the smoke cleared, Quincy asked the nagging question—would his partner still be alive if he had called for the ambulance immediately? Of course it was a question he would never know the answer to.

He didn't have time to dwell on his partner's demise. He came off with over four million dollars in cash and just as much in drugs. The minute he arrived home, he flushed the drugs down the toilet and hid the cash inside the wall of his living room and placed several family pictures to hide any disturbance with the wall. His future was secured. He turned the guns in to his police precinct and was considered a hero when he claimed an informant gave him the weapons.

His future was set. And yes, life was good for him.

Quincy greeted his two dogs in the backyard and fed them their meal before he went into his home. Everything seemed normal and nothing was out of the ordinary. Underneath his winter coat was a holstered Glock 17, plus he carried another ankle holster underneath his jeans. Since he'd heard about the death of the two detectives in Rockaway Park, Quincy moved around cautiously. He had robbed from a heavy-hitting drug dealer, and there was no doubt that they wouldn't hesitate to kill a cop. But in a few days, he wouldn't have to worry about New York City anymore. His permanent residence was about to be the sunny island of Barbados.

Quincy entered his home thinking everything was secured. The alarm hadn't been tripped, and there was no indication of any intruders anywhere. He walked into the kitchen area and was about to turn on the lights. But there was something wrong, something caught his eye—something had been moved on the countertop in the kitchen when it shouldn't have been moved. Instantly, he reached for his holstered weapon, but before he could remove it, he was attacked from behind and felt the needle plunged into his neck, knocking him out cold in the matter of seconds.

Kool-Aid and Phaedra stood over the unconscious cop.

"I'm ready to have some fun wit' this muthafucka," said Kool-Aid.

Two hours later, the detective woke up with the startling shock of cold water thrown into his face and then found himself bound to one of his kitchen chairs, with his arms folded behind him and his hands restrained by his own handcuffs.

Kool-Aid glared at him and said, "Wake up, muthafucka!"

Detective Quincy glared at the young punk standing before him and knew this day would probably come. He had been a cop for too long not to understand when four million in cash and drugs are taken, sooner or later someone was going to hunt it down. He grimaced and sternly warned them, "You're fuckin' with the wrong cop."

"Shut the fuck up!" Kool-Aid shouted, punching him in the face.

Phaedra stood to the side smoking a cigarette. Kool-Aid was ready to administer some serious pain. On the kitchen counter top was a blowtorch, a few knives, and some pliers. Luca had said to them to kill him quick and not to torture him, but Kool-Aid opted to inflict some serious pain and find out where the money, drugs, and guns were stashed.

"You steal from us, muthafucka?" Kool-Aid shouted and struck him again in the face. "Tonight's gonna become a really bad night for you."

Quincy spit out blood and kept his cool. His glared at Kool-Aid and with the urge to break the young kid's neck. They had him bound to a chair with his own handcuffs and it was their first mistake. Kool-Aid reached for the blowtorch.

Phaedra said, "Start wit' his dick. That's every man's worst nightmare."

Kool-Aid smiled. "Yeah, good thinkin', Phaedra."

"I'm glad to be of help."

It was a game to them, murdering people, and Quincy's blood boiled. He refused to die brutally at the hands of two young kids that he could have fathered himself. He was probably old enough to be their grandfather. Well, almost.

Kool-Aid lit the blowtorch, and the hot, blue flame came to life. Quincy started to think. He was an ex-Marine. He had survived it all. He had been through it all, from the military to the NYPD. He was a highly decorated officer and a war veteran. He was skilled in almost everything, even picking handcuffs and plotting his escape.

Subtly, he removed a small safety pin from the sleeve of his shirt, and while Kool-Aid was setting up to torture him, he slipped the angled end of the pin into the thin part of the keyhole. While pressing down, he rotated the pin in the slot. All this was being done unnoticed by his captors. After several short attempts, the lock to the handcuffs popped open. Quincy didn't react right away. He was freed from the cuffs, but he was waiting for the right moment to strike. They'd underestimated him. He was not about to die in his own home. He had come too far, and this was not going to be the final chapter read.

Kool-Aid smiled like a madman as he walked closer with the blowtorch heated up to 2,500 degrees Fahrenheit. He locked eyes with detective Quincy and said to him, "You know, I watched you for weeks and thought you would be my most difficult kill, but I was wrong. So I hesitated, thought about the right moment to strike. Guess what? You're the easiest."

Quincy didn't respond. It was about to get real ugly, but on whose end? Kool-Aid moved the blowtorch closer and added, "We 'bout to make a serious mess of you all over your pretty kitchen floor."

When Kool-Aid was in position, Quincy leaped abruptly from his chair, surprising Kool-Aid and Phaedra. He immediately grabbed Kool-Aid into a crushing chokehold, causing him to drop the blowtorch. Kool-Aid gasped, Phaedra became wide-eyed, and the last thing Kool-Aid heard was, "I told you, you're fuckin' with the wrong cop." And then he snapped Kool-Aid's neck like a twig in his powerful grip.

Snap!

Kool-Aid's body dropped to the floor. Phaedra stood aghast for a fleeting moment. She couldn't believe he was dead.

"Kool-Aid!" she screamed out.

Quincy glared at her. She tried to reach for her gun, but Quincy was all over her like white on rice, knocking the gun out of her hands. He was burly and strong. He grabbed the young female and tossed her across the kitchen and over the countertop like she was paper-thin. Everything on the countertop spilled onto the floor as Phaedra collided with the floor and landed on her side. She was hurt. Quincy ran over to her and roughly yanked her from off the floor with one hand. He wrapped his hands around her slim neck and had her feet dangling mid-air.

"I'm going to kill you, bitch," he growled.

Phaedra struggled for breath. She could feel her neck breaking and the life being pulled out of her. He wasn't going to stop squeezing until she was dead. She didn't want to die.

Sshhhtt…

It was the sound of a knife being thrust into Quincy's stomach. Quincy jolted suddenly from the pain and released her. "Bitch," he hollered.

Phaedra caught her breath and fought to keep her consciousness. Quincy slammed his hand against his stomach, trying to stop the bleeding. He wasn't going down, not yet. He shot a belligerent stare at Phaedra and charged powerfully at her. Phaedra stumbled backwards; it was like a grizzly bear coming after a wolf. He was on top of her, raging mad and trying to overpower her, but she thrust the knife into his stomach repeatedly until his rage slowed down to a dying man on his knees.

"You fuckin' bitch," he whimpered. His stomach was bleeding profusely. He looked faint with his hands pressed against his stomach, everywhere coated in blood. Phaedra stood far from him and watched him die slowly. He collapsed forward, face-first onto the kitchen floor and was finally dead.

She spun around and looked down at Kool-Aid. Her eyes became clouded with tears. She couldn't believe her friend was dead. It was unbelievable.

"Kool-Aid," she sobbed. There was nothing she could do for him. They didn't expect it would turn out like this. Kool-Aid had warned her about this one, and he was right. But it was too late.

Phaedra hurried away from the crime scene with the knife still in her hand. It had her fingerprints on it. A cop dead in his own home and a young gangster too; it was about to be another major headline.

She rushed to the car, not realizing that what they had been killing for was just a couple of feet away, buried in the walls of his Far Rockaway home.

***

Phaedra had nowhere else to go, or couldn't think of anywhere to go. She frantically dialed Luca's number, but her boss wasn't picking up. Phaedra was in anguish and tears. Her best friend was dead. She had fucked up. Everything was falling apart. She was falling apart.

She found herself driving randomly, and then she was on the highway heading toward the city, and then crossing the Brooklyn Bridge and driving into SoHo. Next thing she knew, she was jumping out of her car and walking into Clyde's lounge looking distraught. It was in the wee hours of the morning and the crowd was thin to almost empty. She had cleaned some of the blood off of her, but her hair was in disarray and her eyes red from crying.

Why had she come here, of all places? she asked herself.

Clyde was at the bar talking to one of his bartenders when he noticed Phaedra walk into his establishment. He immediately saw she was in distress. He went over her way to see what was wrong.

"Phaedra," he called out. "Are you okay?"

She looked at him and was completely fucked up. She looked at him and said, "He's dead."

"Who's dead?"

"Kool-Aid."

"Your boyfriend?" he asked.

"He was my best friend. The only person I could really talk too."

Clyde saw that she was in no condition to be alone. She needed his help. "Stay right here for a minute and don't go anywhere," he said.

He went over to the bar and spoke some words to the bartender. He then excused himself, walked over to Phaedra and said, "C'mon, you don't need to be here right now in your condition."

"We're you takin' me?" she asked.

"To my house," he replied.

She didn't argue with him. She climbed into his car and they headed toward his Brooklyn brownstone in Park Slope. During the ride they talked. Clyde was always fond of Phaedra. He told her that he understood how she must have felt to lose her man, and Phaedra was dumbfounded. It finally dawned on her that he'd thought, since they were always together, she and Kool-Aid was a couple.

"He was never my man. He was a friend I grew up with," she said.

She then went on to explain everything to him. As he drove into Brooklyn, her feelings about him just poured out like water from a faucet.

She told him everything, from the first time she saw him and why she began liking women. She talked about Kool-Aid and admitted that the only reason she came to the Paradise lounge was to see Clyde. She talked about how she truly felt about his relationship with Luca.

Clyde was taken aback. He never knew.

When they arrived at his brownstone, Phaedra jumped into the shower right away. She lingered under the cascading water, washing away the blood and trying to wash away the pain she felt. She sighed deeply. She stepped out of the shower, toweled off, wrapped the towel around her body, and knotted it. She felt somewhat refreshed, but the loss of Kool-Aid still lingered.

She joined Clyde in the living room still clad in her towel. It was getting late; daybreak was coming in a few hours. They continued to talk. Phaedra was transfixed by his generosity and hospitality. He gently pressed his lips to her forehead and whispered, "You're a sweet girl, and everything's going to be okay."

The moment felt intimate for them both. Clyde was a gentleman, but Phaedra's young and curvy body scantily clad in a short towel was too enticing. She confessed to not having dick inside of her since her boyfriend died many years ago. It was like she was a virgin all over again.

In a flash, things heated up between them on the sofa. Phaedra undid her towel and revealed her sensuality to him. She undid his pants; he pulled his shirt over his head. She straddled him on the couch. They were almost naked. He was hard, she was wet. She whispered in his ear, "I wanted to love you since the first day I laid eyes on you."

Her pussy throbbed against him. This wasn't right, but the moment felt too good. With precision aim, Clyde was inside her, fucking her closely. There was nothing to hold him back. They fucked like it was meant to be. And they both had reached the point of no return. She wrapped her arms around him and moaned into his ear. She slammed her pussy down onto his hard, big erection. He reached up to play with her nipples as her juices coated him. She rode him on the couch and then they kissed passionately. Phaedra continued moaning in his ear, feeling his dick about to explode inside of her. He gripped her hips and delivered his essence as they exploded together. She made eye contact with him and said, "I want you to be mine."

Clyde knew it was a mistake. But the mistake felt so good.

34

Luca saw the breaking news flash across her TV in the early morning and knew something had gone wrong. She stared at media footage about a police officer and an unidentified male both found dead in a Far Rockaway home. She knew right away that it was Kool-Aid they had found dead, and the home belonged to detective Quincy.

What the fuck happened? she asked herself.

She had been trying to get in touch with Phaedra all morning, but to no avail. Her phone kept going straight to voicemail. She started to worry. Was Phaedra dead too? Luca couldn't help but to think of Phaedra being shot up, bleeding to death and needing paramedic help.

Something was wrong.

Luca got into her car and decided to head over to Clyde's place in Brooklyn. She called his phone too, but he wasn't picking up. *Why isn't anyone answering their damn phone?* she screamed in her mind. It was a nervous morning. Her heart started to beat rapidly. She couldn't help but be worried about her best friend. When she came to a stop in front of Clyde's opulent brownstone on the quiet street, she rushed from her car with the cell phone glued to her ear. She ran up the concrete stairs and banged on his door loudly.

She waited.

He was taking too long to answer. She banged on his door again. Was something wrong? Was it World? Was it Squirrel? Did either one of them get to Clyde, the man she was in love with? She prayed nothing had happened to either of them, Clyde and Phaedra.

The front door opened and Luca exhaled with relief—at least he was still alive.

"Luca," Clyde greeted, looking surprised to see her. "What are you doing here?"

"Something's wrong, Clyde," she uttered. "Kool-Aid is dead, and I can't get in touch with Phaedra. She might be dead, too."

Clyde stepped out of his home fully clothed. Luca wanted to go inside, but for some strange reason, he was blocking her entry.

"Clyde, what is wrong with you? Let me in, I need to talk to you," she said.

Clyde looked at her and heaved a deep sigh. "Luca, I have to tell you something. I have always been honest with you," he started.

Luca gazed at him in confusion. There was something off about everything happening today. She suddenly had a bad feeling. She and Clyde loitered on the front step, and Luca knew something happened. As Clyde was about to tell her the truth, his eyes enlarged with fear in his expression. A lone gunman emerged from behind a parked car with his arm outstretched and at the end of it was a .45 trained at Luca's back.

"Luca, get out the fuckin' way!" Clyde screamed out, pushing Luca aside forcefully and shielding her with his own body.

The gunman opened fire.

Bang! Bang! Bang! Bang!

Four hot slugs tore into Clyde's frame, and he fell over in Luca's arms. Luca snatched out her pistol and returned fire, but missed the gunman completely, shattering car windows in the attempt. She quickly got a glimpse of the muthafucka as he whizzed into an idling car and sped away.

Squirrel!

It was him. She recognized him at once. She had no time to dwell on him; Clyde was shot four times, bleeding in her arms. Luca screamed madly—the day had gone from bad to catastrophic. She was frantic. But things became more bizarre for her when Phaedra came running out of Clyde's place half dressed.

Luca was shocked. But she was too worried about her lover to beef with Phaedra.

"We gotta get him to a hospital," Phaedra said.

EPILOGUE

Luca jumped into her car after they carried Clyde to her vehicle and put him in the backseat. He was bleeding profusely. They sped to the nearest hospital in Brooklyn in haste. It was a very uncomfortable moment for both girls. Luca wanted to know why her best friend was coming out of her man's house in the morning and half dressed. She was too worried about her man's life to ask those questions now. They hurried to Brookdale hospital in a heartbeat. When they reached the emergency room, both ladies spilled out of the car and shouted, "We need help! Help us!"

Quickly, doctors and nurses rushed out of the emergency room wheeling a gurney outside and hurriedly placing Clyde onto it. Both girls rushed behind the medical staff with nervousness.

"He can't die," Luca cried out. "He can't."

They followed behind the hospital emergency staff until they were stopped by security when he was wheeled into a restricted area. They were told to wait there until he was out of surgery. Both ladies were in utter despair. They sat in the waiting area in silence, each in their own thoughts. Luca couldn't even look at Phaedra, and Phaedra felt ashamed.

Hours later, they were told that Clyde was still alive. He had pulled through surgery, but was still in critical condition. Things looked grim.

He was placed in a room alone and every hour was crucial. Luca couldn't wait to see him.

Both women sat on opposite sides of his hospital bed. Luca knew Phaedra had fucked her man. It was written all over her face. She didn't even try to explain herself. Instead, she sat quietly, averting her eyes from her boss. She didn't ask about Kool-Aid. She didn't care what had happened at that moment. It was about Clyde right now.

In her heart, Phaedra knew Luca would possibly want to seek revenge on her. She fucked up and it seemed like she was on a road to hell.

Luca was swamped with nightmare after nightmare. As she sat and worried about Clyde, she knew that World and Squirrel wanted to see her in a grave, and Squirrel had almost succeeded. Clyde saved her life. But she also knew that without Kool-Aid and Phaedra on her team, she was weak. It was a crucial moment. It was very tense in the hospital room— quiet, and nerve-racking as both women refused to leave or get any sleep no matter how many times the nurses or doctors suggested it. They both wanted to be by Clyde's side.

Nine hours later, Clyde came out of surgery for a second time. He was in bad shape, but he was lucky—the bullets had gone straight through and missed all of his vital organs. He managed to open his eyes and noticed both Luca and Phaedra were at his bedside. However, he only managed to say one word, "Luca."

Things were about to get a lot more interesting.

**Don't miss *Bad Girl Blvd 3*
by Erica Hilton, available in 2015
wherever books are sold.**